THE FOUNDLING

THE FOUNDLING

HECTOR MALOT

Translated by
DOUGLAS MUNRO

Illustrated by Alan B. Herriot

HARMONY BOOKS
New York

For Helen

Translated and abridged from *Sans Famille* by Hector Malot,
published by E. Dentu, Paris, 1879.

Translation copyright © 1984 by Douglas Munro
Illustrations © 1984 by Alan B. Herriot

First published in the United States of America in 1986 by Harmony
Books, a division of Crown Publishers, Inc., 225 Park Avenue South,
New York, New York 10003 and represented in Canada by the
Canadian MANDA Group
Originally published in Great Britain in 1984 by Canongate
Publishing Ltd., 17 Jeffrey Street, Edinburgh 1, Scotland

HARMONY and colophon are trademarks of Crown Publishers, Inc.
Manufactured in the United States of America

Library of Congress Cataloging-in-Publication Data
Malot, Hector, 1830–1907.
The foundling.
Translation of: Sans famille.
Summary: A French foundling who is sold to a circus at the age of
eight experiences many adventures before he finally finds
his real home.
[1. Abandoned children—Fiction. 2. Circus—
Fiction. 3. France—Fiction] I. Title.
PQ2346.S4E5   1986   [Fic]   86-18363

ISBN 0-517-56342-8
10 9 8 7 6 5 4 3 2 1
First American Edition

INTRODUCTION

Hector Malot may possibly be regarded by many as one of the best French nineteenth-century novelists, and as a writer of tales for young people he is almost entirely unsurpassed. He was born in 1830 at La Bouille in the Seine Inférieure, and was the son of a notary. He himself studied to become a lawyer but, like many another French writer, abandoned that profession in order to embark upon a literary career.

Malot brought out "Sans Famille", *The Foundling*, in 1878, and followed it with, amongst others, "En Famille" and "Pompon". The book was a great success, and received the high recognition of the Prize of Honour (Couronné) from the Académie Française. Indeed it is today one of the most deeply-rooted and loved of French children's classics, being printed again and again down the years.

The Foundling is a charming and moving story, with a skilful plot in which pathos is blended with humour. Many years ago when I first read it I can remember being very touched by the scene of the death of Joli-Coeur, and excited by the identity-quest side of the plot. One thing has always puzzled me about the book though, and that is where Malot could possibly have obtained his background information for the scenes in London. So far as I know he never visited that city, and he must therefore have culled the descriptions of conditions of poverty in late-Victorian times either from reading Dickens' novels or studying Mayhew's works on the London poor. Or, again, Gustave Doré's vivid portrayals of London may have set his imagination working.

It is my hope that you will enjoy the reading of this book as much as I did the translating, which took me back to my own childhood days and love of books.

The Translator

CHAPTER ONE

I am a foundling.

But until my eighth birthday I thought that I was like other children who had their mothers, for whenever I cried a woman took me in her arms and cuddled me until my tears stopped. I never went to bed without her kissing me goodnight, and when the cold December winds blew snow against the window-panes she would sing to me as she warmed my feet with her hands. And even now I can remember clearly the words of the song that she sang.

When I was out minding our cow as it grazed by the roadside or browsed among the heather, and a heavy shower fell, she would run to me and cover my head and shoulders with her woollen skirt to stop me from being soaked. And if I quarrelled with any of my friends she made me tell her what it was all about, and almost always she would praise me when I was right or, when I was wrong, find a few words to console me.

From these and many other ways, in the way she spoke and looked at me, the gentle way in which she scolded me, I believed she was my mother.

This is how I learned that she was only my adopted mother. The village where I was brought up, for I did not have a village of my own, no birthplace, any more than I had a father or mother, was called Chavanon, and it was one of the poorest in the middle of France. The reason for the poverty was not the laziness of the

1

people who lived there, but the vast stretches of heath and broom which covered the country. Only small patches of land could be cultivated.

We lived together in a cottage by a stream which, in time, joined the Loire, and until I was eight years old I had never seen a man come inside our little house. I should tell you that my adopted mother was not a widow — her husband was a stone-cutter who worked with a lot of others in Paris. He had not come back to the village since I had been old enough to notice what was going on around me. From time to time one of the men who worked with him would bring news.

"Mother Barberin," he would say, "your husband is well. He told me to tell you that he is still working and to give you this money. Do you want to count it?"

And that was all. Mother Barberin was happy that her husband was well and working, earning some money. It should not be thought, because Barberin was away in Paris for so long, that he and his wife were not on good terms with each other. He had to stay in Paris because work was there, and when he was old he would come back to the cottage and they would live on the money that had been put by and so be saved from the poverty of old age.

It was on one November evening when I was on the doorstep breaking some sticks for the fire that a man stopped at the gate, looked at me, and asked if this was where Mother Barberin lived. I told him that it was, and asked him to come in. He pushed open the squeaky gate and walked slowly towards the cottage. Never had I seen such a dirty man. From head to foot he seemed to be covered in mud, and it was clear that he had been walking a long way on bad roads. When she heard our voices Mother Barberin came to the door to see who it was.

"I've some news from Paris for you," the man said.

There was something in the way he said this that frightened Mother Barberin. "Oh heavens," she cried, clasping her hands, "something has happened to Jerome."

"Yes, something has, but don't be alarmed. There has been an accident, but he wasn't killed. Maybe he will be a cripple. He's in

2

hospital now. I used to share a room with him. As I was coming back here he asked me to give you the news. I can't stop now as I have another nine miles to walk and it will be dark soon."

But Mother Barberin wanted to know more, and begged him to stay for supper. The roads were bad and she had heard that wolves were prowling about. He could leave early next morning. He agreed and sat down in a corner by the fire. While he ate he told us both how the accident had happened. Some scaffolding had fallen and Barberin had been badly hurt. He had had no business to be standing where he was, and the builder had refused to pay him any compensation.

The legs of the man's trousers slowly dried out and they became stiff under the coating of mud. "Poor old Barberin," he went on, "he's unlucky. Other fellows might have been given money as the result of an accident like this, but he will get nothing. I told him he ought to sue the builder."

From the way he spoke it was plain that he wouldn't have minded if he had been badly crushed himself as long as it had meant he would get some sort of pension.

"A lawsuit," said Mother Barberin, "but that would cost money."

"Yes, of course, but what if you won!"

Mother Barberin wanted to set off for Paris, but it was such a long journey and would cost so much.

Next morning we both went to the village to have a talk with the priest. His advice was not to go without first finding out if she could be of any help to her husband. He wrote to the almoner of the hospital where Barberin was being looked after, and several days later he received a reply telling him that Barberin's wife was not to come. Instead she should send some money to her husband, for he had decided to sue the builder for his injuries.

Days and weeks went by, and from time to time letters came asking for more money to be sent. The last one was most insistent and said that if there was no money left then the cow must be sold to get the money he needed.

It is only those who have lived in the country with peasants who can understand the distress of those three words: 'Sell the cow'.

The cow has a different meaning for different people, but for peasants it is everything. No matter how big the family, and they have a cow in their byre, they know they can't go hungry. We had our butter, and milk to moisten the potatoes, and until the time I am talking about I had hardly ever eaten meat. Our cow not only gave us nourishment, she was our friend. Some people seem to think that a cow is a stupid beast, but that is not true for a cow is full of intelligence. When we talked to ours and patted her she understood us, and with her big soft round eyes she knew well enough how to tell us what she wanted and what she did not. She loved us and we loved her, and that was all there was about it.

But we had to part with her, for it was only by doing that that we would be able to satisfy Mother Barberin's husband. A cattle-dealer came to the cottage and after thoroughly inspecting Roussette (all the time he was shaking his head and saying that she would be of no use to him, he would never be able to sell her again for she gave no milk and made poor butter) he ended by saying that he would buy her, but only out of kindness to Mother Barberin who was a good woman.

Poor Roussette! As if she knew what was going on she refused to come out of the byre, and started bellowing.

"Get in behind her and chase her out," the man told me, handing me a whip which was hanging around his neck.

"No he won't," Mother Barberin said. She touched Roussette's neck and spoke gently to her: "There now, my beauty, come, come along."

Roussette made no more resistance. When she was on the road the man tied her to his cart, the horse started trotting and she had to follow. We went back to the house, but for a long time we could hear her bellowing. There would be no more milk or butter — in the morning only a piece of bread and in the evening some potatoes with salt.

Shrove Tuesday fell a few days after Roussette was sold. The year before Mother Barberin had made a real feast for me of pancakes and fritters, and I had eaten so many that she was full of

4

Roussette made no more resistance. When she was on the road the man tied her
to his cart, the horse started trotting and she had to follow.

joy. But now there was no Roussette to give us butter to put in the frying-pan, and I was very sad.

But Mother Barberin had a surprise for me. She did not like borrowing; she had asked one of the neighbours for a cup of milk and another for a pat of butter. When I came home at about midday I saw her pouring flour into a big earthenware bowl.

"Oh, flour!" I said, going to her.

"Why, yes, my little Remi," she said with a smile, "it's lovely flour. Come and see what beautiful flakes it makes."

I very much wanted to know what the flour was for, but dared not ask because I didn't wish her to know that it was Shrove Tuesday for fear she might be hurt.

"And what do you make with flour?" she asked, looking at me.

"Bread."

"What else?"

"Why, I don't know."

"Yes you do, but you are such a nice little boy that you don't dare say. You know that today is Pancake Day, but because you think we have no butter or milk you didn't want to talk about it. Isn't that right?"

"Oh Mother Barberin!"

"Look in that bin, little Remi."

I quickly lifted the lid and saw milk, butter, eggs and three apples. While I cut the apples into slices she broke the eggs into the flour, and stirred the mixture adding milk every now and then. When everything was well mixed she put the earthenware bowl on the warm cinders, for it was not until we had supper that we would eat the pancakes and fritters. It was a very long afternoon for me, and I often lifted the cloth that she had thrown over the bowl.

"If you do that you will make the mixture cold," she called out, "and it won't rise."

But, all the same, it was rising well with little bubbles breaking the surface, and the eggs and the milk smelled good.

"Now go and chop some sticks, for we must have a fire that doesn't give off smoke."

6

At last the candle was lit and Mother Barberin said: "Now put some wood on the fire."

She didn't have to say that again for I was waiting to do so. Bright flames were soon leaping up the chimney and the whole room was lit up by the fire. It was then that Mother Barberin took the frying-pan from its hook and put it on the fire.

"Pass me the butter, please."

With the tip of her knife she put a piece as large as a walnut into the pan, where it melted and then sputtered. It had been a long time since we had smelled anything so good. I was watching and listening to its sputtering when I thought I heard footsteps in the yard.

Whoever could be coming at this time in the evening to interrupt us? No doubt it would be a neighbour wanting some firewood. I couldn't let my thoughts wander, for just at that moment Mother Barberin had dipped her wooden spoon into the bowl and was starting to pour some of the mixture into the frying-pan. Then there was a knock on the door with a stick, and it was pushed open.

"Who is it?" asked Mother Barberin, not turning round.

A man came in, and in the bright light I could see that he was carrying a big stick.

"And so you're having a banquet here. Don't disturb yourselves," he said roughly.

"Good heavens! Is it you Jerome?" Mother Barberin cried out as she quickly put the frying-pan on the floor. The she took me by the arm and dragged me towards the man, who was still standing in the doorway.

"Here's your father," she said.

CHAPTER TWO

I went to kiss him but he lifted his stick to stop me.

"What's this?" he said, "You told me..."

"Well, yes, but that wasn't true... because..."

"Not true?"

He stepped towards me with his stick still raised and instinctively I backed away, for what had I done? I had only been going to kiss him.

"So you are keeping Shrove Tuesday," he said to Mother Barberin. "That's good news for I'm starving. What's for supper?"

"I was making some pancakes and fritters."

"I can see that, but you are not going to give pancakes to a man who has just walked thirty miles."

"I have nothing else. I wasn't expecting you."

"Nothing else! Nothing for supper!" He looked round the room. "There's some butter there."

Then he looked at the ceiling where the bacon used to hang, but for a long time there had been nothing there. Only a few ropes of garlic and onions were hanging from the beam now.

"There are onions here," he went on, knocking a rope down

8

with his stick. "With four or five of them and a pat of butter we'll have some good soup. Take those pancakes out of the pan and fry the onions."

Without a word Mother Barberin hurried to do what she was told. Her husband sat down on a chair by the chimney. I had not dared to move and leant against the table looking at him. He was about fifty, with a hard and surly face. Because of his injury his head was bent towards his right shoulder, and this made him look all the more forbidding.

Mother Barberin had put the frying-pan back on the fire.

"Are you going to make soup with that little pat of butter?" he demanded, and grabbing the plate with the rest of the butter on it he threw the lot into the pan.

No more butter, and no more pancakes!

At any other time this would have been a catastrophe which would have upset me, but now I was no longer thinking of pancakes and fritters. All my thoughts were that this man who seemed to be so cruel was my father. My father! I said the word over and over again under my breath. In a vague sort of way I had imagined him to be a kind of mother with a big deep voice, but when I looked at this one who had just fallen out of the sky I felt very sad and frightened.

I had wanted to kiss him, but he had pushed me away with his stick. Why? My mother had never pushed me away when I went to kiss her, indeed, she always took me in her arms and held me tight.

"Instead of standing there as if you're frozen," he said to me, "put the plates on the table."

I nearly tripped in my hurry to obey. The soup was made and Mother Barberin served it. He left the chimney corner, sat down and started eating, only stopping now and then to look at me. I felt so uncomfortable that I couldn't eat. I tried to look at him out of the corner of my eye but quickly looked down when I caught him staring at me.

"Doesn't he usually eat more than that?" he asked, pointing his spoon at me.

9

"Oh yes, he has a good appetite."

"That's a pity. But he doesn't seem to want his supper now."

Mother Barberin did not seem to want to talk, but went about and waited on her husband.

"If you aren't hungry go to bed and go to sleep at once, or I'll be angry."

Mother Barberin gave me a look which warned me to obey without answering. But she need not have done that for I had not thought of saying a word.

Like a great many poor homes our kitchen also served as a bedroom. Near the fireplace were the table, the log-basket, and the sideboard. In a corner was my mother's bed and opposite it an alcove where my bed was, behind a red curtain. I undressed as fast as I could and got into bed, but it was another thing to go to sleep, for I was worried and very unhappy. How could this man be my father, and if he was why should he treat me like this?

I lay facing the wall and tried to drive away these thoughts and go to sleep as he had ordered me to, but sleep would not come. I had never felt so wide awake. After a while, and I could not say how long, I heard someone come over to my bed. The step was slow and heavy so I knew at once that it was not Mother Barberin. A warm breath ruffled my hair.

"Are you asleep?" asked a rough voice.

I took good care not to answer, for the words 'I'll be angry' still rang in my ears.

"He's asleep," I heard Mother Barberin say. "He drops off the moment he is in bed. You can talk without any worry of being overheard."

I should, of course, have told him that I was awake, but I was too frightened. I had been ordered to go to sleep, I was not yet asleep, so I was in the wrong.

"Tell me about your lawsuit," my mother then said.

"I lost it. The judge said it was my fault for being under the scaffolding and the builder was not to blame."

Then he banged his fist on the table and started cursing in words which didn't make sense. After a minute or two he went on:

10

"The case was lost, the money's lost. Everything's gone and poverty's staring us in the face. And as if that's not enough when I come home I find this child. Why didn't you do what I told you to?"

"I couldn't."

"You should have taken him to a home for foundlings."

"No woman could give up a little child like that when she had fed him with her own milk and grown to love him."

"He's not your own child."

"Well, I wanted to do what you told me, but then he fell sick. To have taken him to a home would have killed him."

"When did he get better?"

"Not all at once, for another illness came. He coughed so much it would have broken your heart. Our poor little Nicolas died like that. Time went on and I thought that as I'd put off going I'd put off for a little longer."

"How old is he now?"

"Eight."

"Well, he'll just have to go to the place he should have gone to long ago. And he won't like it so well now."

"Jerome, you can't do that."

"Can't I? Who is going to stop me? Do you think we are always going to keep him?"

There was a silence and I could hardly breathe for I had a lump in my throat that nearly choked me. A little later Mother Barberin went on:

"Paris has changed you. You would never have spoken to me like that before you left here."

"Perhaps you are right, but if Paris has changed me it has also nearly killed me. I can't work now, we've no money, and the cow's sold. When we haven't enough to eat ourselves how can we feed a child that doesn't belong to us?"

"He belongs to me."

"He's no more yours than mine. I was looking at him at supper, he's not a country boy. He's thin and he's delicate, with no arms or legs."

11

"He's the best-looking boy in the village."

"I don't say that he's not good-looking. But he's not strong. He's a city child and this is no place for city children."

"I tell you that he's a fine boy with a good heart, and he'll work for us."

"But in the meantime we've got to work for him, and I'm not much good now."

"If his parents come to claim him what will you say?"

"His parents! Has he any? If he had they would have come for him by now. I was a fool to take him in, and just because he was wrapped up in fine clothes it doesn't mean that his parents will ever hunt for him. Besides, they're dead by now."

"But if they do come?"

"Well then we've sent him to a home. We've talked enough. I'll take him tomorrow. I'm going now to say hello to François. I'll be back in an hour."

The door slammed behind him. I at once sat up in bed and called to Mother Barberin, and she ran to me.

"Are you going to let me go to the home?"

"No, my little Remi, of course not."

She kissed me to cheer me up and I began to feel better.

"And so you weren't asleep?" she said gently.

"It wasn't my fault that I couldn't go to sleep."

"I'm not scolding you."

"You are not my mother, and he isn't my father."

I spoke the last five words in a different tone because although I was unhappy to find out that she was not my mother, I was glad and proud to know that he was not my father. Mother Barberin seemed not to notice.

"Perhaps I should have told you that I am not your real mother," she said, "but you seemed so much my own son that I simply couldn't tell you the truth. Now you should know that Jerome found you one day in a street in Paris. It was in February when he was going to work very early one morning. He heard a baby cry and saw you on a doorstep. He looked around to call someone, and then a man appeared from behind a tree and ran

12

away. While Jerome was wondering what to do some other men arrived, and they agreed that you must be taken to a police station. You never stopped crying, for you must have been very cold.

And when they had made you warm you still cried, and so they found some milk. You were only five or six months old. It was written down at the police station where you were found and what you were wearing, and they decided that you would have to go into a home unless someone would look after you. It was thought certain that the parents would pay anyone well for looking after you, so Jerome said that we would take you. At that time my own baby was the same age as you and I was easily able to feed you both. That was how I became your mother."

"Oh, mother!"

"Yes, but three months later my own boy died and I came to love you even more. But Jerome couldn't forget his child, and when three years went by and your parents hadn't come for you he tried to make me send you to a home. You have heard why I didn't do that."

"Mother Barberin, please don't send me to any home."

"No, you won't go. I'll see to that. Jerome is not really unkind but he has had a lot of trouble and is worried. We'll all have to work, you too."

"Yes, I'll do anything you want me to, but don't send me to a home."

"If you promise me that you'll go to sleep at once you won't go. When Jerome comes back he must not find you awake."

She kissed me and I turned my face to the wall. I wanted badly to go to sleep but what I had been told went round and round in my head. If Mother Barberin was not my real mother, then who was? Then I thought that my real father would not have lifted his stick to me. Could Mother Barberin stop him from sending me away?

In the village there were two boys from the home who were called 'workhouse children', and they each had a metal disc hanging from their necks with a number on it. They were poorly

13

dressed and dirty, and all the other children mocked them and threw stones at them. They chased them just as boys chase a lost dog, for fun, and because a lost dog has nobody to protect it.

How I hated the thought of being like those two boys. I did not want to have a number hung around my neck, and I did not want others to call out at me 'Back to the workhouse'! The thought of all this made me shiver and my teeth chatter, for I just could not go to sleep. And to think that Barberin would be coming back soon!

But luckily he did not return until very late, and I had fallen asleep before he arrived.

CHAPTER THREE

During the night I was very restless, and when I woke up in the early morning I could hardly believe that I was in my own bed. I felt it and then looked around to make quite sure.

Mother Barberin never spoke to me during the morning and I began to think that the idea of sending me to the home had been given up. But at midday Barberin told me to put on my cap and to come with him. I looked at Mother Barberin imploring her to help me, and without her husband noticing she signed to me to follow him as well as to let me know that I had nothing to worry about. Without another nod I did as I was told.

It was some distance from our house to the village; at least an hour's walk. Not a word was said between us, and every now and then he turned to see if I was behind him. I asked myself again and again where he could be taking me, and in spite of Mother Barberin's reassuring sign I was worried and wanted to run away. I tried to lag behind with the idea that I would jump into some ditch where he couldn't catch me.

For a time he seemed happy enough that I should trail along behind, but then somehow or other he seemed to read my thoughts and grabbed me by a wrist so that I had to keep up with him. And that was how we entered the village, with everyone turning round to stare just as if I might have been a snarling dog on a leash.

We were passing the inn when a man who was standing at the

door called out to Barberin inviting him to come in. Barberin took me by the ear, pushed me in ahead of him, and closed the door. I felt happier now because for a long time I had wanted to know what the inside of an inn looked like. I had often wondered what went on behind its red curtains.

Barberin sat down at a table with the man who had called out to him. As for me, I sat by the chimney and had a good look around. In the corner opposite me was an old man with a white beard wearing clothes the like of which I had never seen before. Long hair fell to his shoulders and he wore a tall grey hat on which were green and white feathers. He had a sheepskin tied about him with the woolly side turned inside. There were no sleeves, only two large holes through which his arms were thrust, and they were covered with some sort of velvety material that had at one time been blue. Woollen gaiters which were held in place by a ribbon criss-crossing his legs reached to his knees.

He sat with an elbow on his crossed knees and I had never seen such a quiet, calm man. He reminded me of one of the saints in our church. Lying at his feet were three dogs, a white poodle, a black spaniel, and a pretty little grey-haired thing with a bright and sweet face. The poodle had a policeman's old helmet on its head, fastened under its chin with a leather strap.

While I gazed in wonderment at the old man Barberin and the owner of the inn talked quietly, and I knew in my bones that they were talking about me. Soon I overheard Barberin say that he had brought me to the village to take me to the mayor to ask that the charity home should pay for my keep. Apparently that was all that Mother Barberin had been able to get her husband to agree to, and I had the feeling that if Barberin could get something for keeping me I had nothing to fear.

The old man, without seeming to, had been listening to what was being said. He turned to Barberin and asked him in a foreign accent: "Is this the boy you are talking about?"

"Yes."

"And so you think that the home is going to give you money for his keep?"

"Of course. He has no parents and he has cost me money. It's only fair that I should be paid something."

"I don't say it isn't, but all the same I don't think you'll ever get what you are after."

"Then off he goes into the home to stay there. There's no law that can force me to keep him in my house if I don't want to."

"But if you agreed at the start to look after him then it's up to you to do what you promised."

"Well I'm not going to keep him any longer, and if I want to get rid of him I'm going to."

After a few moments of thought the old man said: "Perhaps there is a way of getting rid of him if you want to, and you could make a little money out of it."

"You show me how and I'll buy you a drink."

The old man got up and sat opposite Barberin. As he did this I saw his sheepskin move and I wondered whether he had another dog under his left arm.

"You won't let this boy eat any more of your bread unless somebody pays for it, is that it?"

"Yes. . . because. . ." and Barberin hesitated.

"Never mind why, that's no concern of mine. If you don't want him just give him to me. I'll look after him."

"You? You'll look after him! Give you a boy like him, the handsomest lad in the village. Look at him!"

"I've looked at him."

"Remi, come over here." I went to the table shaking all over.

"Don't be afraid boy," the old man said gently.

"Just look at him," Barberin said again.

"I've never said he's ugly. If he was I wouldn't want him. I don't want a monster."

"Ah, but what if he had two heads, or was a midget. . ."

"Then you'd keep him to make a fortune. But this boy is neither a midget nor a monster, so you can't put him on show. He's no good for anything."

"He's good for work."

"He's not strong."

17

"Not strong! He's as strong as any man. Look at his legs." And Barberin pulled up my trousers.

"Too thin," said the old man.

"And his arms," Barberin went on.

"Like his legs. He could never stand up against fatigue and poverty."

"Well feel them. Just see for yourself."

The old man felt my legs and arms with his bony hand, shaking his head as he did so and making a face. I had already seen something like this when the cattle-dealer came to buy our cow Roussette. He also had felt over and pinched her; he also had shaken his head and said that it was not a good cow, that it would be impossible to sell her again. And yet he had bought her and taken her away with him. Was this old man going to buy me and take me away too?

If I had dared I would have called out that only last night Barberin had said I was delicate and had thin arms and legs, but I knew that if I did I would get nothing but a thump, so I kept quiet. They argued over my good points, my age and my strength, for quite a long time. I was at the end of the table between the pair of them.

At last the old man said: "Well, such as he is, I will take him. But I'm not going to buy. I'll hire him for twenty francs a year. That's fair and I'll pay in advance."

"But if I keep him the home will pay me more than ten francs a month."

"Perhaps seven or eight — I have a far better idea of these things than you, and in any case whatever you get you will have to buy his food."

"He will work."

"If you knew that he could work you wouldn't be so keen on getting rid of him. And if the charity home instead of letting you keep him, passed him on to someone else you would get nothing at all. If you accept my offer all you need to do is to hold out your hand."

He took a leather purse from a pocket and threw four silver

"Not strong! He's as strong as any man. Look at his legs."

coins on the table, making them ring as they fell.

"But his parents may show up any day," Barberin said.

"What about it?"

"Well, those who have brought him up are bound to get something. If I hadn't thought of that I wouldn't have taken him in in the first place."

When I heard this it made me hate him all the more, the wicked man.

"But it's because you think the parents won't show up that you are throwing him out," the old man said, "and if they do appear they'll go straight to you, not to me. No one knows me."

"What about if you find them?"

"In that case we'll go shares, and I'll give you thirty francs here and now."

"Make it forty."

"No, he's not worth that to me."

"What do you want him for? What are you going to do with him?"

The old man gave Barberin a mocking smile and sipped at his drink. "He'll just keep me company. I'm getting old and sometimes at nights when I'm tired I feel lonely. It will be nice to have a child around."

"At any rate his legs will be strong enough for that."

"Oh, he will have to walk, sometimes for hours; and at the end, when he knows how to dance, then he will perform, for he will be a member of Signor Vitalis's travelling troupe."

"Where's the troupe? And who's Signor Vitalis?"

"I am Signor Vitalis, and now I will show you the troupe."

He opened his sheepskin coat and held out a strange-looking animal in his left hand. This, then, was what had moved several times under the sheepskin. But it was not a little dog as I had thought at first, and when I saw it in full view I could not imagine what it could be. I gazed at it in astonishment. It wore a red coat with gold braid trimmings, and its arms and legs were black and hairy. Its head was as large as a clenched fist and it had a turned-up nose and yellowish lips. But what struck me most was its eyes which were close to each other and glittered like glass.

"Oh, an ugly monkey!" Barberin exclaimed.

I was stupefied. Although I had never seen a monkey I had heard of them. And so this little thing that looked like a black baby was a monkey!

"He is the leading star of my company, and his name is Joli-Coeur," said Vitalis. "Joli-Coeur, my friend, make your bow."

The monkey put a hand to his lips and threw us a kiss.

"Now," Signor Vitalis went on, holding out his hand to the poodle, "this is Capi, and he will have the honour of presenting his friends to the esteemed company assembled here."

At this the poodle, who until now hadn't moved, jumped up quickly to stand on his hind legs. He crossed his front paws on his chest and bowed so low to his master that the policeman's helmet touched the floor. This politeness done he turned to his companions and, with one paw still on his chest, signed to them to come nearer. The other two dogs who were watching the poodle carefully got up and, after giving each one of us a paw to shake, stepped six paces back and bowed to everyone.

"The one I call Capi," said Signor Vitalis, "which, of course, is 'Capitano' in Italian, is the leader of my troupe. He is the most intelligent and he passes on my orders to the others. That black shaggy young fellow is Zerbino, which means 'the sport' — look at him and you will see what I mean. As for that modest young person, she is the Signora Dolce, and she is called that because of her lovely nature. With this remarkable troupe I travel all over the country earning my living. My luck is sometimes good, sometimes bad. Capi!"

The poodle crossed his paws.

"Capi, my friend, come here and be on your best behaviour. These people are well brought up and they must be spoken to very politely. Will you be kind enough to tell the time to this young lad who is staring at you with such big round eyes?"

Capi then uncrossed his paws, went to his master, brushed the sheepskin to one side, felt in a waistcoat pocket, and pulled out a big silver watch. He looked at the dial and gave two distinct barks and followed these with three quiet little barks. The time was a quarter to three.

"Excellent," said Vitalis. "Thank you Signor Capi. Now will you ask Signora Dolce to give us the pleasure of seeing her skipping."

Once again Capi felt in one of his master's pockets and this time pulled out a rope. He gave his signal to Zerbino who quickly faced him. Capi then tossed one end of the rope to him and they both picked it up in their mouths and began to turn it. As soon as the turning became regular Dolce started to skip, all the time with her gentle soft eyes on her master.

"You see how intelligent my pupils are," Vitalis said. "But their intelligence would be appreciated even more if I had a clown to act with them. That is why I want your boy in my troupe."

"And so he's going to be a clown," Barberin interrupted.

"It takes a clever person to be a clown, and the boy will be able to act the part after a few lessons. If he has the intelligence I think he has he will know that with me he will be able to see France as well as other countries. But if he stays here all he will do will be to look after cattle in the same fields from morning to night, and then go back to a home where he will not get enough to eat."

I somehow knew this was true. The dogs were very clever and it would be fun to be with them. But I would have to leave Mother Barberin, and even if I refused I might still not be able to stay with her. I was so unhappy that my eyes filled with tears. Vitalis gave my cheek a gentle tap.

"Oh, the boy understands. He is not crying because he does not want to come with us, for he is reasoning things out. Tomorrow..."

"Oh, monsieur," I cried out, "please let me stay with Mother Barberin."

Before I could say anything more Capi's loud barking interrupted me, and at the same time he sprang towards the table where Joli-Coeur was sitting. The little monkey, taking advantage of everyone talking about me, had grabbed his master's glass of wine and was about to drink it. But Capi, the good watchdog, had seen what he was doing and wanted to stop him.

"Joli-Coeur," Vitalis said severely, "you are a glutton and a rogue. Go to the corner and face the wall, and you, Zerbino, keep watch — if he moves give him a slap. As for you, Capi, you are a good dog. Give me a paw so that I may shake hands with you."

The monkey, with little stifled cries, did as he was told, and Capi, happy and proud, held his paw out to his master.

"Now," Vitalis continued, "let's get back to business. I'll give you thirty francs for him."

"No, forty."

The argument started again, but Vitalis soon stopped it by saying: "The boy's bored here. Tell him to go into the courtyard and amuse himself." And as he said this he turned towards Barberin.

"Yes, go out there," Barberin ordered, "but don't you dare move or I will deal with you."

I had to do as I was told and went to the courtyard, but I had no heart to play. I sat on a large stone and waited, wondering. So they were deciding what was to become of me. The cold and worry made me tremble. They talked for a long time, and it was not until an hour later that Barberin came out. He was by himself. Had he come to fetch me and to hand me over to Vitalis?

"Come along you," he said, "we're going home."

Home! Then I wouldn't be leaving Mother Barberin. I wanted to ask questions, but I was afraid for he seemed to be in a very bad temper. We walked all the way in silence, but just before we reached the cottage Barberin who was walking ahead of me stopped. He seized my ear and said:

"If you say one single word of what you have heard today then you will pay for it. Understand?"

CHAPTER FOUR

"Well, and what did the mayor have to say?" Mother Barberin asked when we went in.

"We didn't see him."

"Why was that?"

"I met some friends at the Notre-Dame Café and when we left it was too late. The boy and I are going back tomorrow afternoon."

So Barberin had decided against making a bargain with the man with the dogs. On the way back I had been wondering if returning to the cottage like this he was not up to some trick, but after what he had said I had no more suspicions. It seemed certain that Barberin had not agreed to Vitalis's offer.

In spite of his threats, I would have spoken to Mother Barberin if I could have found a few minutes to be alone with her. But during the whole of the evening Barberin never left the cottage and so I went to bed without getting the chance. I fell asleep thinking that I would tell her the next day, but when I got out of bed she was nowhere to be seen. As I was running around trying to find her Barberin asked me what I was looking for.

"Mother."

"She has gone to the village and won't be back until the afternoon."

I didn't know why but this made me worried, for she had not told me the previous evening that she was going to the village. If we were to go in the afternoon why hadn't she waited for us? Would she be back before we left? Without knowing why I began to feel frightened, and Barberin gave me a look which didn't reassure me. So as to escape from him I went into the garden.

The garden wasn't very big, but it meant a great deal to us for there was no ground wasted and in it we grew almost all we ate — potatoes, beans, cabbages, carrots and turnips. But Mother Barberin had let me have a corner for myself where I had grown different plants that I had pulled up in the lanes while feeding our cow. My garden was not beautiful, but I loved it and it was mine, and I always spoke of it as 'my garden'.

Now the jonquils were in bud, the lilac was about to burst into flower, and the primulas would soon be out. Every day I came to watch them. And there was another part of my garden that I always looked at a little anxiously, for it was here that I had planted a vegetable that someone had given me, and which was almost unknown in our village — it was a Jerusalem artichoke. I had been told that it would produce a lot of tubers like potatoes but tasting much better, for they would have the flavour of French artichokes, turnips and other vegetables all combined. I wanted what I had grown to be a surprise for Mother Barberin, and had not breathed a word about this present I had for her.

When they came through the ground I would let her think that they were some sort of flower, and then when everything was ready, pull them out and cook them myself. How? I wasn't too sure about that, but I didn't worry too much over such a small matter. Then when she came in for supper I would serve her a dish of my own new vegetable. It would be something to replace those everlasting potatoes, and it would help Mother Barberin to forget the sale of poor Roussette. And who would be the inventor of this new dish? Why, me, Remi! I would be of some use in the house after all.

My head was so full of this plan that I had to give very special care to my Jerusalem artichokes. Every day I used to go to where they were planted, and it seemed to me as if they would never grow. I was kneeling down with my nose almost touching the ground where they were when I heard Barberin shouting to me. I ran back to the house and you can imagine how surprised I was when I saw standing in front of the fireplace Vitalis with his dogs.

I understood at once what had been in Barberin's mind.

Vitalis had come to collect me, and so that Mother Barberin would not be able to stop me from leaving he had sent her to the village. I knew only too well that I could expect nothing from Barberin, so ran to Vitalis.

"Oh, monsieur, please don't take me away," and I burst into tears.

"Now, little fellow," he said gently, "you won't be unhappy with me. I never hurt children, and you will have for company my clever dogs. Why should you be sorry to come with me?"

"Anyway you are not going to stay here," Barberin said, pulling my ear. "You either go with Monsieur Vitalis or into the home."

"No, no! Oh, Mother Barberin!"

"So you are trying to make me angry." Barberin was in a terrible temper. "I'll chase you out of here with a stick if I have to."

"The child is upset at leaving his mother, so don't beat him for that. He has feelings and that's a good sign." As he said this Vitalis put eight five-franc pieces on the table, and Barberin very quickly swept them into his pocket.

"Where's his bundle?" Vitalis asked.

"Here it is," replied Barberin, handing him a large blue cotton handkerchief tied at its four corners. "There are two shirts and a pair of linen trousers."

"That's not what was agreed. You said you'd give him some clothes — these are only old rags."

"He has nothing else."

"If I ask the lad I'm sure that he will say that that's not true. But I've no time to argue. We must be off. Come on my boy. Now, what's your name?"

26

"Remi."

"Well, Remi, pick up your bundle and walk beside Capi."

I held out my hand to Barberin, I don't know why, but he turned away. Vitalis took me by the wrist and so I had to go. I looked all about me, my eyes blurred with tears, and called out "Mother Barberin." But there was no answer and my voice ended in a sob. I had to follow Vitalis, for he wouldn't let go of my wrist.

"Good luck," Barberin shouted, and went back into the house. It was all over.

"Come, Remi, you must hurry." Vitalis then took hold of my arm and we walked away side by side. Luckily he was not a fast walker, but when I think back I am sure that he suited his pace to mine.

The road we followed went uphill and at each turn I could see Mother Barberin's house, always getting smaller and smaller. I had walked along this road lots of times, and I knew that when we reached one bend I would be able to see it no longer. Before me was the unknown, and gone was the house where I had spent so many happy days. Perhaps I would never see it again.

When at last we reached the top of the hill Vitalis would still not let go of my arm, and I asked him if we could have a rest.

"Of course," he replied.

He let go of me, but I saw him make a sign to Capi which the dog understood, for he came close to me. Capi was to be my guardian and I knew that he would jump at me if I tried to run away. I went to a high mound covered with turf and sat down with Capi beside me. I looked, my eyes full of tears, for Mother Barberin's cottage, and I could make it out away in the distance. Little puffs of smoke were coming from the chimney, going straight up into the air. I could even make out the rubbish heap and see our big hen pecking about, but she did not look as big as usual; if I had not known it was our hen I would have thought she was a pigeon.

At the side of the cottage I could also see the twisted pear tree on which I used to ride imagining it was a horse, and I could see the outline, too, of the drain running from the stream, which I had

had so much trouble in digging so that it would turn a mill I had somehow made, but which would never work. Who would see the flowers bloom, and who would eat my Jerusalem artichokes? Barberin probably, the horrible man.

When I went back to Vitalis the cottage and the garden would again be hidden from me, but suddenly I saw on the road that led to our cottage from the village a white sun-bonnet which, like a butterfly, disappeared behind some trees and then came into sight again. The distance was great but I was sure that it could only be Mother Barberin.

"Well," Vitalis called out, "shall we go on now?"

"Oh no, monsieur, please."

"Then it must be true what he said, your legs are weak and you are tired already. That doesn't sound very promising for the days ahead."

I didn't reply and just kept on watching. It *was* Mother Barberin wearing her bonnet and blue petticoat. She was walking quickly as if she was in a hurry to get home. When she reached our gate she pushed it open and went quickly through the yard. I jumped up and stood on the highest part of the mound at once, without giving a thought to Capi who sprang towards me.

Mother Barberin didn't stay long in the cottage. She came out and began running about the yard with outstretched arms. She was looking everywhere for me. I leaned forward and cried out with all the strength of my lungs:

"Mother, Mother!" But my voice could not reach her.

"What's the matter? Have you gone crazy?" Vitalis asked.

I didn't answer him, for I was still gazing at Mother Barberin. But she could not know that I was there and did not look up. Then she looked in both directions along the road. I called out louder, but it was no use. Vitalis came up beside me, and it was not long before he, too, saw the white bonnet.

"Poor little lad," I heard him murmur.

"Do let me go back," I said to him, for I was encouraged by what he had said.

But all he did was to take me by the wrist and lead me down to the road.

"Now that you are rested we must move on."

I tried to get free, but he was holding me too firmly.

"Capi! Zerbino!" And the dogs came near me, one behind and the other in front. After walking a little further I turned round; we had passed beyond the crest of the hill and I could no longer see either the valley or the cottage.

CHAPTER FIVE

It does not mean because a man buys a child for forty francs that he is an ogre and intends to eat him. Vitalis had no wish to eat me and although he bought children he was not by any means a bad man. Indeed, I soon had proof of this. We had reached the top of a mountain overlooking the Loire and Dordogne, and after walking for about a quarter of an hour he let go of my arm. I gave a sigh of relief.

"I know how you feel," he said. "You may cry as much as you like, but try and think that this is for your own good. Those people were not your father and mother. The wife was good to you and you loved her, and she loved you — that is why you are feeling so bad. Remember that she couldn't have kept you if her husband didn't want you about the place. He is sick and he can't work any more, and life will be hard for him. But he may not be such a bad chap after all."

No doubt what he said was true, but there was only one thought in my mind and that was that I would never see Mother Barberin again. I loved her most in the world for she had always been so kind and good to me.

"You will not be unhappy with me," Vitalis went on, "and don't ever try to run away, because if you do you will soon be caught by Capi and Zerbino."

Me run away? Where could I go if I did? After all, this old man with his white beard might turn out to be a kind master. It was the

30

first time I had walked so far, and all around us were barren hills and valleys.

My master strode along carrying Joli-Coeur on his shoulder or sometimes in his bag, and the dogs trotted along beside us. Vitalis now and then said a friendly word to them, sometimes in French and sometimes in a language which I couldn't understand. Neither he nor his animals seemed to get tired, but I was worn out and could hardly put one foot after the other. It was all I could do to keep up with them.

"It's those clogs that are the trouble," Vitalis said. "When we get to Ussel I will buy you a pair of boots."

I was cheered up. I had always wanted to wear boots — the mayor's sons and the innkeeper wore them so that on Sundays when they came to mass they seemed somehow to glide along the flagstones, while we others in our clogs made such a dreadful din.

"Is Ussel very far away?"

"Ah, that's spoken from your heart," Vitalis said with a laugh. "So you would like a pair of boots? Well, you'll have a pair, and with big nails too. I'll also get you a pair of velvet trousers, and a jacket and a hat. That will dry your tears and give you the strength to walk the miles that are left."

Boots with nails! I was dazzled at the thought of them. Velvet trousers, a jacket and a hat! If Mother Barberin could see me how happy and proud she would be. But all the same I was beginning to wonder if I would ever reach Ussel.

The sky had been blue when we started off, but now grey clouds were coming up, and soon it started drizzling. Vitalis was well enough protected in his sheepskin and was able to shelter Joli-Coeur, who at the first drop of rain had got quickly into his bag. But the dogs and I had nothing to cover us and soon we were soaked. The dogs could shake themselves, but I had to tramp on with wet clothes which made me shiver.

"Do you catch cold easily?" Vitalis asked.

"I don't know. I can't remember ever having a cold."

"That's good. But I don't want you to run any risks. There is a village not very far away and we will sleep there."

31

There was no inn in the village when we reached it, and nobody would give shelter to an old beggar who was trailing along with him a small boy and three dogs, all soaking wet.

"No lodgings here," they said, and closed their doors in our faces.

Must we trudge another few miles to Ussel without sleeping? Night fell, the rain was cold, and as far as I was concerned my legs felt like blocks of wood. Oh, for Mother Barberin's cottage! In the end a peasant who was more kindly disposed than his neighbours agreed to open a barn for us on condition that we went to sleep without any light.

"You give me your matches," he said to Vitalis, "and I'll give them back to you tomorrow when you leave."

At least we had a roof over our heads. From the bag slung over his shoulders Vitalis took a hunk of bread, and it was then that I saw again how well-trained his troupe was. When we had been going from door to door asking for shelter Zerbino had gone into one of the houses and come out again almost at once carrying some bread in his jaws. I had thought no more of this until I saw Vitalis dividing his bread, and Zerbino looked very dejected. Vitalis and I were sitting on two bundles of bracken with Joli-Coeur between us. The three dogs sat in a row in front of us, Capi and Dolce with their eyes fixed on their master and Zerbino with his ears drooping.

"Zerbino the thief will go into a corner and sleep without any supper," Vitalis commanded. At once Zerbino left where he was sitting and dejectedly went to the corner Vitalis pointed to. He crouched out of sight under some bracken, but we could hear him giving little whimpers every now and then.

Vitalis then gave me a piece of bread, and while eating his own broke off pieces for Joli-Coeur, Capi and Dolce. I longed for Mother Barberin's hot soup, the warm fire, and my bed with the blankets pulled up to my nose. I sat there tired out and my feet nearly raw from the clogs. I was shaking with the cold from my wet clothes. It was quite dark now but I had no thought of sleeping.

"Your teeth are chattering," Vitalis said, and I heard him open his bag. "I haven't much of a wardrobe," he continued, "but here's a dry shirt and vest you can change into. Then get under some bracken and it won't be long before you are warm and asleep."

But I didn't get warm as quickly as all that and for a long time I kept turning over, too unhappy to sleep. Would it always go on like this, tramping along in the rain, sleeping in some barn, shaking with cold and only a piece of dry bread for supper? I was feeling very sorry for myself and tears rolled down my cheeks. Then suddenly I felt a warm breath on my face. I stretched out a hand and my fingers touched Capi's woolly coat. He had crept softly over to me, and soon he was close beside me gently licking my hand. I sat up, and throwing my arms around his neck, kissed his cold nose. He gave a little whine, put his paw in my hand, and then remained quite still.

I forgot all my tiredness and sorrow. I was alone no longer for now I had a friend.

Early next morning we started again. The rain had stopped, the sky was blue, and during the night the wind had dried the mud. Birds were singing happily and the dogs gambolled about us — indeed, every now and then Capi stood on his hind paws and barked to show how pleased he was. He understood everything, and he knew how to make you understand.

I had never left my village and was looking forward to seeing what a town looked like. But what I most wanted to see was a bootmaker's shop. I looked about me in every direction as we walked through the old streets of Ussel. The only memory that remains with me of the town is of a shop close to the market-place. In the front of it hung some old guns, a number of lamps, and a lot of old rusty keys. We walked down three steps and were in a large room which I don't think ever saw the light of day.

How could such lovely things as boots with nails be sold in such a dismal place? But Vitalis knew, and it was not very long before I had the joy of wearing the kind of boots he had promised me, and which were three times heavier than my clogs. And as he had also

Vitalis explained the actions in the comedy as it was acted.

promised me, Vitalis then bought for me a blue velvet shirt, a pair of woollen trousers, and a felt hat.

Velvet for me who had never worn anything better than cotton! Vitalis was certainly the most generous man in the world. True the velvet was creased, the wool a little worn, and the hat had been so soaked with rain that it was difficult to know its original colour, but I was dazzled by so much finery and anything else meant nothing to me.

When we got to an inn Vitalis, to my astonishment, took a pair of scissors from his bag and shortened the legs of my trousers so that when I put them on for the first time they came to only just above my knees. I looked at him round-eyed.

"I am doing this because I don't want you to look like every other boy," he explained. "While we are in France you will dress like an Italian boy, and if we go to Italy like a French boy."

I was even more astonished when he continued: "We are travelling players and we don't dress like ordinary folk. If we went about dressed like them do you think that anyone would stop to watch us? No, for appearances count more than you think, as you will learn."

My trousers shortened Vitalis then criss-crossed lengths of red cord about my legs above my ankles to my knees, and twisted red ribbons over my hat which he then decorated with a sort of posy of woollen flowers. I don't know what other people imagined I looked like, but I thought I looked wonderful. Capi thought so too for he gazed at me for a long time and then held out his paw. I was glad that Capi approved. While I was being dressed Joli-Coeur had been sitting opposite me and when everything was finished he put his hands on his hips, threw back his head, and made mocking little cries of laughter.

I suppose it is a matter of guesswork as to whether all monkeys do really laugh, but I lived close to Joli-Coeur for quite a time and I know that he, at any rate, certainly did laugh — often in a way that humiliated me. Of course his laugh was not like yours or mine, but when something really amused him he would screw up his eyes, draw back the corners of his mouth, and move his jaws as

35

if he were going to burst into laughter.

"Now that we are ready," Vitalis said as I put on my hat, "we'll get to work. Tomorrow is market-day and we will give a grand performance for your first appearance. You will play in a comedy with the dogs and Joli-Coeur."

"But I don't know how to play in a comedy," I said nervously.

"You don't know unless you learn. These animals have studied hard to know their parts. It has been difficult for them but you can see how clever they are. The piece we are going to play is called 'Monsieur Joli-Coeur's Servant; or, the simpleton is not always the one you think.' Now, I'll explain everything to you. Monsieur Joli-Coeur has until now had a servant and he has been very pleased with him. The servant is Capi and he is leaving because he is getting old, but Capi has promised that before he goes he will get Joli-Coeur another one. His successor is not to be a dog, but a boy — a country-boy named Remi. You have just come from your village to enter Monsieur Joli-Coeur's service."

"But monkeys don't have servants."

"In comedies they do. Well, you have come straight from your village and your new master thinks you are a fool."

"But I am not a fool and I don't like that idea at all."

"It doesn't matter if it makes everyone laugh. Well now, you have come to this gentleman to be his servant and been told to set the table. Here is one just the same as we shall use in the comedy. Go and set it."

On the table were a white cloth, plates, and a knife and fork. How could I set them properly? As I pondered and leant forward with outstretched hands, my mouth open, and with no idea of how to begin, Vitalis clapped his hands and burst out laughing.

"Excellent," he said, "that's perfect."

"But I don't know what I have to do."

"That's why you are so good. You are natural, and that is splendid. After you do know you will have to pretend and if you get the same look on your face, and stand as you were standing then, you'll be a great success."

As you can imagine 'Monsieur Joli-Coeur's Servant' was not a masterpiece. Its performance lasted no longer than twenty minutes. Vitalis made us all rehearse over and over again, and I was surprised to see how patient he was for in my village I had seen performing animals treated badly. Although we rehearsed for a long time I did not once see him get angry. When a mistake had been made all he would say rather sternly was: "Now we'll do that all over again. Capi, you didn't do that well." And: "Joli-Coeur, I'll scold you if you don't pay attention."

And that was all, but it was enough.

When the rehearsals were ended he said to me, "You are intelligent and attentive. But look at the dogs and compare them with Joli-Coeur. Probably he is intelligent too, but he's impatient. He learns easily enough but he forgets almost at once what he has been taught, and he never willingly does what he is told. It's his nature to do the opposite and that's why I don't get angry with him. Monkeys have not the same understanding as a dog has and that is the reason why they are inferior to a dog when it comes to obedience. Do you understand what I am saying?"

"I think I do."

"Well, be obedient and do your best whatever you have to do. Remember that all your life."

I summoned up courage then to ask him what had astonished me so much during rehearsals — how he could be so very patient with Joli-Coeur, the dogs and me. He smiled.

"It is clear that you have lived among peasants who often are unkind to animals and think that they can only be made to obey by threats. That is stupid. Nothing can ever be gained by cruelty and a lot, if not everything, by gentleness. It is because I am never unkind to my animals that they are what they are. If I had beaten them they would be frightened creatures, for fear paralyses intelligence. As I have given lessons to my animals so I have received lessons from them. I have developed their intelligence and they have formed my character."

This seemed strange to me and I laughed.

"You think that odd," Vitalis continued, "odd that a dog should be able to teach a man, but it's true. Think a little. Then

37

you will understand that the master must watch what he does when he teaches his dog, for that dog will take after the master. Show me your dog and I'll tell you what you are. The criminal's dog is a scoundrel, the burglar's dog a thief, and the peasant's dog is stupid. A kind man has a friendly dog."

My comrades in the troupe had the great advantage over me of having appeared before in public, and I was very nervous at the thought of the next day. I didn't sleep soundly. We marched off in procession to the market-place with Vitalis leading the way. Holding his head high and with his chest out he kept time with his hands and feet as he played a lively tune on his flute. Behind him trotted Capi with Joli-Coeur on his back wearing the uniform of a British general and a helmet topped with a plume. Next, at a respectful distance, came Zerbino and Dolce stepping delicately side by side. I brought up the rear. The sound of the flute brought the people, filled with curiosity, running from their houses, and windows opened. Lots of children followed us and by the time we reached the square we had attracted quite a crowd. Our theatre was quickly set up, for all that was needed was to tie a rope to four trees and we took our places in the middle of the space.

The first part of the programme was made up of various turns performed by the dogs, but what they were I cannot remember because I had an attack of stage-fright. All that I can recall now was that Vitalis had put his flute down and taken up his violin to play an accompaniment — sometimes dance music and sometimes rather sentimental tunes.

The audience pressed against the ropes. When each turn was ended Capi took a wooden bowl between his jaws and, walking on his hind legs, went among the crowd. When anyone did not drop a coin in he tapped the pocket of the spectator two or three times with one of his front paws. At this everyone laughed and called out with delight.

"That's a clever poodle, that one, he knows whose pockets are well-lined."

"Put your hand in your pocket!"

"He'll give something!"

38

"No, he won't."

"And that one has just had a legacy from his uncle!"

In the end something was always thrown into the bowl. While all this was going on Vitalis, without saying a word but always with an eye on Capi, played his violin. Capi returned to his master proudly carrying a full bowl.

Now it was time for my turn with Joli-Coeur.

"Ladies and gentlemen," Vitalis announced, waving his bow in one hand and the violin in the other, "we are going to present a delightful comedy called 'Monsieur Joli-Coeur's Servant; or, the fool is not always the one you would think.' A man with my reputation does not need to lower himself by praising his plays or his actors in advance. All I shall say is that you should watch, listen and be ready to applaud."

Of course, what Vitalis called 'a delightful comedy' was really a pantomime. It had to be, for the good reason that its two principals, Joli-Coeur and Capi, couldn't speak, and the third, me, was too nervous to say more than two words altogether. However, so that the audience could understand what was going on on the stage, Vitalis explained the actions in the comedy as it was acted. For instance, when he announced the entrance of General Joli-Coeur, who had gained his high rank through battles in India, he took on a martial air. Until his promotion to General Joli-Coeur had only been able to afford to have Capi waiting on him, but now he wanted a man-servant as well.

While Joli-Coeur waited for his new servant to arrive he walked up and down smoking his cigar, and you should have seen the way he blew the smoke into the faces of the audience. Then, becoming impatient, the General began to roll his eyes as if he were about to lose his temper — he bit his lips and stamped about. At the third stamp I had to make my entry, led by Capi. If I had forgotten, the poodle would have given me a reminder for at a given moment Capi held out his paw to introduce me to the General who, seeing me, held up his hands in despair. What was all this? Was this the servant they had found for him? Then he came and looked closely at my face, and walked all round me shrugging his shoulders.

39

His expression was so comical that everyone burst out laughing for they understood perfectly that Joli-Coeur thought I was a fool, and so did they. The act was intended to show how awkward and slow-witted I was, while every chance was given to the monkey to display his cleverness and shrewdness. After a thorough examination the General took pity on me and decided to keep me.

"The General thinks that after his new servant has had something to eat he won't be such an idiot," Vitalis explained.

I was seated at a little table which had already been set, with a napkin on my plate. But what did I do with a napkin? Capi signed to me to unfold it. I looked thoughtful for a moment and then used it to blow my nose. The General held his sides laughing, while Capi rolled over on his back waving his paws in the air at my stupidity.

Seeing that I had made a mistake I stared again at the napkin wondering how I should use it. Then I had an idea. I rolled it up and made it into a tie. There was more laughter from the General, and once again Capi rolled over with his paws in the air. Finally, overcome with exasperation, the General pulled me from my chair, sat down at my place, and ate the meal that had been meant for me. He knew what the napkin was for! Elegantly he tucked it into a buttonhole in his uniform and spread it over his knees. With what beautiful manners he broke his bread and emptied his glass!

Lunch ended, he gestured for a toothpick which he used to the manner born. At this there was applause from everyone. What an intelligent monkey, and what a fool of a servant!

On the way back to the inn Vitalis praised my performance. I was already a good comedian, and I was so very proud of myself.

CHAPTER SIX

While Vitalis's troupe was certainly full of talent it was not very versatile, and so we gave at the most only four performances in each town. Three days after our arrival at Ussel we were on the road again. I had now become bold enough to ask my master where we were going.

"Do you know this part of France?" And he looked at me.

"No."

"Then why do you ask where we are going?"

"Just to know."

"To know what?"

I could not answer and could only look at the road which stretched ahead of us. He looked at me thoughtfully for a moment and then asked: "Can you read?"

"No."

"In a book I will show you when we sit down for a rest you will find the names and history of the towns and countries we are going to travel through. It will be like having a story read to you, and you will learn from it."

It is true that I had been sent to the village school but it was only for a month, and during that time I had never once held a book in my hands. I was really brought up in ignorance. At the time I am talking about there were large parts of France where there were

41

no schools, and where there were the teachers were either poorly educated themselves or had some other part-time work, and so could do little in the way of teaching the few pupils they had. This was certainly true of the schoolmaster in our village. We learned nothing, not even the alphabet, for he was a clog-maker by trade, sitting most of the time at his bench shaping beechwood and walnut.

After we had been walking in silence for some time I said to Vitalis: "Is it difficult to read? I would love to learn if you would teach me."

"Well, we shall see. We have plenty of time ahead of us."

Time ahead of us! Why not start at once? I did not know how difficult it was to learn to read, for I thought that I had just to open any book to know what was inside. As we continued on our way the following day Vitalis stooped down and picked up a thin piece of wood covered in dust.

"Look, this is the book from which you are going to learn to read," he said.

A piece of wood a book! I looked at him to see if he was joking, but he seemed quite serious so I stared at the wood. It was a piece of beech as long as my arm and as wide as my two hands. There were no marks of any kind on it.

"Wait until we get to that clump of trees down there where we will have a rest," he said, "and I'll show you how to read from this."

We soon reached the trees, threw what we were carrying on the ground, and sat down where daisies dotted the grass. Joli-Coeur, who had been unchained, sprang into a tree and shook the branches as though he was trying to make nuts fall. The tired dogs settled down beside us. Then Vitalis took out his knife and when he had smoothed both sides of the wood started to cut out twelve pieces all the same size. I never took my eyes off him. I knew that a book was made up of pages on which were black signs — but where were the pages and the signs?

"Now, I am going to cut a letter out of each piece of wood, and you will learn these letters from their shapes. When you are able to tell at a glance what they are I'll then make them into words, and when you are able to read the words then you will learn from a book."

I soon had my pockets full of bits of wood and was not long in learning the alphabet. But to know how to read was a very different thing. I could not get along very fast and often I was sorry that I had said that I wanted to learn. It was not because I was lazy, it was really pride — for while teaching me my letters Vitalis had the idea of teaching Capi at the same time. If a dog could learn to tell the time from a watch why couldn't he learn the alphabet? The bits of wood were all spread out on the grass and Capi was taught that he must pull towards him the letter that had been pointed out to him.

At first my progress was faster than Capi's but if I had quicker intelligence he had a far better memory. Once he learnt a thing, he never forgot it. When I made a mistake Vitalis would say: "Capi will learn to read before you, Remi."

And Capi, obviously understanding, proudly shook his tail.

I was so put out by this that I applied myself with all my heart. So, while the poor dog could get no further than pulling out the four letters which spelt his name I, at long last, learned to read from a book.

"Now that you can read words how would you like to read music?" Vitalis asked me.

"If I knew how to read music would I be able to sing like you?"

"You like hearing me sing don't you?"

"I like it more than anything else. Sometimes I want to cry and sometimes to laugh when I hear you singing. Don't think I am being silly but when you sing your songs I think that I am back with Mother Barberin, for if I shut my eyes I can see her again in our cottage. But I don't understand the words because they are all in Italian."

As I spoke I looked up at him and saw that his eyes were filled with tears, so I stopped and asked him if what I had just said had hurt him.

"No, my child," he replied, his voice trembling, "you haven't

43

hurt me. Quite the contrary, for you have taken me back to my happy childhood days. Don't worry, I will teach you to sing and as you are so understanding you, too, will one day make people weep, and applaud you."

He stopped suddenly, and I am sure that for the time being he did not wish to say anything more. I could not have known then the reason why he felt so sad, but I did learn why some time afterwards, and I will tell you the reason later in my story.

Next day Vitalis cut out little pieces of wood for the music notes just as he had done for my letters. The notes were much more complicated than the alphabet, and I found them a great deal harder to learn. Vitalis, so patient with the dogs, lost patience with me more than once.

"With an animal," he cried, "one can control oneself because it is a dumb creature, but you are enough to drive anyone crazy," and he would wave his arms about.

Joli-Coeur always took particular delight in imitating gestures that he thought funny and so he mimicked Vitalis. As the monkey was always there when I was being given my lessons I had the humiliation of seeing him also lifting his arms in despair whenever I hesitated or made a mistake.

"You see," said Vitalis, "even Joli-Coeur is mocking you."

I suppose that if I had dared I would have said that Joli-Coeur was mocking Vitalis as well as me, but my respect for him stopped me. Finally after weeks, months, of hard work I was able to sing a tune that Vitalis himself had composed. That day my master did not wave his arms about in the air but, instead, he patted my cheek and said that if I continued to do so well I would one day most certainly become a great singer.

Our way of travelling had no sort of plan — we simply followed the road in front of us and when we were near a village which did not look too poverty-stricken we began our preparations for a triumphal entry. It was my job to dress up the dogs. I combed Dolce's hair, got Zerbino ready, put a plaster over Capi's eye when he was acting the part of a grumbling old man and, finally, made Joli-Coeur get into his General's uniform. This last was the

"When you are able to tell at a glance what they are I'll then make them into words."

most difficult thing to do, for the monkey knew only too well that this was the start of work for him and he thought up the oddest tricks to stop me from dressing him. More often than not I had to call on Capi for his help, and between the two of us we were able in the end to defeat all his tricks.

When everything was ready Vitalis took his flute and we marched into the village. If enough people started following us we would give a performance, but if there were only a few stragglers we simply continued on our way. If we stayed several days in a town Vitalis would let me go out in the morning for a walk, but always Capi was with me.

Vitalis once said to me: "You are travelling through France, when most boys of your age are at school. Open your eyes and look around you and learn. If you see something you don't understand don't be afraid to ask me questions. I have not always been leading a troupe of animals, and I have learned a lot of other things."

"What are they?" I asked.

"We will talk about them some other time. For the present just listen to my advice, and when you are much older I hope that you will remember gratefully the poor musician you were so afraid of when he took you from your adopted mother, for that may not have done you any harm after all."

I often wondered what my master had been in earlier days, and who his family was.

After we had left the Auvergne we plodded on until we reached the desolate plains of Quercy. There was not a river, nor a brook, nor a pond to be seen. In the middle of the plain we came to a large village called Bastide-Murat, and we spent the night in a barn belonging to the inn.

"It was here," Vitalis told me that evening, "and quite possibly in this inn, that a man was born who would lead thousands of soldiers to their deaths. He started life as a stable-boy and later became a prince and a king. His name was Murat. They called him a hero and this village was named after him. I knew him and we often talked together."

"When he was a stable-boy?"

46

"No," answered Vitalis with a laugh, "when he was a king. This is the first time I have been in this part of the country, and it was in Naples that I knew him when he was King."

"You have known a king!"

The tone in which I said this must have sounded rather comical for Vitalis burst into long and loud laughter. We were sitting on a bench in front of the stable with our backs against the wall, which was still warm from the sun. In a great sycamore which sheltered us the cicadas were clicking away. The full moon had just risen over the tops of the houses, and the evening seemed all the more peaceful after a scorchingly hot day.

"Do you want to go to sleep, or would you rather I told you the story of King Joachim Murat?" Vitalis asked.

"Oh yes please, do tell me the story."

Then he told me all about Murat while we sat on the bench for hours. As he talked the moonlight fell on him and I listened with my eyes fixed on his face. I had never heard of Murat, and who else could have told me? Certainly not Mother Barberin, for she had been born in Chavanon and would probably die there.

My master had seen a king and this king had talked to him! I wondered what he could have been when he was young, and how he had come to be like this, as I saw him now in his old age.

We continued our travels, seeing the river Dordogne and reaching Bordeaux, where we gave several performances. From Bordeaux we followed the banks of the Garonne and came to the Landes, which seemed like a desert. We saw the ocean, and we walked, and walked. At last Vitalis said to me that we should reach somewhere that evening where we could sleep. But night fell and there was no sign of any village, nor even smoke to show that we were near a house.

I was very tired and longed to go to sleep, and Vitalis was tired too, for we had been tramping since early morning. He decided to stop and rest for a while on the roadside, but instead of sitting down beside him I wanted to climb a small hill which was covered with broom and some distance from the road. From there I might be able to see a village. I called to Capi, but he was tired too and

47

wouldn't move, which was unusual.

"Aren't you afraid to go alone?" Vitalis asked.

This made me set off at once. There was no moon and it was a bit misty, but the stars were shining. Looking to right and left I saw what strange forms the things around me took in the mist. The higher I climbed the thicker the broom and bracken became, their tops often being over my head; and sometimes I had to make my way on my hands and knees. But I was determined to get to the top of that hill.

When at last I did and gazed about me I could see no light anywhere — nothing but weird shapes and forms, and broom which seemed to hold out long branches to entangle me. I listened for a noise somewhere, the mooing of a cow or the barking of a dog. I stood quietly for a minute, hardly breathing so that I could hear better. Then I started to shiver, for the silence scared me. What could I be frightened of? The silence of the night probably, but anyhow I was gripped by a fear I could not understand.

I looked around and in the distance I could see an enormous shadow moving among the broom, and then at the same time I heard branches rustling. I tried to tell myself that it was only fear that made me imagine I had seen something unusual, and that it could, somehow, be only some shrub I had not noticed before. But there was not even a breath of wind, and branches don't move unless there is some sort of breeze or someone touches them.

Someone? No, this big black form that was coming closer could not be a man. Perhaps it was some kind of animal that I did not know of, or an enormous night bird, or even an immense spider hovering over the trees. Whatever it was it was moving towards me quickly. Strength came back to me and I raced down the hill to Vitalis. But curiously I was slower going down that when I was coming up. I threw myself into some broom and heather and, crawling along, I was torn and scratched. Scrambling out of a thicket I looked back, only to see whatever it was was coming closer and almost upon me.

By good luck the ground was now covered only with brushwood and I could run quicker. Although I ran as fast as I possibly could the thing kept gaining on me. There was no need for me to look behind for I felt that it was almost on my back. I made one last effort and fell among the dogs at my master's feet. I was only able to say "The beast! The beast!"

Above the barking of the dogs I heard peals of laughter. At the same time Vitalis put a hand on my shoulder and made me turn round. I opened my eyes and looked where he was pointing. The apparition that had frightened me so badly had stopped and was standing still on the road. At the sight of it I began to tremble again, but I was with Vitalis and the dogs were near. I was no longer on the hilltop.

Could it be an animal or a man? It had the body, the head and the arms of a human, but the hairy skin that covered it and its two long skinny legs with funny feet like paws looked as if they belonged to some strange sort of beast. Although it was a dark night I could distinguish all this. I would have stayed staring for a long time if Vitalis had not spoken to it.

"Can you tell me if we are very far from a village?" he asked.

So it was human, and you can imagine my astonishment when the reply came that there were no houses near, only an inn and he would lead us to it. If he could talk why did he have paws? If I had had enough courage I would have gone to see what the paws were made of, but I was still more than a little scared and so I picked up my bag and followed Vitalis without saying a word.

"You see now what gave you such a fright," he said.

"But I still don't know what it is. Are there giants in this part of the country?"

"Yes, when men walk on stilts."

Then he explained to me that in the Landes, in order to cross the sandy or boggy ground and not sink to their hips, people strode about on stilts like giants with seven-league boots.

CHAPTER SEVEN

I have happy memories of Pau, where the wind hardly ever blew. We stayed there for the whole of one winter for Capi's collecting bowl was almost always filled to overflowing. Our audiences were mainly children and they never tired of us giving the same performances time and time again. They were mostly British children, and it was from them that I acquired a taste for sweets, for they came with their pockets full of them and generously shared them with Joli-Coeur, the dogs and me.

But when spring came with its warmer days our audiences became smaller, and after performances they would come to say goodbye and to shake hands with us all. And so we had to leave too. For a long time, I cannot remember for how many days or weeks, we tramped through valleys and over hills leaving behind the blue peaks of the Pyrenees.

Then one night we reached a very big town beside a river. All its houses seemed to be made of red brick, and the streets were paved with small pointed cobblestones which were very hard on the feet of travellers like us who had walked many miles each day. My master told me that this was Toulouse, and that we would be staying there for some time. As usual, the first thing we did after we had arrived was to look for a suitable place where we could perform. There were any number of these, especially near the Botanical Gardens with its beautiful lawns shaded by big trees and with avenues leading to and through it. It was near one of these avenues that we gave our first performance to a quite large audience.

By ill-luck a policeman saw us arranging our things and seemed annoyed, perhaps because he did not like dogs or because he thought we had no business to be there. At any rate he tried to send us away. It would probably have been wiser if we had packed up and gone, for we were certainly not strong enough to hold out against the police. But Vitalis was a proud man, even though he was old and wandering about the country with his animals. He felt that he was not breaking any law and that the police should protect him, so when he was told that we must move on he refused.

Vitalis was very polite, indeed he carried his Italian politeness to extremes, addressing the policeman as if he were someone who held a very high position in the city. "Can the illustrious gentleman who represents authority," he said, raising his hat, "show me the regulation which states that it is forbidden for strolling players like ourselves to carry on their miserable profession in a public place?"

The policeman answered that he was not going to enter into any discussion and that he must be obeyed.

"Certainly," Vitalis replied, "and I promise that we will do so as soon as you can show me what authority you have to move us."

On that particular day the policeman turned away from us and Vitalis, hat in hand and bowing, gave a quiet chuckle. But on the following day the same policeman returned and jumped over the ropes that made our stage. As it happened he arrived in the middle of one of our acts called 'Illness cured'.

"Muzzle your dogs," he said in a rough voice to Vitalis.

"Muzzle my dogs?"

"It's a police regulation. You ought to know that."

The audience started to protest. "Don't interrupt!" and "Let him finish the show!" were some of the things they called out.

Vitalis put up his hand asking for silence. Then he took off his hat, and with its plumes sweeping the ground he made three deep bows to the policeman.

"Does the illustrious gentleman representing the law say that I

51

must muzzle my comedians?"

"Yes, and be quick about it."

"Muzzle Capi, Zerbino and Dolce?" Vitalis called out, more to the audience than to the policeman. "How can the wise Doctor Capi, known all over the world, prescribe a cure for Joli-Coeur if he wears a muzzle on the end of his nose?"

At this children and parents started to laugh. Encouraged by this Vitalis went on: "And how can the delightful nurse Dolce use her eloquence to persuade the patient to take the medicine that will cure if *she* has a muzzle on the end of *her* nose? I ask my audience, can this be fair?"

The audience roared with laughter and Vitalis was given a cheer. Everyone was amused, above all by Joli-Coeur who had gone behind the policeman and was making faces at him. The policeman crossed his arms, then uncrossed them and put one fist on his hip and threw back his head — and Joli-Coeur did exactly the same. This brought more laughter. Provoked by Vitalis's little speech and very annoyed by all the laughter the policeman, who did not give the impression of being a very patient man, turned round suddenly to see what all the laughter was about, only to see the monkey's imitations of him. For some moments monkey and policeman stared at each other, and it became only a question of time as to who would lower his eyes first. The crowd yelled with delight.

"If your dogs are not muzzled tomorrow you'll be arrested. That's all I have to say." And the policeman angrily shook his fist.

"Until tomorrow then, signor," Vitalis replied.

As the policeman strode away Vitalis almost bent in two in an attitude of respect. Then the performance continued.

I thought that he would buy muzzles for the dogs, but not a bit of it, and the evening passed without any mention of his quarrel with the policeman. At last I decided to speak about it.

"If you don't want Capi to tear off his muzzle during the performance tomorrow," I said, "I think it would be a good idea to put it on soon so that he can get used to it. We can easily teach him that he must keep it on."

"So you think I am going to muzzle my dogs?"

"Well it seems to me that if you don't we're going to have trouble with that policeman."

"You're only a country lad, and like all people who live in towns you are afraid of policemen. But don't worry, I'll arrange things tomorrow so that I can't be arrested and at the same time see that the dogs won't be too unhappy. And the audience will be amused too. What I am going to do is see that this policeman brings in more money and plays the comic role in the act that I'm thinking up into the bargain.

"Now, tomorrow you will go along with Joli-Coeur, attend to the ropes, play some music on your harp, and when there is a big enough audience you can be sure that our policeman will come on the scene. Just then I will arrive with the dogs — and the fun will start."

I was not at all happy about this arrangement but I did what I was told. By now I could play the harp quite well and, I like to think, sing very well. Among the songs I knew was a Neapolitan 'canzonetta' which was always applauded. But that day I knew only too well that the crowd had not come to hear me. All those who were there the day before had come along and brought their friends with them, for policemen in Toulouse are not popular favourites and people were curious to see how the old Italian would come out of the affair, and what was meant by his words "Until tomorrow then, Signor." Indeed, one of the audience seeing me alone there with Joli-Coeur interrupted my singing to ask if the 'old Italian' would be coming.

"He will arrive soon," I answered.

The policeman appeared. Joli-Coeur saw him first, and at once repeated his previous imitations and started trotting about in a ridiculously important way. The crowd laughed at these antics and clapped. The policeman was disconcerted by this and glared at me, which caused more laughter. I was beginning to feel uncertain and was wondering how it would all end. If Vitalis was there he could stand up to the policeman, but I was alone, and what if I should be ordered away. Joli-Coeur could not be

53

expected to understand how serious the situation was and continued to strut along inside the ropes side by side with the policeman, copying every movement he made. And as the monkey passed me he looked at me over his shoulder and made such comical faces that the crowd laughed even louder.

I was beginning to feel that matters had gone far enough so I called to Joli-Coeur to stay beside me. But he was in no mood to obey and continued his perambulations, dodging me when I tried to grab hold of him. I can't tell you exactly how it happened but the policeman, who was becoming more and more angry, thought I was encouraging the monkey and jumped over the rope. In seconds I had been knocked to the ground with a blow from his fist. When I had got to my feet again I saw Vitalis, who had sprung from I don't know where, standing between me and the policeman and holding his wrist.

"You are not to hit that boy. What a cowardly thing to do!"

The policeman tried to free his wrist but Vitalis would not let go. For some little time the two men glared at each other. The policeman was purple in the face, but Vitalis was superb — he held his beautiful white head high and his face was full of indignation. I thought that the policeman would disappear into the earth but he did nothing of the sort. With a sudden movement he wrenched his wrist free, grabbed Vitalis by the collar and gave him a push. Vitalis stumbled and nearly fell, but he quickly regained his balance and lifting his right arm he struck the policeman sharply on a wrist. My master was an old man and still quite strong, but the policeman was young and much stronger. Any struggle could only be brief, but there was no struggle.

"You are under arrest. Come along with me."

"Why did you hit that boy?"

"No more talking. Follow me."

Vitalis did not reply and, instead, turned to me. "Go back to the inn," he said, "and stay there with the dogs. I will send word to you."

Vitalis had no chance to say any more for he was dragged away. So ended the performance that my master had wanted to be funny

54

and which had ended so sadly. The dogs started to follow him, but I ordered them back and they returned to me. It was then that I saw that they were muzzled, but not with the usual kind of muzzle — all they had on was a silk ribbon with a rosette and tied under the chin. Capi, who was white, wore red; Zerbino, who was black, white; Dolce, who was grey, blue. Vitalis had obeyed the law.

The audience, except for a few stragglers, quickly dispersed.

"The old man was in the right."

"He was wrong."

"Why did the policeman hit the boy? He hadn't said a word and had done nothing."

"It's a bad business and the old man will go to gaol."

I went back to the inn feeling very depressed. Every day I had grown more and more fond of Vitalis. We had lived the same life together, and at night we had often shared the same bed of straw. No father could have shown more affection. He had taught me to read, sing, write and count. During our long tramps he had given me lessons, and on hot days he had always helped to carry the bags and other things which I was supposed to. When we ate he never kept the best food for himself, but shared it out equally. Sometimes, it is true, he pulled my ears more roughly than I liked, but if I needed correcting what of it? I loved him, and he loved me.

For how long would they send him to prison? What would I do while he was there? How would I live? Vitalis had always carried the money on him and he hadn't had time to give me anything before he was dragged away. I had only a few sous in my pocket, and how would I feed Joli-Coeur, the dogs, and myself? The next two days were agony for me, and I did not dare to leave the inn's yard. The animals were downcast too. At last on the third day a man brought me a letter from Vitalis, and it said that on the following Saturday he was to come before the judge for resisting arrest and for attacking a policeman.

This is what he wrote: 'I was wrong to fly into a temper and it may cost me dear. But it is too late now. Come to the trial. You will learn a lesson.' Then he added some advice and sent his love, and told me to look after the animals.

55

While I was reading the letter Capi, who was sitting between my legs, put his nose to the paper and sniffed at it. By the way he wagged his tail I could tell he knew that it had come from his master. It was the first time in three days that I had seen him happy.

At nine o'clock on that Saturday morning I arrived at the court. Quite a lot of people who had watched the scene with the policeman were there too. I was so scared at being in court that I squeezed behind a large stove that stood near the wall, making myself as small as I could. The first to be tried were men who had been arrested for robbery or for fighting. They all said they were innocent, and were all found guilty. At last Vitalis was brought in and he sat down on a bench between two policemen. First he was asked where he came from but I never heard his reply for I was too overcome with emotion. I gazed at Vitalis who was now standing straight-backed and with his white head thrown back. He looked ashamed and sad. I then looked at the judge.

"You struck the policeman who arrested you?"

"I hit him only once, sir. When I reached the place where we were to give our entertainment I was just in time to see the boy fall to the ground from a blow — the little boy who travels with me."

"He is not your son?"

"No, sir, but I love him like a son. When I saw him struck I lost my temper and grabbed the policeman's wrist so that he could not strike again."

"You struck him?"

"When he laid hands on me I thought of him as a man, not a policeman. Any movement I made was by instinct."

"At your age you should have known better."

The policeman then said what he had to say. Vitalis listened without paying much attention, his eyes roaming round the room. I knew that he was looking to see if I was there so I decided to come out from where I was hiding. I elbowed my way through the crowd that had come out of curiosity and stood beside him. His face shone with pleasure when he saw me.

The trial soon ended. Vitalis was sentenced to two months in prison and a fine of one hundred francs. Two months in prison! Through my tears I saw him follow a policeman, and a door slammed behind them. Two months separation, and where could I go?

I went back to the inn with a heavy heart and red-eyed. The landlord was standing in the yard and as I was passing him to go to the dogs he stopped me.

"Well, and what is the news of your master?" he asked.

"He was sentenced to two months in prison and a fine of one hundred francs."

"Two months and a hundred francs!" he repeated two or three times. "What are you going to do during the two months?"

"I don't know, monsieur."

"Oh. I suppose you have money to live here and pay for the feeding of the animals?"

"No, monsieur."

"Are you expecting me to keep you?"

I told him perfectly truthfully that I expected nobody to do that.

"Your master already owes me money," he went on, "and I cannot give you board and lodging for two months without knowing whether I will be paid. You'll have to leave."

"But where shall I go, monsieur?"

"That's not my business."

I was dumbfounded for a moment or two, but he was right — why should he keep me?

"Take your dogs and monkey and get out. But give me your master's bag. When he comes out of gaol he will have to come here for it and then he can pay what he owes me."

Then I had an idea. "Since you know he will pay his bill when he comes out why can't you keep me till then and add onto it what I cost?"

"Your master might be able to pay for your keep for a few days, but two months is a very different thing."

"I'll eat as little as you give me."

"And what about the animals! Now be off. You'll pick up

"At your age you should have known better."

enough to eat in villages."

"But, monsieur, how will my master find me when he comes out of gaol? He's certain to look for me here."

"All you have to do is to come back on that day."

"And what if he writes to me?"

"I'll keep the letter. No more talking. I've told you to go, and be quick about it. You have five minutes to get out of here."

I knew it was no use going on pleading with him so I went to the stables to get the dogs and Joli-Coeur. Then I picked up my bag, slung my harp over my shoulder, and left the inn. The innkeeper watched me go.

I was in a hurry to get out of the town because of the dogs not being muzzled. What would I say if I met a policeman? That I had no money to buy muzzles? It would be true, for all I possessed was eleven sous and that wouldn't be enough. They might arrest me, and if both of us were in prison what would then become of the animals. I felt terribly responsible.

As I hurried along the dogs looked at me in their own way of telling me that they were hungry and Joli-Coeur, who I was carrying, pulled my ear every now and then to make me look at him. Then he rubbed his stomach in a way no less expressive than the looks the dogs gave me. I was hungry too, for none of us had had breakfast.

My eleven sous could not buy enough for midday and evening meals, so we just had to be satisfied with one meal a day. I did not care where we went for it was all the same to me, and so when we were well away from Toulouse we just wandered along. The question of where to sleep brought no worries, for the open air would do. But how to eat was my great concern. We must have walked for all of two hours before I dared to stop. At last I felt that I was far enough from that hated city to have nothing more to fear so I went into the first bakery that I saw and asked for a pound and a half of bread.

"It would pay you better to take a two-pound loaf," the woman said. "With that menagerie of yours it wouldn't be too much. You must feed the poor animals."

It was certainly not too much for my 'menagerie', as she called it, but it was too much for my purse. The bread was five sous a pound, and I thought it best to be careful for I could not know what the next day would bring. So I bought the pound and a half, and that left me with three sous and two centimes. I went out of the shop clutching my bread; the dogs jumped with joy and Joli-Coeur made little cries as he pulled at my hair.

We didn't go far, for at the first tree we came to I put my harp against the trunk and we sat together on the grass, except Joli-Coeur, who wasn't tired, and stood ready to snatch the first crumbs that dropped. I cut the bread into five portions as equally as I could and passed them round, but I kept some of Joli-Coeur's share as he needed less food than the dogs, and hid it in my bag for later on.

After we had eaten I felt that I should explain our grave situation to my companions. "My friends," I said, "I have bad news for you. We shan't see our master for two months."

Capi gave a bark, and I went on: "It's sad for him and it's sad for us, for we depended on him for everything and now he's not with us we haven't any money."

Hearing the word money, which he understood perfectly, Capi rose on his hind legs and started to trot around as if he were taking a collection.

"Capi, I see that you want to give a performance, and that's good advice. But would we make any money? We have only three sous left, so you mustn't get hungry, and you must be obedient and help me all you can, you dogs and Joli-Coeur. I want to feel that I can depend on you."

I wouldn't go as far as to say that they understood all I said, but I certainly think they got the general idea. They knew by Vitalis's absence that something serious had happened, and they had expected some explanation from me. Their satisfaction was shown by the attention they gave me, except for Joli-Coeur for it was impossible for him to keep still for very long. During the early part of my talk he had listened with lively interest, but he soon jumped into the tree and was happily swinging from branch to branch.

If Capi had behaved like that my pride would have been hurt, but I was never astonished at anything Joli-Coeur might get up to for he was so empty-headed. But, after all, it was perfectly natural that he should want to amuse himself, and I must admit that I would have liked to do the same — but my new importance and dignity could not allow me to do any such thing.

After we had rested for a while I gave the signal to start. We had to find a place where we could rest for the night and then earn our next day's food. We walked for nearly an hour before we came to a village. I quickly dressed my troupe and in as good order as possible we made our entry. Unfortunately we had no flute and we also missed Vitalis's commanding presence for, like a drum-major, he always attracted attention. Moreover, I had not the advantage of being tall; indeed, I was small and rather thin and I would have had an anxious look on my face.

While we were marching I glanced to right and left to see what sort of effect was being made. Very little I regret to say, for no one followed us. When we reached the small square with a fountain shaded by trees I unslung my harp and started to play a waltz. The music was gay, my fingers were nimble, but my heart was heavy. I told Zerbino and Dolce to waltz together, and they obeyed me at once and started to whirl about in time to the music. But no one came to their doors to watch us, although inside I could see quite a few women either knitting or talking. I went on playing and the two dogs went on dancing, for perhaps if anyone decided to come over to watch us others would follow.

I played on and on and Zerbino and Dolce went round and round, but some of the women didn't even look at us. However, I was determined not to be discouraged. I went on playing with all my might, making the strings of my harp vibrate and nearly breaking them. Suddenly a small child toddled over towards us. I thought that its mother would follow, and after her a friend, and then we would have an audience and a little money. So as not to frighten the child and to entice him nearer I played softer. A few steps more and he would have reached us, but just then the mother looked up and saw her child. Instead of running after it as

61

I thought she would she called out and obediently the child went back to her. Perhaps these people didn't like dance music for, after all, I thought that was quite possible.

I told the two dogs to lie down and then began to sing my 'canzonetta', and never did I try so hard to please. I had not gone very far when I saw a man coming towards me. At last! And I sang with more fervour.

"What are you doing here, you young rascal?" he asked.

I stopped with my mouth open and watched him come nearer.

"Singing, monsieur."

"Have you permission to sing in our village square?"

"No, monsieur."

"Then off you go or I will send for the police."

"But, monsieur..."

"Be off, and hurry up, you little beggar."

I knew that after what had happened to Vitalis it was no use arguing so I hurried away. Beggar! That wasn't fair. I hadn't begged, I had sung. In five minutes I had left behind me that unfriendly village. The dogs followed me with their heads down and their tails between their legs, for they understood that some bad luck had just befallen us. From time to time Capi went ahead, turning round every now and then to look at me with his intelligent eyes. Capi was too well-bred to question me, but I saw his jaws tremble as if he was trying to keep back his protests.

When we were far enough off not to worry about the village policeman I signed to the dogs to stop and they formed a circle around me, with Capi in the middle watching me.

"As we had no permission to give a performance we were sent away," I explained to them.

"And now?" Capi seemed to ask, wagging his tail.

"Well, we'll have to sleep in the open with no supper."

At the word supper all the dogs barked. I showed them my three sous. "You must know that that is all we have, and if we spend them tonight there will be no breakfast tomorrow. So, as we have had something to eat today it is better to save these." And I put the three sous back into my pocket.

Capi and Dolce resignedly bowed their heads, but Zerbino who was not always so understanding and a bit of a glutton, growled.

"Capi, please explain to Zerbino."

Capi at once tapped Zerbino with his paw, and you would almost think that there was a bit of an argument between them. Animals have a language of their own, and as for dogs they not only know how to speak but also how to read. Watch them with their noses in the air, or with their heads lowered sniffing the ground and smelling stones and shrubs. Suddenly they'll stop at a tuft of grass or a wall and stay there for a while — we can see nothing on that wall, but a dog can read all sorts of curious things which could be written in mysterious letters that we don't understand.

What Capi said to Zerbino I cannot tell you for although dogs can understand men's language men do not understand the language of dogs. All I could see was that Zerbino would not listen to reason and insisted on the sous being spent at once. Capi became angry and it was when he showed his teeth that Zerbino, who was not very brave, became silent. By 'silent' I mean that he lay down.

The weather was fine and the day was warm so that to sleep in the open air would not be a terribly serious matter. The only thing was to keep out of the way of wolves, if there were any in this part of the country. We walked straight ahead along the white road until we came to a wood with a lot of very large stones strewn about in it. The place looked mournful and deserted but there was nothing better, and I thought that we might find shelter from the night air among the stones. I say 'we' but I mean Joli-Coeur and myself, for the dogs were all right. I had to be careful of myself for I was well aware of all my responsibilities, for what would become of Vitalis's troupe if I fell ill, and what would become of me if I had to be a nurse to Joli-Coeur?

We found a kind of grotto which was strewn with fallen pine-needles which would make a good mattress. All that was needed was something to eat, and I tried not to think of how hungry we all were. What does the proverb say — 'He who sleeps, dines'? Before

63

going to sleep I told Capi that I relied on him to keep watch, and instead of lying down with the rest of us on the pine-needles that excellent dog stayed outside our shelter as a sentinel. I could now sleep in peace. I did not drop off at once. Joli-Coeur was asleep beside me wrapped in my coat, and Zerbino and Dolce were stretched out at my feet. My worries were greater than my tiredness.

This first day had been bad and I wondered what tomorrow would bring. I was hungry and thirsty and I had only three sous — how could I possibly feed my troupe if I could not give any performances? And what about muzzles? Perhaps we would all die of hunger. While I was thinking of all this I looked up at the stars shining in the dark sky. Everything was quiet; there was not a breath of wind, no rustling of leaves nor a bird's call, and no rumble of a cart on the road. How alone we all were, and tears welled up. Poor Mother Barberin! Poor Vitalis!

I was lying on my stomach when suddenly I felt a breath on the back of my neck and hair. I turned quickly and a big warm tongue licked my face. It was Capi. He had heard me weeping and had come to comfort me just as he had done on the first night of our wanderings. I took hold of his neck and kissed his wet nose. He gave two or three sad little snuffles, and it seemed as if he was crying with me. I went to sleep and when I woke up it was daylight. Capi was sitting beside me and gazing at me. Birds were singing, and I could hear far away a church bell ringing the angelus. The sun was already high in the sky throwing its warm rays to comfort heart and body.

CHAPTER EIGHT

We set off in the direction from where we could hear the church bell. Surely we would find a baker, and I decided to spend our three sous. After that we would just have to see what would happen. When we reached the village there was no need for me to ask where the bakery was, for my sense of smell was now as keen as that of the dogs. We couldn't get much for three sous, as bread was five sous a pound. Each of us had a little piece and so our breakfast was soon over.

We simply had to make money that day. I walked about the village to find a good place for a performance as well as to look at the people and try to guess whether they might be friendly or not. I did not intend to give a performance at once for it was too early. After I had found a place we would come back at a better time and then take our chance.

I was wrapped up in my thoughts when all of a sudden I heard shouts behind me. I turned quickly and saw Zerbino racing towards me and being chased by an old woman. It did not take me long to know what had happened. While I was deep in my thoughts Zerbino had seized the chance to run into a house and steal a piece of meat, which he now had in his jaws.

"Thief!" the old woman cried. "Catch him! Catch them all!"

When I heard her shouting I felt that somehow I was guilty, or at least responsible for Zerbino's crime, so I began to run. What could I answer if she demanded the price of the stolen meat? How could I pay her? Seeing me running Capi and Dolce were soon on my heels, while Joli-Coeur clung tightly round my neck so that he would not be jolted off.

Others joined in the chase, but fear made us run faster. We raced down a side-road and soon we had left our pursuers behind, but I didn't stop running until I was out of breath. I think we must have gone about two miles before I turned round, but no one was now following us. Capi and Dolce were still with me, while as for Zerbino he had stopped some distance back to eat his piece of meat. I called him, but he knew very well that he would be punished so instead of coming to me he ran away as fast as he could. Of course he was very hungry, but I could not accept this as an excuse.

If I wanted to keep discipline in my troupe he would have to learn his lesson or he would steal again in the next village, and then Capi might follow his example. So his punishment would have to be in front of them all, but to do this I would first have to catch him and that would not be at all easy. So I turned to Capi: "Go and find Zerbino."

He left at once to do what I told him, but it seemed to me that he was not as keen as usual to obey me. From the look he gave me I saw that he was on Zerbino's side. I sat down to wait for their return for I was only too happy to rest after all the running I had done. We had stopped on the banks of the Midi canal with its shady trees and fields on both sides. An hour passed. The dogs did not come back and I was beginning to feel worried when at last Capi appeared alone with his head down.

"Where is Zerbino?"

Capi cowered, and when I looked closely at him I saw that one of his ears was bleeding. I knew the reason for that — Zerbino had put up a fight. Although Capi had obeyed my order he had felt that I was being too severe and had allowed himself to be defeated. What was the use of scolding him? I could only wait until Zerbino decided to return, for I knew that sooner or later he would feel sorry and would come back to take his punishment.

So I stretched out under a tree holding Joli-Coeur tight in case

66

he should take it into his head to go and find Zerbino. Capi and Dolce lay at my feet. Time passed and still Zerbino did not show up. At last I dropped off to sleep and when I awoke the sun was setting. There was no need for the sun to tell me that it was getting late, my stomach had been saying so for a long time. And I could tell from the looks of the dogs and Joli-Coeur that they were famished. Capi's and Dolces's eyes were piteous and Joli-Coeur was making faces to show how hungry he was. Zerbino still hadn't come back. I called to him, and I whistled, but it was no use. Having eaten well he was probably curled up somewhere under a bush.

Things were getting serious for if we left where we were Zerbino might not be able to find us. And if we stayed there was no chance of making a little money to buy something to eat. Our hunger was becoming acute, and the dogs were looking at me more and more imploringly while Joli-Coeur was rubbing his stomach and making angry squeals. I decided to send Capi to look for the truant once again but in half an hour he returned alone. What was I to do now? Although Zerbino was guilty and it was through him we were in this predicament I couldn't abandon him. I wondered what Vitalis would say if I did not bring back all his dogs to him. In spite of everything I was very fond of that rascal Zerbino so I decided to wait on into the evening; but it was impossible to sit about doing nothing. If we were all doing something I knew that somehow we would not feel so terribly hungry.

Then I remembered that Vitalis had told me that when a regiment was tired out by a long march its band played lively music so that the soldiers would forget their fatigue. If I played tunes like that on my harp perhaps we could all forget our hunger; the dogs could dance with Joli-Coeur and time would pass quicker. I picked up my harp and turning my back on the canal spoke to my animals and started to play a dance tune.

At first none of them seemed very keen to dance. All they wanted was something to eat and my heart ached for them, but they simply had to forget their hunger. I went on playing and then, little by little, the music had its effect. They danced, and so I

67

played more and different tunes. Suddenly I heard a child's clear voice call out: "Well done!" The voice came from behind me and I turned round quickly.

A barge was moored to the canal bank and the two horses that pulled it were on the opposite side. It was a curious barge and I had never seen one like it. It was much shorter than the boats which usually travel on canals, and the deck was made to look like a verandah shaded by climbing plants. I could see two people, a lady who was still young with a beautiful sad face and a boy of about my own age who seemed to be lying down. It was plain that it was the boy who had called out 'well done'.

I was very surprised, and I raised my hands in thanks for the applause.

"Do you play for your own amusement?" the lady asked in a foreign accent.

"I like to keep my dogs in practice and, besides, it's a relaxation for me and them."

The boy made a sign and the lady bent over him.

"Will you play something again?" she said, turning towards me.

Would I play? Play for an audience that had arrived out of the blue? It was too good to be true.

"What would you like, a dance? Or would you like to see a little comedy?"

"Oh, a comedy!" the boy answered, but the lady said she would prefer a dance.

"A dance is too short," the boy exclaimed.

"After the dance, if the 'distinguished audience' wishes it we will perform our different roles as they do in the circuses in Paris." This was one of Vitalis's favourite replies and I tried to say it in the grand manner that he did. On second thoughts I was not sorry that the lady didn't want a comedy, for I don't see how I could have given a performance with Zerbino still missing. I started to play a waltz. Immediately Capi took Dolce by the waist with his two front paws and they whirled about keeping good time. Then Joli-Coeur danced alone, and we went through our whole repertoire. We no longer felt tired, for the animals knew as well as I did that they would be rewarded with a meal, and did their very best. To our great surprise, in the middle of a dance, Zerbino came out from behind a bush and as Capi and Dolce and Joli-Coeur passed near him he boldly joined in.

As I played my harp and watched my performers I glanced every now and then at the little boy. He was getting a great deal of pleasure from what we were doing, but I saw that he didn't move. It looked as though he must be paralysed for his only movement was when he clapped his hands. The barge had drifted closer to the bank and soon I could see him clearly. He had fair hair and his face was very pale with blue veins showing on his forehead. He certainly did not look strong.

"How much do you charge for seats at your performances?" the lady asked.

"You pay according to the pleasure we have given you."

"Then my mother must pay you a lot," the boy said, and added something in a language I didn't know.

"My son would like your actors to come nearer so that he can see them properly."

I signed to Capi who delightedly sprang onto the barge.

"And the others too!" the boy cried out.

Zerbino and Dolce also jumped aboard.

"And the monkey!"

Joli-Coeur could easily have jumped the distance, but I was never quite certain of him. Once on board he might get up to some tricks which wouldn't please the lady.

"Is he bad tempered?" she asked.

"No, madam, but he doesn't always do what I tell him and I am afraid he might misbehave."

"Well, you carry him onto the barge yourself."

She nodded to a man who was standing near the steering-wheel and he came and threw a plank across to the bank. With my harp on my shoulder and Joli-Coeur in my arms I stepped aboard.

"The monkey! The monkey!" the boy repeated.

I went over to him and while he stroked and petted Joli-Coeur I

69

was able to see him properly. He was strapped to a board.

"Have you a father?" the lady asked.

"Yes, but I am alone just now. I have been for two months."

"For two months, at your age! Why is that? Does your father make you take him money at the end of every two months?"

"No, madam, he does not force me to do anything. He is happy if I can make enough to live on with my animals, that's all."

"And you can do that?"

I hesitated before replying. Somehow I felt a kind of awe and respect in her presence. Yet she talked to me so kindly and in such a gentle voice that I decided to tell her the truth, for after all there was no reason why I shouldn't. I told her of how Vitalis and I came to be parted, of how he had gone to prison because he had defended me, and of how since then I had not been able to make any money. While I was talking the boy, whom the lady called Arthur, was happy fondling the dogs; but all the same he was listening to what I was saying.

"But you all must be very hungry," he cried out.

Hearing the word 'hungry' the dogs started barking and Joli-Coeur, of course, rubbed his stomach with great vigour. The lady said a few words to a woman whose head I could see through a half-open door. She soon reappeared with some food.

"Sit down here my child."

Putting my harp to one side I did not hesitate and quickly sat down at a table with the dogs grouped about me. Joli-Coeur jumped on my knees.

"Do your dogs like bread?" Arthur asked.

Did they like bread! I gave each of them a piece which they swallowed at a gulp.

"What about the monkey?"

But there was no need to worry about Joli-Coeur, for while I was attending to the dogs he had taken a piece of crust from a meat pie and was nearly choking himself under the table. I helped myself to the pie and although I did not choke like Joli-Coeur I gobbled it up. Arthur was watching me with wide-open eyes astonished at how hungry we were, even Zerbino who should not have been after eating the meat he had stolen.

"What would you have eaten tonight if you hadn't met us?" Arthur asked next.

"I don't think we would have eaten at all. Perhaps tomorrow we might have had the luck to meet someone like you."

Arthur turned to his mother and for some little time they talked together in the language I didn't know. He seemed to be asking for something which she did not seem willing to agree to. Then, his body still not moving, he turned his head to me.

"Would you like to stay on the barge with us?"

I was so taken aback that I could not reply.

"My son is asking if you would like to stay with us," the lady repeated.

"On this lovely barge?"

"Yes, my son is not well, as you have seen, and the doctors have said that he has to be strapped to a board. We travel on the barge so that the days will pass faster and more pleasantly for him. If you would like to you may stay with us. Your dogs and monkey can perform every day and Arthur and I will be their audience. Whenever you want to you can play your harp for us. You will be doing us a kindness and, you never know, we may be helpful to you."

I had always wanted to live on a barge. What marvellous luck! I did not know what to say, but just took the lady's hand and kissed it. She had said I might like to play my harp and this I had great pleasure in doing at once to show how grateful I was. I took the harp to the bow of the barge and started to play softly.

At the same time the lady put a little silver whistle to her lips and blew it. I stopped playing wondering why she had whistled. Was it to tell me that I was playing badly or to make me stop? Arthur, who saw everything that went on about him, had seen how worried I was.

"Mother blew the whistle for the horses to pull the barge," he said.

And in fact the barge had started to glide over the calm water which lapped gently against its hull. On both sides of the canal there were trees, and behind us was the setting sun.

"Now please go on playing," and Arthur with a movement of his head beckoned to his mother to sit beside him. He took her hand and held it in his, and I played to them all the tunes that Vitalis had taught me.

Arthur's mother was English, and her name was Milligan. She was a widow. Arthur was her only child, for later I learned that her first son had been lost in some mysterious way; apparently when the child was only six months old he had been stolen and no trace of him had ever been found. At the time of his disappearance Mrs Milligan had been very ill indeed and her husband was dying. Her brother-in-law, James Milligan, had searched everywhere, fruitlessly, for the missing boy, and there being no heir at that time had expected to inherit his brother's property. He was to be disappointed, for seven months after his father's death Arthur had been born.

The doctors, however, said that the frail little child could not be expected to live long, indeed he might die at any time. In the event of his death James Milligan would succeed to the fortune. He waited and hoped, but the doctors' predictions did not come true, for his mother's nursing saved Arthur's life. When he had to be strapped to a board because of his diseased hip she could not bear the thought of her son always being confined to a house so she decided to have a barge built and to travel with him through France along its canals. The barge was called 'Le Cygne'.

Of course I did not learn all this at once. I was told the details little by little while I was with her.

I was given a small cabin. The only piece of furniture was a sort of low chest-of-drawers, the top of which when pulled out was a bed with a mattress, pillow and covers combined. Lower down were more, and smaller, drawers which held brushes and combs, and so on. There was no table and there were no chairs, but against the bulkhead were two small planks which, when they were pulled forward, made a tiny table and chair. There was a porthole which opened to let in fresh air.

It was good to get into that bed, and it was the first time in my life that I had slept between soft sheets, for Mother Barberin's had been stiff and coarse. Vitalis and I had often slept in inns where the sheets were even coarser than Mother Barberin's, and in some there were no sheets at all.

I woke up early next day for I wanted to find out how my animals had passed the night. I found them where I had left them the night before, and sleeping just as though the barge had been their home for months. The dogs jumped up when I came near, but Joli-Coeur, although he had one eye half-open, did not move — instead he started to snore making a noise like a trombone. I soon guessed what was the matter with him. Joli-Coeur was a sensitive creature, and could get angry quickly and then sulk. He was annoyed now because I had not taken him to my cabin, and he showed how displeased he was by pretending to be asleep. I could not explain to him why I had to leave him on deck, and as I felt that I had hurt his feelings I took him in my arms and cuddled him to show that I was sorry. He continued to sulk for a while but he soon thought of something else, and with his signs made me know that if I would take him for a walk on land he would perhaps forgive me.

The man who was cleaning the deck had already lowered the plank to the bank and I went off into the field with my troupe. Time passed quickly as I played with the dogs and ran after Joli-Coeur. When we got back the horses were harnessed and they were only waiting for a touch of the whip to start off again. Not long after we were all on board the rope holding us to the bank was untied, the sailor took his place at the helm, and we were on our way. We glided along without feeling the movement, and the only sounds were the gentle swish of the water against the hull and the tinkle of the bells around the horses' necks.

At times the water was nearly black, as if it was very deep, but then it would become as clear as crystal and we could see shiny pebbles and velvety grass below. I was gazing into the water when I heard my name being called. It was Arthur. His mother was with him and he was being carried out on his board.

"Did you have a good sleep?" he asked me. "Better than in a

field?"

I went over to him and after I had said good morning to Mrs Milligan said that I had.

"What about the dogs?"

I called to them, and they came running up with Joli-Coeur who was making faces as he usually did when he thought we were going to give a performance. But there was no question of any performance just then for Mrs Milligan moved her son into the shade and sat down beside him.

"Now," she said to me, "you must take the animals away for we have work to do."

I did as she told me and we all went to the bow. But what sort of work could Arthur do? I turned round and saw that his mother was repeating a lesson from a book she was holding. Arthur seemed to be having great difficulty in mastering it, but his mother was very patient with him. At last she said, "You have made many more mistakes today than yesterday."

"I just can't seem to remember, Mother," he said plaintively. "You know how sick I am."

"Your head isn't sick. I can't let you grow up in this way just because you are an invalid, Arthur. You make me very unhappy when you don't learn your lessons."

That seemed to me a very unkind thing to say even although she had spoken gently.

"I can't Mother," and he began to sob. But Mrs Milligan took no notice of his tears. "Let's try again." She read to him a fable called 'The Wolf and the Sheep' and Arthur repeated the words after her. She went through it three times, then handed the book to him telling him it learn it alone, and then left him.

I could see Arthur's lips moving for he really was trying very hard. But soon his eyes left the book. Suddenly he saw me and I made a sign to him to go on with his lesson. He smiled back, but he couldn't keep his mind on what he was doing and his eyes began to wander from one side of the canal to the other. A kingfisher flew over the barge as swift as an arrow and Arthur raised his head to follow its flight. By then I had come up to him, and when it was out

74

of sight he looked back at me.

"I can't learn this," he said, "and I do so much want to."

"It's not very difficult," I replied.

"Oh but it is. It is awfully difficult."

"It seems to me to be quite easy. I listened while your mother read it and learned nearly all of it myself."

He smiled as if he didn't believe me.

"Do you want me to repeat it? You take the book."

He picked up the book again and I began to recite. I was almost word-perfect.

"What! You know it."

"Not quite, but next time I think I could repeat it without a mistake."

"How did you do that?"

While your mother was reading I listened carefully without looking to see what was going on around me."

He reddened and looked away.

"I will try, like you," he said, "but tell me what did you do to remember the words?"

I didn't quite know how to explain but I tried my best.

"Now what is the fable about? Sheep — well first of all I thought about sheep, and the sheep were in a field. I could imagine them lying down and sleeping there. Picturing them like that I did not forget."

"Yes," he said, "I can see them too, white and black ones, in a field with a fence around it."

"And what usually guard the sheep?"

"Dogs."

"And...?"

"A shepherd."

"The sheep thought they were quite safe, and what happened then?"

"The dogs went to sleep, while the shepherd played his flute in the shade of a big elm with the other shepherds."

Little by little Arthur had the whole fable pictured in his mind. As well as I could I described every detail, and when he was

75

thoroughly interested we went through the story together and in about a quarter of an hour he was almost word-perfect.

"I know it now," he called out, "and how pleased Mother will be."

Mrs Milligan had now joined us and looked at me in surprise for she thought that we had been playing, but before she could say anything Arthur had started reciting the fable to her. I glanced at her and saw her lovely face break into a smile. Then I thought I saw tears in her eyes but she bent her head quickly and put her arms around her son.

"The words don't mean anything," Arthur said, 'they're silly, but the things that one can picture! Remi made me see the shepherd with his flute, the field, the sheep and the dogs. I could even hear the tune the shepherd played. Would you like to hear the words of the tune, Mother?"

And he sang a sad little song in English.

This time Mrs Milligan really did cry, for when she got up from her seat I saw that Arthur's cheeks were wet with her tears. Then she came to me, took my hand and pressed it.

"You are a good boy," she said.

If I have told you this story at some length it is only to emphasise that only the evening before I had come onto the barge a little tramp with his performing animals to amuse a sick child, but now because of this lesson I had become a companion, almost a friend, to him. From then on there grew a strong feeling of real companionship between us all, and I never felt any difference in our positions — this may have been because of Mrs Milligan's kindness, for she often spoke to me as if I were her own child.

When the countryside was interesting we would take our time and travel slowly, but if the landscape was monotonous we would quicken our speed. We always ate at the same time every day and would watch the banks of the canal moving past us. At sunset the barge was stopped, and at dawn we would be on our way again. The evening hours were all too short, for if the weather was fine I would take my harp, walk a short distance from the barge and sit behind a tree. There, hidden by the trunk, I would play and sing

*Mrs Milligan had now joined us and looked at me in surprise, for she thought
we had been playing.*

all the songs I knew. For on calm nights Arthur liked to hear the music without being able to see who played, and when I played a favourite tune of his he would call out "Encore" and I would play that particular piece again.

This was a wonderfully happy life for me, the country boy, who had sat by Mother Barberin's fireside and who had tramped the highroads with Signor Vitalis. What a difference between the dish of boiled potatoes that was all my poor foster-mother had been able to give me and the delicious tarts, jellies and pastries made by Mrs Milligan's cook. What a contrast between the long tramps in the mud in pouring rain or under the scorching sun, trudging along with Vitalis, and this voyage on a barge.

Yes, the pastry and all the other lovely foods were delicious, and yes, it was wonderful not to be hungry, or to be too cold or too hot; but I must say that it was the kindness and love of this lady and her little boy that I valued most. Twice I had been separated from those I loved — first from Mother Barberin, and then from Vitalis to be left alone with the animals and to take care of them.

Often as I looked at Arthur strapped to his plank, pale and drawn, I felt myself envying him — I who was so full of health and strength. My envy of him was not for being surrounded by so many comforts, nor for the barge, but for having such a wonderful mother. He could put his arms around her whenever he wished, but I scarcely dared to touch her hand when she held it out to me. I thought sadly that I would never have a mother who would hug me and whom I could hug back.

Perhaps one day I would see Mother Barberin again, and that would make me very happy, but I could not call her 'Mother' now for she was not my mother. I was alone, and I knew I would always be alone. I was old enough now to understand that one should not expect too much from this world and to know, too, that as I had no mother or father and no brothers and sisters I should be grateful to have friends. And I was happy, absolutely happy, on that barge. However it could not be expected to last long, for the day was coming nearer when I must go back to my old life again. Time had passed quickly, and soon there would be no more nice bed, no more nice pastry, and no more sitting round the table in the evenings.

One day I decided to ask Mrs Milligan how long it would take to get to Toulouse, for I wanted to be waiting at the prison door when Vitalis came out. When Arthur heard me he started to weep, and called out: "I don't want Remi to leave us!"

I told him that I was not free to stay on the barge because Vitalis had paid a sum of money for me, and so I had to go back to him. I had spoken about my foster-parents but had felt ashamed to admit that I was a foundling, for I knew how the children at the home in my village had been treated with contempt. It seemed to me that it was the most shocking thing in the world to be a foundling and I did not want Mrs Milligan and Arthur to know. Would they turn from me in disdain?

"Mother, we must keep Remi," Arthur went on.

"I would be very happy to keep Remi with us for we are so fond of him," Mrs Milligan answered. "But there are two things. First, Remi would have to want to stay."

"Oh, he does," Arthur said. "Don't you, Remi? You don't want to go back to Toulouse?"

"And the second is," Mrs Milligan continued, "will his master agree to let him go, to give him up so that he can stay with us."

"Remi comes first," Arthur insisted.

Vitalis had been a good master and I was very grateful for all he had taught me, but my life with him could not be compared with the life I would have with Arthur; moreover, there was no comparison between my respect for Vitalis and my affection for Mrs Milligan and Arthur. I knew in my heart that it was wrong to prefer these strangers to Vitalis, but all the same I had grown to love my new friends.

"If Remi stays with us it will not be all pleasure," Mrs Milligan said. "He will have to do lessons the same as you, and to study hard. It cannot be the free life that he would lead tramping along the roads.

"You know how much I would like..." I began.

"There you see, Mother," Arthur interrupted.

79

"What we have to do is to get his master's agreement. I will write to him and ask if he will come here, for we cannot take the barge all the way to Toulouse. I will send the money for his fare and explain why we cannot take the train. I do hope so much that he will accept, and if he agrees to what I am going to suggest then I will make arrangements with your parents, Remi, for you know they must be consulted too."

Consult Mother Barberin and her husband! They would only tell her what I had been trying to keep secret, that I was a foundling, and then neither Arthur nor Mrs Milligan would want me. I gave Mrs Milligan a frightened look, not knowing what to say. She looked at me in surprise, probably thinking that I was upset at the thought of Vitalis coming, but she did not insist.

I was glad when bedtime came and I could lock myself in my cabin. That was my only bad night on 'Le Cygne'. What could I do and what could I say? All sorts of ideas went through my brain. Perhaps, after all, Vitalis would not give me up, then they would never know the truth. My dread of them finding out the truth was so great that I began to hope that Vitalis would insist on me staying with him.

Three days later Mrs Milligan received a reply to her letter. Vitalis said he would be delighted to come and see her, and that he would arrive on the following Saturday by the two o'clock train. I asked for permission to go and meet him at the station, and to take with me the dogs and Joli-Coeur. That morning the dogs were restless as if they knew that something was going to happen; only Joli-Coeur was unconcerned. I was terribly excited for my fate would soon be decided. If I'd had the courage I would have implored Vitalis not to mention that I was a foundling, but I felt that I could not utter that word even to him.

I stood at the corner of the station-yard. The dogs were on a leash and Joli-Coeur was tucked under my coat. I waited, and saw little of what was going on about me. It was the dogs who warned me that the train had arrived, for they had scented their master. Suddenly there was a tug at the leash and as I was taken unawares they broke loose, bounding forward and barking. I saw them spring upon Vitalis — Capi had jumped straight into his arms, while Zerbino and Dolce leapt about at his feet. I walked towards him and when Vitalis saw me he quickly put Capi down and threw his arms around me. He said again and again: "Buon di, povero caro."

Vitalis had never been really hard on me, but neither had he ever been affectionate so I was not used to this sort of thing. I was touched and tears came to my eyes. I looked at him and saw that prison had aged him, his back was bent, his face pale, and his lips bloodless.

"You find me changed don't you, Remi," he said. "I was not at all happy in prison, but I'll be better now that I'm out." Then he changed the subject and added, "Tell me about this lady who wrote to me. Where did you get to know her?"

I told him how I had met Mrs Milligan and Arthur on their barge, and of what we had done and seen. I rambled on hardly knowing what I was saying. Now that I was able to speak to him I found it impossible to tell him that I wanted to leave him to stay with Mrs Milligan. By the time I had finished my story we had arrived at the hotel where Mrs Milligan had said she would meet him. Vitalis had not mentioned what she had written in her letter.

"Is this lady waiting to see me now?" he asked as we went into the hotel.

"Yes, I'll take you up to the room."

"There's no need to do that. You wait here with the dogs and Joli-Coeur."

I never argued with Vitalis, but now I felt that it was only fair to accompany him when he met Mrs Milligan. However, with a wave of his hand he stopped anything that I was going to say, and I had to wait downstairs. Why didn't he want me to be present? I was asking myself this and still pondering over it when he returned.

"Go and say goodbye to the lady," he said abruptly. "I'll wait for you here. We are leaving in ten minutes."

I didn't know what to say.

"Haven't I made myself clear? You're standing there as if you are stupid. Hurry up."

He had never spoken so roughly to me. When I had gone a few steps I turned. "What did you say to her?"

"I told her that I needed you and that you needed me, and that I was not going to give up my rights to you. Go now, and come back quickly."

The fact that I was a foundling was so engraved on my mind that I imagined that if I had to leave immediately my master must have told Mrs Milligan all about me. When I entered her room I found Arthur in tears and his mother bending over him.

"Oh, Remi, you won't go. Tell me you won't go," he sobbed.

Mrs Milligan answered for me, telling Arthur that I must do as I had been told.

"Your master would not allow us to keep you," she said to me sadly.

"He is a wicked man," Arthur called out.

"No, Arthur, he is not. He loves you Remi, and he needs you. He speaks like an educated man and, in his words, this is what he told me. 'I am fond of this boy, and he is fond of me. The start in life that I am giving him is good for him, and far better than he would have with you. It is true that you would have him taught lessons, but you would develop his mind and not his character. Only the hardships of life can do that. He cannot be your son, and he would only be a companion for your own boy'."

"But he's not Remi's father," Arthur said.

"That is quite true, but he is Remi's master and for the time being at any rate Remi must obey him. But I will write to his parents and see what I can do."

"Oh no, don't do that," I cried.

"Why not?"

"Please don't."

"But that is the only thing to do, Remi."

If Mrs Milligan had not mentioned my parents I would have stayed much longer than the ten minutes Vitalis had allowed me.

"They live in Chavanon, don't they?" she asked.

Without answering her I went over to Arthur and, putting my

82

arms around him, I clung to him for a few minutes. Then freeing myself from his weak grip I turned to Mrs Milligan and kissed her hand.

"Poor boy," she murmured and kissed my forehead.

I hurried to the door.

"I will be thinking of you, Arthur," I said, my voice choking, "and I will never, never forget you, Mrs Milligan."

"Remi! Remi!" Arthur called out.

I went out and closed the door. A moment later I was with Vitalis.

"Off we go," was all he said.

And that was how I parted from my first friend of my own age.

CHAPTER NINE

Once again I was tramping along with Vitalis, through rain
and sunshine and mud and water, with my harp strapped to
my shoulder. I had once more to laugh and amuse the audiences.

The fresh change in my life was abrupt but I quickly became
used to it. All the same, more than once in our long walks I lagged
behind thinking of Arthur, Mrs Milligan and 'Le Cygne'. At
night when we were staying at some dirty village inn I would long
for my cabin on the barge. How rough the sheets were now! And
to think that I would never again play with Arthur, and never
again hear his mother's soft voice.

Happily I had one consolation in my sadness, which was very
deep, for Vitalis was so much kinder than he had ever been before.
His manner had changed and I felt that now he was more to me
than just a master. Often, if I had dared, I would have given him a
hug but I hadn't the courage, for Vitalis was not a man with
whom one could be familiar. I suppose that at first it had been fear
that kept me at a distance, but now it was something vague which
I suppose could better be called respect.

When I left my village Vitalis was, as far as I was concerned, the
same as all the other men I had met; but in the two months I had
spent with Mrs Milligan my eyes had been opened and my
understanding had developed. Now, looking at Vitalis with more
attention, it seemed to me that in his manner and bearing he was
greatly superior to the men I have mentioned. Indeed, his ways

were like Mrs Milligan's ways. For some time we never spoke about her or 'Le Cygne', but little by little our conversation came round to my stay on the barge. On our tramps my eyes always turned in the direction of water, and I was always hoping that I would see the barge, but I never did. It was the end of my dream.

We spent several days in Lyons and then went on to Dijon. Winter was coming nearer now and we had to trudge wearily along in the rain and the mud, wet to the skin. Some nights when we reached a wretched inn or barn I was so tired out that I couldn't sleep, and Joli-Coeur was just as sad and mournful, and he had a cough.

Vitalis's idea was to get to Paris as fast as possible, for it was only there that we would have the chance to give performances in winter. We had been making very little money and so we couldn't afford to travel by train. After the rain the wind changed to the north. At first we didn't mind the biting wind in our faces, but soon the sky started filling with heavy black clouds and the sun disappeared. It was plain that a snowstorm was approaching, and fast.

My master was most anxious to get to the next big town, which was Troyes, before the really bad weather overtook us, for there we could stay and give several performances.

"Go to bed soon," he said when we got to an inn that particular night, "We are going to start very early tomorrow. We don't want to be caught in this snowstorm."

He did not go to bed immediately but sat down by the fireplace in the kitchen to warm Joli-Coeur who was feeling the cold terribly. Although we had wrapped him up well he had not stopped coughing. I got up early as I had been told. It was not yet daylight — there was not a star to be seen and the sky was black and lowering. When we opened the door the wind was roaring.

"If I were you I wouldn't venture out," the inn-keeper said to Vitalis. "There's a terrible storm coming up."

"I'm in a hurry and we must get to Troyes before it's really bad."

"You can't walk thirty miles in an hour."

All the same we started off. Vitalis held Joli-Coeur close to him so as to give him some of his warmth, while the dogs were only too pleased to run ahead of us. Vitalis had bought me a sheepskin in Dijon and I wrapped myself in it like him with the wool against my body.

It soon became almost painful to open our mouths so we plodded along in silence, hurrying as much to get warm as to get ahead. Although it was long past dawn the sky was still dark. To the east there was a sort of white band and yet the sun couldn't show through. But looking across the country things were becoming more distinct. We could see the trees stripped of their leaves and hear the bushes with their dry foliage rustling in the strong gusts of wind. There was no one else on the road, no one in the fields, and there was not the sound of a cart nor the crack of a whip. The only living things were birds sheltering in the bushes.

Suddenly in the north we saw a pale streak which grew larger and larger as it came closer, and we heard the hissing of wild geese flying south. They flew quickly over us, but before they were out of sight snowflakes no larger than butterflies fluttered around us, whirling incessantly without touching the ground. We could make little headway, and it seemed quite impossible for us to reach Troyes before really heavy snow started falling. The clouds were becoming heavier and heavier, and the flakes no longer hovered and soon fell straight and fast to cover us from head to foot.

"We will have to shelter in the first house we come to," Vitalis said, "We can never reach Troyes now."

I was pleased to hear him say so, but where would we find a house? As far as the eye could see, and that was not very far, there was no sign of human habitation, nor anything to show that we were near a village. Ahead of us was a sombre forest and on either side of us hills. The snow was falling faster and thicker. Every now and then Vitalis would lift his sheepskin to let Joli-Coeur have a breath of air. Silently we tramped on, from time to time turning our heads so that we could take a deep breath. The dogs no longer ran ahead, but walked at our heels asking for the shelter we could not give them.

Slowly and painfully, blinded, soaked, and frozen, we continued on our way and, although we were now in the heart of the forest, the road through it was exposed to the full blast of the wind. From time to time it abated and then the snow fell more heavily. Soon the road was so covered that our steps made no sound. Several times I saw Vitalis glance to the left as if he was looking for something, but he said nothing. As for me I kept looking straight ahead, and I thought we would never come to the end of that forest.

Until then I had only seen snow falling when I was looking through the window of a warm kitchen, and that seemed a long time ago. It was now becoming more difficult to walk because of the depth of the snow, but all of a sudden and without saying a word Vitalis pointed to the left — I looked, and saw not very clearly a small hut made of branches. Now we had to find a track leading to the hut, and this was difficult for the snow was already thick enough to wipe out all traces of any path, if one had ever existed. However, there seemed to be a ditch and we scrambled along it and managed at last to reach our shelter. The dogs were the first to arrive and they rolled over and over in their joy. That hut was a veritable mansion!

"I had the feeling that there must be a woodcutter's shelter somewhere in the forest," Vitalis said, "and now it can snow as much as it likes."

"Yes, let it snow," I replied defiantly.

I went to the door, or rather to the opening, into the hut and shook my coat and hat, for I didn't want the inside of our mansion to get wet. The hut was simply and strongly built and its furniture, if it could be called that, consisted of some big stones which could serve as seats. All the same it was all that we wanted or needed.

A fireplace could be built and fuel was not difficult to find for all we had to do was to pull out sticks here and there from the walls and roof. This was quickly done and soon we had a bright fire. Certainly the hut filled with smoke but what did that matter if we had warmth. I crouched and blew on the fire while the dogs sat gravely around me with their necks outstretched facing it. Soon Joli-Coeur peeped out from under Vitalis's coat and took in what he saw about him. Evidently satisfied he jumped to the ground and, taking the best place in front of the fire, held out his two trembling little hands to the warmth.

Vitalis was a man who from experience always worked out things in advance in case of an emergency, so on the following morning we ate only a very little bread and cheese, for we did not know how long we might be forced to stay in our shelter. He wisely thought it best to keep something for supper.

When I asked him he said that he did not know this forest road nor whether we would find an inn before we reached Troyes. I understood then why he was rationing the food, but the dogs did not, and when they saw the rest of the bread being put back in his bag when they had scarcely eaten they held out their paws to their master, scratched his knees, and stared at the bag. But he took no notice of them and they settled down to sleep, Capi with his nose almost in the fire. Through the opening into the hut I could see the snow still falling, and I decided to go to sleep too.

I don't know for how long I slept but when I woke up the snow had stopped falling. I looked outside and saw that it was so deep that if we continued on our way to Troyes it would be over our knees. I wondered what time it could be. I couldn't ask Vitalis because his big silver watch, from which Capi told the time, had had to be sold when he had bought my sheepskin at Dijon, and all his money had gone in payment of the fine. Nothing outside could help me to even guess the time for everything except the snow was dark and there was not a sound to be heard nor a sign of any movement.

"Do you think we should get on our way?" Vitalis called out to me.

"I don't know. Whatever you say."

"Well, I think we should stay here. At any rate we have shelter and warmth."

That was true, but I remembered about the food and said nothing.

"I feel it is going to start snowing again soon," Vitalis went on, "and if we are caught again on our way before nightfall. . ."

He divided the very little remaining bread between the six of us for supper and we gobbled up every crumb. When this frugal meal was finished Vitalis put his knife back in his trouser pocket, and Capi got up and smelled the bag the bread had come from. Then he put his paw on the bag to feel it and, now sure that there was nothing more to eat, he went back to his place in front of the fire and gazed at Zerbino and Dolce as if to tell them they were getting nothing more. With a sigh of resignation he stretched himself out.

"It is useless to beg," he seemed to have said to them, as plainly as if he had spoken out aloud. The other two understood and they too stretched out beside the fire with sighs. But Zerbino's sigh was the loudest for he had always had a big appetite and this shortage of food hurt him more than the others.

The snow started to fall again, and we could see the white carpet on the ground getting deeper and deeper until the shrubs and bushes were completely hidden. When night came big flakes were still falling from the black sky. Since we had to spend the night there the only thing to do was to go to sleep as quickly as possible. I wrapped myself in my sheepskin which I had dried in front of the fire during the day and lay down beside the fire with a stone for a pillow.

"Yes, you go to sleep," Vitalis said, "and I'll wake you when it's my turn. We have nothing to fear but one of us must be awake to see that the fire doesn't go out. We must be very careful not to get cold, for it will be really bitter when the snow stops."

Early in the morning my master woke me. The fire was still burning and it had stopped snowing. "As the fire dies down," he said, "throw on it the wood that I've put ready here."

Vitalis was a much lighter sleeper than me so he had piled up a heap of wood so that I would not disturb him by pulling sticks from the walls every time I needed them. It was a wise thing to do but Vitalis, alas, could not know the consequences. He stretched out before the fire with Joli-Coeur huddled against him and soon I knew from the way he was breathing that he was fast asleep. I got up as quietly as I could and went to the opening to see what it looked like outside. The snow covered everything, bushes and trees, and all about was a dazzling white. The sky was dotted with stars and it was freezing hard. I wondered where we would have been in all this snow and bitter cold if we had not found the hut.

Even though I had walked on tiptoe I had wakened the dogs and Zerbino had followed me. The beauty of the night meant nothing to him and all he wanted to do was to get out. I ordered him back to where he had been lying and told him to stay there by the warm fire. He obeyed me with a very bad grace and kept his nose pointed towards the opening. I stayed there for a few moments, for the snow looked very beautiful, but somehow I felt a vague sadness as my eyes were held by the white mysterious night.

I returned to the fire at last and, having put three or four pieces crosswise on it, I sat down on the stone I had used for a pillow. Vitalis was sleeping peacefully, and so were the dogs and Joli-Coeur. The flames leapt from the fire, swirling up to the roof and throwing out sparks. The silence of the night was unbroken. For a long time I amused myself by watching the sparks, then little by little I became drowsy.

If I had been kept occupied in tending the fire I could have stayed awake, but sitting in front of it with nothing to do my head must have dropped lower and lower even though at the same time I thought I would be able to keep awake. I jumped up suddenly, roused by furious barking. It was still night and I must have been asleep for some time because the fire was almost out and no flames lit the hut. Capi was barking his head off, but strangely there was no sound from Zerbino or Dolce.

"What's going on?" Vitalis called out, raising himself on an elbow.

"I don't know."

"You've been asleep and the fire's gone out."

Capi bounded to the opening and stood there still barking. He was answered by two or three mournful howls and among them I recognised Dolce's voice. The howls were coming from behind the hut and were not very far away. I wanted to go out but Vitalis put his hand on my shoulder and stopped me.

"First," he ordered, "put some wood on the fire."

While I was doing this he took a half-burned stick from the fire and blew on it until one end was alight, making a torch.

"Come along," he said, "Walk behind me and you, Capi, lead the way."

As we stepped out of the hut there was the most frightening howl, and Capi drew back cowering.

"Wolves! Where are Zerbino and Dolce?"

What could I answer? The two of them must have gone out while I was asleep. Being Zerbino he would have crept out and Dolce would have followed him. Had the wolves carried the two off, for there was fear in Vitalis's voice when he asked me where they were?

"Make another torch," Vitalis said, "We must find them."

When I was young I had heard people in our village tell terrible stories about wolves. I did as I was told and then followed my master. But outside, except for the dogs' paw-marks, there was no sign of either dogs or wolves. We followed the tracks about the hut, then some distance away we could see in the snow where animals had been rolling about.

"Capi, go and hunt," Vitalis ordered. Then he whistled to attract Zerbino and Dolce.

But there was no answering bark. No sound disturbed the intense mournful silence of the forest. Capi, instead of doing what he had been told, stayed beside us quivering with fear. Brave Capi, who was always so obedient. There wasn't enough light for us to follow the paw-marks for any distance. The snow was dazzling, but further away everything else seemed vague and confused. Vitalis whistled again and shouted for the missing dogs, but once again there were no anwering barks. Poor Zerbino and poor Dolce!

"The wolves have carried them away. Why did you let them out?"

I could not reply, but after a pause I said: "We must try and find

91

them." I stepped in front of him, but he stopped me.

"Where will we look?"

"I don't know, everywhere."

"In this poor light and in all this snow we can't tell where they've gone." That was quite true. The snow was over our knees and our two torches together could not pierce the shadows.

"If they don't reply to our whistles and shouts," Vitalis went on, "it's because they must be a long way away. We mustn't go any further for the wolves might attack us too, and we have nothing to defend ourselves with."

It was terrible to have to abandon the poor dogs, our two friends. The worst part of it for me was that I knew I was to blame, for if I hadn't fallen asleep they would never have gone out. Vitalis turned to go back to the hut and I followed him, looking back as I plodded through the snow and every now and then stopping to listen. I saw nothing and heard nothing.

Another surprise was awaiting us when we got back. The sticks that I had thrown on the fire were blazing and lighting up the darkest corners, but Joli-Coeur was nowhere to be seen. The coverings to keep him warm were there in front of the fire, and that was all. Both Vitalis and I called to him but he didn't show up. So, once again, holding our torches we set out but we could find no sign of him. We came back to the hut to see if he could be hiding among some sticks. We searched for a long time, looking in the same place and in the same corners time and again. I climbed onto Vitalis's shoulders to see if he could be among the branches forming the roof, but it was all no use.

Vitalis was very angry and I was in despair. I asked him if he thought that the wolves had taken Joli-Coeur too.

"No, wolves would never dare come into the hut. I'm quite sure that when Zerbino and Dolce ran out the wolves were waiting. Quite likely Joli-Coeur became so very frightened while we were out there he has hidden somewhere. That is why I am so worried, for in this terrible weather he will catch cold, and you know that cold is fatal to him."

"Well, let us have another good search."

We went all over the hut again, but it was no use.

"We will have to wait for daylight," Vitalis said.

"When will that be?"

"In about two or three hours I should think."

Vitalis sat down in front of the fire with his head in his hands. I didn't dare disturb him but stood close to him, only moving every now and then to put more wood on the fire. Once or twice he got up and went to the opening to the hut to look at the sky and to listen attentively, and then came back and sat down. I would have preferred him to be angry with me than that he be so quiet and sad.

Those hours passed so slowly that I thought the night would never end. However at last the stars started to fade and the sky became lighter. But at daybreak the cold grew more intense, and the air that came through the opening froze us to the marrow. If we should find Joli-Coeur would he be alive? And what hope would we have of even finding him?

The snow had stopped falling now and there was a pink light in the sky which promised better weather. As soon as it was light enough to see we both found stout sticks and went out. Capi did not seem to be as frightened as he had been before and with his eyes on Vitalis he waited only for a sign from him to bound ahead. As we were looking for Joli-Coeur's footprints Capi threw back his head and started to bark happily to tell us to look up, and not along the ground.

We raised our eyes to a big branch which hung over our hut, and there we saw him. Yes, there was Joli-Coeur. Frightened by the noise made by the dogs and wolves he had first jumped onto the hut's roof and from there had climbed up the tree to hide. Feeling he was safe he had stayed there huddled and crouching and ignoring our calls to him. The poor frail little creature must have been frozen. Vitalis called to him in a gentle voice, but he didn't move and we began to think that he might be dead. Vitalis went on calling for several minutes, but there was still no movement. I had to do something to atone for all my negligence.

"If you want me to I will climb up and get him," I said.

"You'll only break your neck."

"No, there's no danger."

That was not quite true, for there was danger. It would be very difficult because the branches and part of the trunk were covered with frozen snow.

When I was a very small boy I had learned how to climb trees and I was now quite good at it. I jumped and grabbed hold of one of the lowest branches and held on, even though I was nearly blinded by falling snow. I somehow managed to clamber up to a fork, and once I was there it became easier although I had to be careful not to skid. As I got higher I spoke softly to Joli-Coeur who didn't move, but watched me with those shining eyes of his. I had almost reached him and was still stretching out my hand to take hold of him when he sprang up onto another branch. I followed, but humans are not made like monkeys when it comes to tree-climbing. Quite possibly I would never have caught him but for the fact that the snow was making his feet wet. Not liking this he soon became tired of dodging me, and then, dropping from branch to branch, he jumped straight onto his master's shoulders and hid inside his coat.

It was marvellous finding Joli-Coeur, but now we had to find the two dogs.

By now it was broad daylight and easier for us to see, and we could follow their footsteps in the snow for about thirty yards. They had come out of the hut one behind the other. Then we saw other footprints, and on one side there were signs of a struggle where the wolves had leapt on the dogs. All around there were footprints where the wolves had trotted off bearing their prey with them to eat when they wanted to. The only trace of the dogs was a trail of blood staining the snow.

There was no need to look any further so we returned to the hut to warm Joli-Coeur and look after him. While Vitalis held out the little fellow's feet and hands to the fire, just as if he were holding a baby, I warmed his coverings. When this was done we wrapped them around him, but what he needed most was a warm drink and we had nothing to give him.

Vitalis and I sat in front of the fire saying little and just watching the flames. Poor Zerbino and Dolce, our poor friends. Each of us murmured their names, first him then me. The dogs had been our good companions in fair weather and foul, and to me in my loneliness they now meant so very much. I reproached myself deeply for not having stayed awake and kept watch, for now I knew that the wolves would never have attacked us in our hut but would have stayed well away, frightened by the fire.

If only Vitalis had scolded me, even beaten me. Instead he said nothing, not even looking at me — he just sat with his head bent over the fire, probably wondering what would become of us without Zerbino and Dolce.

CHAPTER TEN

Next morning there was bright sunshine and the snow which during the night had looked so bleak was so dazzling that it was almost blinding. From time to time Vitalis felt Joli-Coeur under his coverlet but he did not seem much warmer, and when I bent over him I could feel him still shivering. The blood in his veins seemed frozen.

"We must get to a village as soon as possible," Vitalis said, "or Joli-Coeur will die. Let's start off at once."

The little creature was wrapped up as warm as we could make him, and now my master put him under his coat and held him to his chest. We were ready to leave.

"This has been a shelter that has made us pay dearly for its hospitality," Vitalis said, and his voice shook.

He went out from the hut first and I followed. We had to call Capi for he had stayed outside the hut with his nose pointing to where his friends had been snatched by the wolves. In about ten minutes we reached the main road where a cart passed us and the driver told us that in about an hour we would reach a village. This cheered us up but it was difficult, almost painful, for me to walk because the snow reached almost to my waist. I often asked Vitalis how Joli-Coeur was, and each time he answered that the monkey was still shivering. At long last we saw the white roofs of a large village.

It was unusual for us to stay at better-class inns — we always went to an ordinary sort of place where we were sure we would not be driven away and it would not cost too much. But this time Vitalis walked on until we came to an inn with a gilded sign hanging over its front door. The kitchen door at the back was open and we could see a large stove covered with polished copper saucepans from which steam was rising. How good the soup smelled to us standing outside with our empty stomachs.

Vitalis put on his most gracious manner and, with his hat on and his head thrown back, went into the kitchen and asked the innkeeper's wife, a fine-looking woman, for a good room with a fire. At first she had not condescended to take any notice of us but Vitalis's grand manner evidently impressed her for she called a maid and told her to take us up to a room.

"Hurry, get into bed," Vitalis said to me while the maid was lighting the fire.

I looked at him in astonishment. Why should I go to bed? I would much rather have sat down beside the fire to have something to eat.

"Hurry," Vitalis said again.

There was nothing to do except obey. An eiderdown was on the bed and he pulled it up to my chin.

"Try and get warm, for the warmer you are the better."

It seemed to me that Joli-Coeur needed warming far more than I did, for I was not feeling nearly as cold now. Then, to the maid's amazement, Vitalis took hold of poor little Joli-Coeur and turned him round and round before the fire as if he was going to nearly roast him.

"Are you warm now?" he asked me after a few minutes.

"I'm suffocating."

"That's good," and he hurried to the bed. He popped Joli-Coeur in beside me and told me to hold him close to my chest. The little creature, who usually rebelled when he was made to do

97

something he didn't want to do, seemed resigned to everything. He let me hold him close to my body without making any fuss or protest. He was no longer cold, indeed his body was very hot.

Vitalis went down to the kitchen and soon came back carrying a bowl of warm, sweetened wine. He tried to make Joli-Coeur drink a few teaspoonfuls, but gently as he tried he could not unclench his teeth. With his brilliant eyes the monkey looked imploringly at us as though asking us not to torment him. Then he pulled out an arm and held it towards Vitalis. I wondered what he meant by doing that; I looked enquiringly at Vitalis and he explained that before I had met them Joli-Coeur had suffered from inflammation of the chest and he had had to be bled, the blood being taken from his arm. Knowing that he was sick now Joli-Coeur wanted us to bleed him so that he could get better as he had done before. Vitalis was very touched, but this made him more anxious — it was clear that Joli-Coeur was ill, and he must be very ill indeed to refuse the sugared wine that he liked so much.

"Drink the wine, Remi, and stay in bed with Joli-Coeur," Vitalis said. "I'm going for a doctor."

I must admit that I, too, like sweetened wine, and I did not have to be told twice. When I had emptied the bowl I slid down again under the bedclothes where the warmth helped by the wine almost overpowered me.

Vitalis hadn't been gone long before he came back with a man wearing gold-rimmed spectacles — the doctor. Thinking, with good reason, that the doctor might not put himself out for a monkey Vitalis had not told him who was the patient. When he saw me in bed, and I must have been as red as a peony, the doctor put his hand on my forehead and said one word: "congestion". Then he shook his head.

It was time for me to clear up any misunderstanding in case he might want to bleed me, so I called out: "I'm not the one who's ill."

"Not ill! The child's delirious."

Without replying I lifted the bedclothes a little and showed him Joli-Coeur, who put his arm around my neck. "He's the one who

98

is ill," I said.

The doctor took two steps back and turned angrily to Vitalis. "A monkey! You've brought me out in this weather to visit a monkey!"

Vitalis was a man who thought quickly and did not easily lose his head. Politely, and in his grand manner, he explained the position, how we had been caught in a snowstorm and how in fear of wolves Joli-Coeur had jumped into a tree where he had been almost frozen to death. The patient might only be a monkey, but what a monkey — a genius, and a friend and companion to us both. How could we confide such a talented creature to the care of an ordinary veterinary surgeon, for everyone knew that the fellow in this village was a fool while everyone knew that the doctor, even in the smallest village, was a man of science. If you rang at a door bearing a doctor's name you could be sure of finding a man of knowledge and, even more, a man of generosity. He wound up by saying that although a monkey is just an animal he is, according to naturalists, so like a human that any illness is often treated in the same way.

The doctor was so flattered by what Vitalis had said that he returned from the door where he had been standing and came back to the bed. While Vitalis had been talking Joli-Coeur had almost certainly decided that the man wearing the spectacles was a doctor, and several times he held out an arm.

"Look," said Vitalis, "he wants you to bleed him."

That was enough for the doctor. "Most interesting," he murmured. "A most interesting case."

But, alas, it was a sad business for us, for the doctor decided that poor little Joli-Coeur once again, had an inflammation of his chest. The doctor took his arm and cut a vein without Joli-Coeur giving the slightest moan for he knew that this would cure him. After the bleeding Joli-Coeur needed a good deal of attention. Naturally I no longer stayed in bed, for I was the nurse carrying out Vitalis's instructions.

Joli-Coeur was happy with me nursing him, and he rewarded me with smiles which were almost human. He who was normally so lively and at times petulant, always playing tricks on us, was now quiet and obedient. In the days that followed he tried to show us how friendly he felt towards us, even to Capi who had so often suffered from his tricks.

As is usual with this sort of complaint he soon began to cough, and the coughing made him very tired for his tiny body shook with convulsions. All I owned was five sous and with this I bought him some barley-sugar to suck. He soon grew to know that every time he coughed I would give him a little piece of the sweet, and he quickly took advantage of this to get as much as he could, but instead of helping to make him well again it seemed to make him worse. Of course I stopped giving him any more, but he would not be put off. First he begged most appealingly, then when he saw that I would not give him any more he would sit up, put a hand on his stomach, and cough as hard as he could. The veins on his forehead stood out and the tears ran from his eyes, and he finished up nearly choking himself.

Vitalis never spoke to me about money matters, for it was only by chance that I had learned that he had sold his watch to get me my sheepskin. One morning while I was looking after Joli-Coeur he came back to the inn and told me that the innkeeper's wife had asked him to pay our bill; he said that all he had was fifty sous, and so the only thing to do was to give a performance that same evening.

A performance without Zerbino, Dolce and Joli-Coeur! That seemed to me quite impossible, but we had at any price to save Joli-Coeur's life and somehow pay for our board and lodging.

Forty francs were needed. But forty francs in this village, in this cold! While I looked after Joli-Coeur Vitalis went out and found a hall in the market-place, for any out-door performance was clearly out of the question. He wrote out announcements and posted them up all over the village. With a few planks of wood he fixed up a stage, and with those last fifty sous he bought candles, cutting them in half to double the lights.

I watched him from our bedroom window trudging back and forth in the snow, and wondered anxiously what sort of a programme he could stage. I soon knew, for the village town-crier wearing a scarlet cap stopped in front of the inn. He gave a magnificent roll on his drum and then read out the programme. Vitalis had made the most extravagant promises — there were to perform a world-renowned artist, that was Capi, and a marvellous young singer. The singer was myself! But the most interesting part was that there were to be no fixed prices, and we relied on the audience's generosity; the spectators need only pay after they had seen, heard and applauded the entertainment.

The idea seemed to me to be a very bold one, but who was going to applaud us? Capi certainly deserved to be celebrated but as for me, I wasn't at all sure that I was a marvel. Ill as Joli-Coeur was he tried to get up when he heard the roll of the drum, and from Capi's barks he seemed to guess that there was to be a performance. I had to hold Joli-Coeur back but then he made signs for me to give him his general's uniform — the red coat and trousers with gold braid, and the plumed hat. Poor Joli-Coeur, he clasped his hands and went on his knees to beg me.

When he saw that he could get nothing from me by begging he tried what a show of anger would do, and then finally melted into tears. It was quite clear that we would have a lot of trouble convincing him that he had to give up all ideas of performing that night, and I thought it best not to let him know when we left the inn.

Vitalis did not know what had gone on while he was out. When he came back he told me to get my harp ready as well as all the other things we needed for our performance. Joli-Coeur understood what he was saying and turned to his master to renew his entreaties to him. He could not have expressed himself better, for they were real tears rolling down his cheeks and real kisses on Vitalis's hand.

"And so you want to perform?" Vitalis asked him.

"Yes, yes," Joli-Coeur's whole body seemed to cry out. He tried to show that he was no longer sick, but we knew very well that if we took him with us it would mean his certain death.

It was time for us to go. Before we left I made up a good fire and wrapped Joli-Coeur up well. He cried again and held on to me. Then we started off. As we tramped through the snow Vitalis told me what he expected of me. We could not, of course, give our usual full repertoire but Capi and I could vie with each other in doing our best. It was most urgent to collect forty francs. Forty francs! It was impossible.

Vitalis had got everything ready, and all we had to do now was to light the candles. However, we couldn't do this until the hall was full for our illuminations would have to last out until the end of the performance. Meantime the town-crier with his drum was going through the streets for the last time. After I had dressed Capi and myself I went outside and stood behind a pillar to watch the audience arrive.

Before long the beating of the drum came nearer and I could hear the murmur of voices. These came from twenty or so children who were marching in step with the drum's beat. Still sounding his drum the town-crier stood beside the two large lamp-posts that were lit at the entrance to our theatre. The audience had only to walk in and take their seats for the performance to begin.

The drum continued its happy rat-a-tat-tat, and all the village children must have been inside. But it was not they who between them were likely to pay the forty francs, and there would have to be some well-to-do grownups who were generous with their money. At last Vitalis decided that we must start even though the hall was far from full. We simply couldn't wait any longer because of the worry over the candles.

I had to appear first and sing two songs accompanying myself on the harp. I must admit that what applause I received was not very loud or enthusiastic. I had never considered myself much of an entertainer, but the coolness of the audience discouraged me more than I can tell you. It was not for any sort of glory that I was singing — it was for poor Joli-Coeur, and I had so much wanted to warm the audience up. Capi was more successful, and received several encores. His part in the entertainment ended in a burst of applause, with a lot of handclapping and stamping of feet.

The decisive moment had arrived. While I performed a

Spanish dance to Vitalis's accompaniment Capi, with the wooden bowl in his jaws, ran through the audience. Would he collect forty francs? That was the question that made my heart beat as I smiled at the public as nicely as I could. I was out of breath but I went on dancing, not stopping until Capi had come back. He didn't hurry himself, and when he saw that he hadn't been given a coin he, as usual, put his paw against the person's pocket or purse.

At last I saw him return and I thought that I might stop, but Vitalis signalled me to go on. So on I went, and going a few steps nearer Capi I saw that the bowl wasn't anywhere near full. Vitalis had seen this too, and bowing to the audience he said:

"Ladies and gentlemen, I think that without flattering ourselves we have conscientiously carried out our programme. However, as the candles are still burning I will, if you wish, sing some songs myself. Capi will make another tour among you, and those who have not made a contribution yet will perhaps give this time. Please have your money ready."

Although Vitalis had taught me to sing I had never really heard him sing, or at least not as he sang that evening. He chose two songs, an air from 'Joseph' and one from 'Richard Coeur-de-Lion'. I was only a very young boy then and was no judge as to whether anyone was a good singer or not but Vitalis's singing affected me strongly and I went to a corner of the stage, my eyes filled with tears.

Through my tears I saw a young lady who was sitting in the front row clap her hands with all her might. I had already noticed that she was quite different from the rest of the audience. She was rather beautiful, and from her fur coat I took her to be the richest person in the village. She had with her a child who had loudly applauded Capi. He was very probably her son, for the likeness was striking.

When the first song had ended Capi did his rounds again and I saw with surprise that the lady put nothing in his bowl. As soon as Vitalis's second song was finished she beckoned me to her.

"I would like to speak to your employer," she said.

I was even more surprised, for it seemed to me that it would

103

have been better if she had dropped a coin into the bowl. However, on Capi's return after collecting very little more than the first time, I told Vitalis what she had said.

"What does she want me for?"

"Just to speak to you."

"I have nothing I want to say."

"She never gave anything to Capi and perhaps she would like to give it to you."

"It is for Capi to go to her, not me."

However, in the end he decided to go over to her taking Capi with him, and I followed. By now a servant had appeared carrying a lantern and a rug. He stood behind the lady and the child. Vitalis bowed coldly to her.

"Forgive me if I am being a nuisance," she said, "but I want to congratulate you."

Vitalis bowed but said nothing.

"I am a musician," she went on, "and I am telling you this so that you will know how much I appreciate your great talent."

My master with a great talent! The dog-trainer! I was stupefied.

"An old man like me has no talent."

"Please do not think I am inquisitive."

"I am quite ready to satisfy your curiosity, madam. You are surprised that a dog-trainer is able to sing a little. But I have not always been what I am now. A long time ago, when I was young, I was the servant of a great singer and like a parrot I imitated him. I used to sing over and over again some of the songs he practised while I was in his room. That is all."

The lady did not reply but only looked at him. Vitalis stood looking embarrassed.

"Au revoir, monsieur," she said at last, with a curious emphasis on the 'monsieur'. "Au revoir, and let me thank you once again for the great pleasure you have given me this evening." And, bending towards Capi, she dropped a gold coin into the bowl.

I thought that Vitalis would have escorted her to the door. He did nothing of the sort and when she was out of earshot I heard him swear softly in Italian.

"She gave Capi a gold coin," I said.

I thought he was going to hit me, but he let his raised hand fall.

"A gold louis," he said, as if he were coming out of a dream. "Ah yes, poor Joli-Coeur, I had forgotten him. We must go back at once."

I climbed the stairs of the inn first and ran into the room. The fire hadn't gone out but there were no flames. I quickly lit a candle to look for the little creature for I hadn't heard any sound from him. I found him lying under his coverings, stretched out at full length and still dressed in his general's uniform. He seemed to be sleeping, so I bent over him and gently took his hand to waken him. His hand was cold.

Just then Vitalis came into the room, and I turned to him.

"Joli-Coeur is cold," I said.

Vitalis came over to me and also bent over the bed.

"Alas, he's dead," he said. "It had to happen. Listen, Remi, I did wrong when I took you away from Mrs Milligan, and I have been punished for doing so. Zerbino, Dolce, and now Joli-Coeur. And this is not the end."

We were still a long way from Paris. From morning to night we had to tramp along roads covered with snow with the wind blowing in our faces. How sad and weary this continual trudging made us. Vitalis went on ahead with me at his heels and Capi following on behind. For hours and hours, our faces blue with cold, our feet wet and our stomachs empty, we pushed on. People who passed us turned round to stare, obviously puzzled and wondering where the old man could be leading his child and dog.

To me the silence of our march was almost painful for I would love to have talked just for the sake of companionship, but when I did venture to make some remark Vitalis replied only briefly without even turning his head. Fortunately Capi was more sociable and I often felt his warm tongue on my hand as much as to say "I, your friend Capi, am here." Then I gave him a pat — we understood and loved each other. I like to think that my patting helped him to forget the death of his friends Zerbino and Dolce.

"Joli-Coeur is cold," I said.

When night fell we found either a barn or a sheepfold to sleep in. A small piece of bread was our evening meal — indeed it was our dinner and supper all in one. A sheepfold was the better place for the sheep helped to keep us warm against the cold. We didn't tell the shepherds that we were famished, but Vitalis would cleverly hint that "the young boy when he was a baby was very fond of sheep's milk to drink." This story was not always believed but it was a happy night for me when it was, and I always felt stronger next day.

So, mile after mile, from one sleeping-place to the next, we slowly came nearer to Paris. But what astonished me was the fact that the country became ever less beautiful. I had always heard what a wonderful place Paris was, and I suppose in my ignorance I expected something quite different, but what I didn't know. I wouldn't have been a bit surprised to see trees made of gold, marble palaces along the streets, and everyone wearing clothes made of silk.

What were we shabby people going to do when we did arrive in Paris? I wanted to ask Vitalis but didn't dare for he was so gloomy and wrapped in his own thoughts. But when we finally came in sight of the roofs and steeples of the city Vitalis slackened his pace to walk beside me.

"In four hours we should be in Paris," he said, and at that very moment a ray of sunshine came through the clouds as if to fulfil my thoughts of seeing trees of gold. "We are going to part when we get there," he went on, and at once all the brightness changed to gloom. I stared at him and he looked back at me. For a moment I couldn't speak. My sudden paleness and trembling lips told him how what he had just said had affected me.

"Going to part?" I murmured at last, and tears came to my eyes.

"You poor little chap."

It was so long since I had heard a kind word. "You are so good," I stammered.

"It is you who are good. You're a brave boy. You know, when everything is going well one can go through life without giving

107

much thought to a companion, but when things start going wrong and above all when age creeps up a person wants to lean on somebody. You may be surprised to know that I have wanted to lean on you, but it's true. Only to see your eyes fill with tears as you listen to me gives me comfort, little Remi. I, too, am very unhappy. The tragedy is that we have to part just as we are getting closer to each other."

"But you're not going to leave me all alone in Paris are you?" I asked timidly.

"No, of course not. What would you do all by yourself, my child? You must remember that I have no right to do that. The day I would not allow that good lady to keep you and bring you up as her son I gave my word that I would do the best I could for you, and that is why I think it is best for us to part. But it is only for a short time, perhaps a few months. What could we do in Paris with all of our troupe gone except Capi? It is better that we should separate during the last months of the bad weather."

When he heard his name spoken Capi came up beside us. He sat, put a paw to his ear in a military salute and then placed it on his heart, as though to tell us that we could count on his devotion. Vitalis patted the dog's head affectionately.

"Yes, Capi, you are a good, brave dog. But without the others we can't do much, can we? Everyone would jeer at us."

"But what about my harp? I can play that."

"If I had two boys like you things would be different. But an old man with only one of your age is no good. If I were a very old man, and blind, people might stop and pay attention and listen to us. So, Remi, I have decided to leave you with a 'padrone' until the end of winter. He will take you in with the other children he has, and you will then be able to play your harp."

"And what about you?" I asked.

Vitalis took no notice of my question.

"I have stayed several times in Paris," he continued, "and I'm known there. I will give violin lessons to Italian children. It will be easy for me to find all the pupils I want and in my spare time I will find and train two dogs to take the place of Zerbino and Dolce.

Then Remi in the spring we will be together again and I will take you to Germany and England and you will grow, and your mind will develop. I'll educate you in all sorts of things, and make a man of you. I promised Mrs Milligan that I would do this, and I am a man of my word. I will teach you to speak English; you already know how to speak Italian as well as your own French, and that is something for a boy of your age."

As Vitalis said, perhaps it was all for the best but I could think of only two things — we were to be parted, and I was to have another 'padrone'. In the course of our wanderings I had met several of these who ill-treated children, even thrashing them. They were not the slightest bit like Vitalis, for they were cruel, they cursed and very often they were drunk. Would I fall into the hands of one of these awful men?

And if fate did give me a kind master it was to be another change. First it was Mother Barberin, then Vitalis, and then... Would it be always like this? Would I never find anyone whom I could love and live with always? Little by little I had become fond of Vitalis, for he seemed almost what a father should be like. Would I never have a father, a family, and always be alone in the world?

Vitalis had asked me to brave and to accept what had to be. I had no wish to add to his worries, but it was very hard having to leave him.

We continued walking and came finally to a river crossed by a bridge covered with dirty snow. We then came to a village, and again more open country with some miserable houses dotted about. All sort of vehicles were passing us, going and coming I supposed from Paris. Suddenly the countryside stopped and we were in a road with houses on each side, poorly-built houses and nothing like those I had seen in other towns. Soon we were walking down an awful street with heaps of snow on either side covered with ashes and rotting vegetables, and smelling horribly. I asked Vitalis:

"Where are we now?"

"In part of Paris, Remi."

Where were the marble houses and the people dressed in silk? Was this the Paris I had so much wished to see, and was I to spend the rest of the winter here separated from Vitalis and Capi?

CHAPTER ELEVEN

W e went on walking for some time along a street much cleaner than the first one that had smelt so horribly and then Vitalis, who plainly knew his way, turned to the right, pushing his way through groups of people who were blocking our path. "Mind you don't lose me," he said.

There was no need for him to give me that warning for I was treading on his heels, and to be doubly sure was holding on to a flap of his coat. We crossed a large courtyard to a dirty and dismal-looking house which I was quite certain never saw a ray of sunlight — it was the ugliest and most scaring house I had ever seen.

"Is Garofoli at home?" Vitalis asked a man who could be seen in the light from a lantern hanging rags on nails stuck into a wall.

"How should I know. Go and see for yourself, his door's facing you at the top of the stairs."

"Garofoli is the 'padrone' I told you about, Remi, and this is where he lives."

The street, the house, the staircase, did nothing to reassure me and I could not help wondering what my new master would be like. We climbed to the fourth storey and without knocking Vitalis pushed open the door at the top of the stairs and we found ourselves in a kind of big attic. The centre of the room was empty, but all around the walls were about a dozen beds. The walls and ceiling, once white, were now grimed with smoke, dust and dirt.

On the wall were hanging drawings, some of them funnily enough of flowers and birds.

"Are you there, Garofoli?" Vitalis called out. "It's so dark in here I can't see anything. It's Vitalis."

He was answered by a child in a weak and plaintive voice, "Signor Garofoli has gone out and won't be back for another two hours."

Then a boy of about twelve came towards us out of the gloom. I could not help noticing how strange he looked, and I can see him now as I saw him then. He seemed to be all legs and head, and his head was out of all proportion to the rest of him. He could never have been called good-looking, but there was something in his face which attracted one strongly — an expression of sadness and hopelessness. His big eyes were as gentle and soft as a dog's.

"Are you sure he will not be back before then?"

"Quite sure, signor. It will be dinner-time then and no one serves dinner except Signor Garofoli."

"When he comes back tell him that Signor Vitalis wants to see him."

"Yes, signor."

I was going to follow Vitalis as he was leaving but he stopped me.

"Stay here," he said, and then noticing how worried I was, "I'll be back," to reassure me.

When Vitalis's steps on the stairs could no longer be heard the boy turned to me.

"Are you Italian?" he asked, speaking in that language.

"No," I replied in French. "I'm French."

"Ah, so much the better."

"Do you like the French better than the Italians?"

"Oh no, I was thinking when I said 'so much the better' that if you were Italian you would probably be coming here to work for Signor Garofoli, and then I'd be sorry for you."

I was not very happy to hear this and so I asked: "Is he a bad man then?"

The boy did not reply, but the look he gave me was enough. As

112

though he did not wish to go on with the conversation he turned his back on me and went over to a fireplace. I followed him to warm myself and I noticed that on the fire was a very big cast-iron pot. Its lid had a spout sticking from it to let steam escape, and the lid was hinged to the pot on one side. The lid was padlocked. I was inquisitive.

"Why the padlock?" I asked.

"So that I can't take any of the soup. I have to guard it, but the 'padrone' doesn't trust me."

I couldn't help laughing.

"It's all very well for you to laugh," he said sadly, "because I suppose you think I am a glutton. Perhaps if you were me you would have done the same as I did. I was starving one day and the smell of the soup as it came out of the spout made me even hungrier, and I had some."

"So Signor Garofoli put on a padlock?"

"Yes, as a punishment, and I will tell you everything because if he's going to be your 'padrone' it will be a warning to you. My name is Mattia, and Garofoli is my uncle. My mother is a widow and very poor, and has only enough for herself and my little sister Christina. When Garofoli visited us in Italy last year he brought me back here with him. But that's another story. There are twelve boys here, some are chimney-sweeps, and those who are not strong enough to do that work are sent to sing and beg in the streets. Just to show you, Garofoli gave me two little white mice for people to see and I was told to bring back thirty sous at the end of each day. That was hard to do, and as many sous as I was short so many blows would I get from him. And the blows are hard, too, when Garofoli orders them.

"Nearly all the boys had their money when they came back at night, but I scarcely ever had mine. There is another boy here who shows mice and he's expected to bring back forty sous, and he does so every night. Quite a lot of times I have gone with him to see how he does it, and heard ladies say 'Give it to the pretty little boy, not to the ugly one.' The ugly one, of course, is me. A blow hurts you but it hurts more to hear things like that said, and in front of a lot of people too. You wouldn't know because I'm sure that nobody has ever called you ugly. When Garofoli saw that beating me didn't do any good he tried another way. Each night he took away some of my supper. I can't say to people in the streets who are watching my mice: 'Please give me something or I won't get anything to eat tonight.' They don't give for that reason."

"Why *do* they give?"

"Because you are good-looking, or because you remind them of some child of theirs who has died, and not because you are cold and hungry. Oh, I know their ways. Isn't it cold today?"

"Yes, very cold."

"After about six weeks I became so pale that I often heard people say 'that poor child is starving to death', and I learned that a suffering look does what good looks can't do. But you have to be very starved for that, and I would be given food, sometimes bread sometimes soup. That was a good time for me because Garofoli had stopped hitting me just to see if it would hurt me more going without supper. So when I got something to eat outside I didn't care. But one day Garofoli saw me with a bowl of soup that a fruiterer had given me, and then he knew why I didn't mind going without supper at home. It was after that he made me stay here and look after the soup. Every morning before he leaves he puts a small bit of meat and a few vegetables in the pot and locks the lid on, and all I have to do is see that it keeps hot. I smell the soup, but that's all. Smell doesn't fill your stomach, it only makes you hungrier. Am I very pale? As I never go out I don't hear people say so, and there's no mirror here."

"You don't seem any paler than other boys I've seen," I answered.

"You're saying that so as not to frighten me, but I'm glad I'm sick, and I want to be very ill."

I couldn't help staring at him.

"You don't understand," he said, and he smiled. "When someone's very ill they either take good care of you or let you die. If they let me die it will be all over — no more hunger, no more beatings. And I have been told that when we die we go to heaven

114

and live with God. Then, if I'm up there I can look down on Christina and I can ask God not to let her be unhappy. But I shall be just as pleased if they send me to the hospital."

No matter how sick I had felt while we were tramping across the country, and even when I thought I might have to go into a hospital, I had always summoned up enough strength to go on. I was quite amazed to hear Mattia speak like this.

"I'm really quite ill now, but not ill enough to make Garofoli worry," he went on in his quiet rather drawling voice. "By good luck he hasn't entirely given up hitting me. A week ago he hit me on the head and see how I have swollen up now, look at the lump. Yesterday he told me that it was a tumour and by the way he said it I think it might be something serious. At any rate it hurts, and at night when I go to bed I cry with the pain. I think that in two or three days he'll decide to send me to the hospital because he doesn't like being put about here by me. Yes, I think I am almost bad enough now to be sent there."

He came and stood quite close to me with his big eyes staring at me. I somehow did not like to tell him how dreadful he looked with those glittering eyes, hollow cheeks and bloodless lips, but I said all the same: "Yes, I think you are ill enough to go to the hospital."

Then he walked slowly over to the table, dragging his legs as he went, and began to wipe it down.

"Garofoli will be here soon, and we'd better not talk any more."

He hobbled about the table putting down plates and spoons. I counted twenty plates. So Garofoli must have twenty boys. As there were only twelve beds some of them must sleep two to a bed. And what beds! The covers must have been bought at stables when they were too old and not warm enough even for horses.

"Don't come here, try to find somewhere else to stay," he said.

"But where can I go?"

"I don't know. Wherever it is you'll be far better off than here."

While I was thinking over what he had said the door opened and a child came in carrying a violin, and in his free hand a big

115

piece of wood.

"Give me that wood," Mattia said going towards the boy. "Give it to me for the fire so that the soup'll be hotter."

"What makes you think I brought it back for the soup? I've been given only thirty-six sous today, and this bit of wood might save me from being beaten. It'll make up for the four sous I'm short."

"It won't do you any good." Mattia said this in a matter of fact way, almost as though he was pleased at the thought of the child being punished. I was very surprised to see such a hard look come into those big soft eyes, but it was only later that I learned that you get like the people you live with.

The boys then started to return one by one, and each as he came in hung on a nail above his head whatever musical instrument he was carrying. Those who weren't musicians and had simply shown animals put their mice and guinea-pigs into a cage. Just then there were steps on the stairs and a little man wearing a grey overcoat came into the room. I knew that this must be Garofoli and the moment he entered he gave me a look that froze my heart. Quickly and politely Mattia told him what Vitalis had said.

"So Vitalis is here," he said. "What does he want?"

"I don't know," Mattia answered.

"I'm not speaking to you. I'm speaking to this boy."

"My 'padrone' is coming back, and will tell you himself what he wants," I replied.

"Here's someone who knows the value of words. You're not Italian?"

"No, I'm French."

As soon as Garofoli had entered the room two small boys had moved to stand on each side of him, and then waited until he had finished speaking. Then one took his felt hat and very carefully put it on a bed, while the other brought a chair. They did this with all the gravity and respect that you see when choir-boys attend to the needs of a priest at mass. As soon as Garofoli had sat down another boy jumped to bring him an already-filled pipe, while a fourth gave him a lighted match.

116

"It stinks of sulphur, you animal," he shouted, throwing the match into the grate.

The culprit hurried to light another match and let it burn for a while before giving it to his master, but Garofoli wouldn't take it.

"Not you, you imbecile," he said in his harsh voice. He turned to another boy and said with a simper: "Ricardo, my pet, you give me a match," and the 'pet' hurried to obey.

"Now," Garofoli went on after he was comfortably settled in his chair and his pipe burning, "now to business my little angels. Mattia, bring me the book."

Mattia fetched a very dirty notebook, and Garofoli beckoned to the boy who had lit the first match.

"You owe me a sou from yesterday, and you promised to bring it today. How much have you got?"

The boy hesitated for a long time before he replied, for he was distressed. At last he blurted out: "I'm one sou short and it's not the sou for yesterday but for today."

"But that makes two sous. I've never come across anyone like you."

"It's not my fault."

"No excuses. You know the rules. Take off your coat. Two strokes for yesterday, two for today, and no supper for your cheek. Ricardo, you're my good boy and you deserve some fun, so go and get the whip."

Ricardo went to a wall and took down a short-handled whip with two knotted leather straps. While he was doing this the boy who was two sous short started taking off his coat, baring his body to the waist.

"Wait a minute," Garofoli said with a nasty smile, "you won't be the only one, and it's always nice to have company."

All the children were standing motionless before him but somehow they managed to force a laugh at this cruel joke of his.

"The one who laughed loudest is sure to be the one who is short the most. Now tell me, who was it who laughed?"

Everyone pointed to the boy who had come home first and had brought the piece of wood.

117

"You, how much do you owe me?" Garofoli demanded.

"It's not my fault."

"Never mind about that. Anyone who says 'It's not my fault' will get an extra stroke. How much are you short?"

"I brought back a piece of wood, a lovely piece of wood."

"Well, I suppose that that's something. But try going to the baker's and asking him for bread in exchange for your lovely piece of wood! How many sous are you short? Speak up."

"I made thirty-six sous."

"You wretch, you're four short. And you stand there in front of me like that. Off with your coat. Ricardo, you are going to have a very happy time."

"But what about the wood?" the boy cried out.

"I'll give it to you for your supper."

All the children who were not going to be punished burst out laughing again. Ricardo stood holding the whip until five of Garofoli's victims stood in a row before him.

"You know, Ricardo," Garifoli said with a groan, "I don't like to watch because a scene like this always makes me ill. But remember that I can hear and from the noise I can judge the strength you are putting into your blows. Go at it with a will, my pet, and remember that you're working for your supper."

He turned towards the fire, pretending that he could not watch the punishments. I stood forgotten in my corner and was shaking with anger and fear. So this was the man who was going to be my new master, and if I did not bring back to him his thirty or forty sous I would be whipped by Ricardo. Now I understood how Mattia could speak of illness and death so calmly.

The first lash of the whip as it cut into a boy's flesh made my eyes sting. I thought that I had been forgotten, but I was mistaken for Garofoli was looking at me out of the corner of one eye.

"Now, there's a boy who has a good heart," he said, pointing to me. 'He's not like you other wretches who laugh when your comrades suffer. This new companion of ours is an example to you."

Their companion! I was shaking more than ever.

At the second blow one of the victims gave a wail, and at the third a shriek. Garofoli raised a hand, and Ricardo stopped with his whip lifted. I thought that Garofoli was going to show some sort of mercy, but I was wrong.

"You know how much it hurts me to hear you cry," he said gently to the unfortunate boy. "You know that if the whip tears your skin your cries go to my heart. So let me warn you that for each yell you will get another stroke, and that will be your own fault. If you have any affection or gratitude for me you will be quiet." Then a pause. "Go on, Ricardo."

Ricardo went on with the whippings.

Thank goodness I saw little more of this shocking torture for just then the door was pushed open and Vitalis appeared. He took everything in at a glance, for he had heard the cries of pain as he was climbing the stairs. Running to Ricardo he grabbed the whip from him and then quickly turning to Garofoli he stood in front of him with folded arms. It had all happened so fast that Garofoli was dumbfounded. But he quickly recovered himself, and said weakly: "Isn't it terrible, that boy has no heart."

"This is dreadful," Vitalis cried.

"That's just what I say," Garofoli murmured.

"Enough of that!" Vitalis shouted, and I had never seen him like this. "You know only too well that it's not the boy I'm talking about. It's you, you who torture these poor children who can't defend themselves."

"Don't you meddle in what doesn't concern you, you old fool," Garofoli answered, his voice changing.

"It's a matter for the police."

"The police! You threaten me with the police?" And Garofoli got up from his chair.

"Yes, I do," my master replied, not at all frightened by the bully.

"Vitalis, do you want to talk to the police?" and Garofoli almost hissed. "If you do I can talk too. Your affairs are no concern of mine, but there are a lot of people interested in you and if I talk, if I say just one name... Then, you tell me, who will have need to worry?"

119

My master did not answer. I was shocked, but before I had time to think he had taken me by the arm.

"Come along with me, Remi." And he pulled me to the door.

Garofoli was laughing now. "I thought you wanted to talk to me, my old friend."

"I don't wish to speak to you."

Without another word we went down the stairs. He still held me tightly, and you can imagine the relief I felt, for I had escaped from Garofoli. If I had dared I would have thrown my arms around Vitalis's neck.

For as long as we were in the street Vitalis didn't say a word, but when we came to an alleyway where there was a boundary-stone he sat down on it and wiped his forehead — a sure sign of embarrassment with him.

"So now we are in the gutters of Paris," he muttered, as if he were talking to himself, "without a sou and with nothing to eat." Then, "Are you very hungry?" he asked, looking up at me.

"I haven't eaten anything since the piece of bread you gave me this morning."

"Poor Remi, and I have nothing for us or for Capi. And where are we going to sleep?"

"You thought I would be sleeping at Garofoli's didn't you?"

"Yes, and he would have given me about twenty francs for you for the rest of the winter, while I could have got along somehow for the time being. But when I saw the way he treated those other children I couldn't let you stay with him."

It was already late and getting colder. The wind was from the north and when it dropped there was going to be a hard frost. Vitalis sat on the stone for five minutes or more, and Capi and I stood motionless and silent facing him, waiting for him to say what we would do. At last he got up.

"We are going to Gentilly," he said. "We will try and find a stone-quarry where I slept a long time ago. Are you very tired?"

"There was nowhere for me to sit at Garofoli's."

"The pity is that I have been walking ever since I left you there, and I can't go on much longer. But we must get on our way now.

120

Forward, my children!"

This had been his good-humoured signal to the dogs and me when we were about to start in the morning, but this time he said it sadly.

Here we were, wandering in the back streets of Paris. It was a dark night and the gas-lamps flickering in the wind gave little light to the alleys we walked through. At almost every step we slipped on the ice-covered pavements. Vitalis held my hand and Capi followed at our heels. Every so often the poor dog stopped to smell among a heap of rubbish to see if he could find a bone or a crust of bread, but the heaps were covered with frozen snow and he had no luck. Then, with drooping ears, he would trot along to catch up with us.

More streets and alleyways, and the few people we met stared at us in astonishment. Was it the way we were dressed, or was it the tired way we plodded along that made them stare? The policemen we passed turned round and watched us as we tramped on. Vitalis never said a word; his back was bent almost double, and in spite of the cold his hand holding mine was burning. It seemed to me that he was trembling, and sometimes when he stopped to lean for a minute on my shoulder I felt his whole body shaking. Normally I would never have dared to question him, but that night I felt I must. Besides, I had a great wish to tell him that I wanted to help him.

"You are ill," I said when he paused to rest again.

"I'm afraid I am. I'm certainly very tired. This cold is too much for me at my age. What I would like most is supper in front of a fire and a warm bed. But that's just a dream."

We were now in the outskirts of Paris. We met no people nor policemen and there were no street lights, only a few lighted windows; over our heads the dark sky was dotted with a few stars. The wind, which now blew more bitterly and strongly, made our clothing cling to our bodies. By good luck it was at our backs, but as my coat-sleeves were torn near the shoulders it blew down my arms chilling me to the bone. Although it was very dark and the streets continually criss-crossed each other Vitalis walked like a

121

man who knew his way and was quite sure of the direction he was taking. So I followed on feeling certain that we would not get lost. Suddenly he stopped.

"Do you see a clump of trees ahead of us?" he asked.

"I can't see anything."

"You're sure you don't see anything tall which could be trees?"

I looked and looked but could see nothing; there were no trees, not even houses, and there was no sound except the whistling of the wind. I was afraid to say that I couldn't see anything like a clump of trees. He trudged on again and for some minutes nothing was said. Then he stopped once more and asked me the same question. I had a vague feeling of fear which made my voice shake when I gave the same reply that I could see nothing.

"Then we must have gone wrong somewhere on our way."

I didn't know where we were or even where we were going, so I didn't answer.

"We'll walk on for another five minutes and if we don't see the trees I remember we'll come back to where we are. I might have made a silly mistake on our way."

Now that I knew that we had lost our way I seemed to lose any strength left to me and stumbled. Vitalis grabbed my arm.

"I can't go any further."

"Do you think I'm going to carry you? Tell me, are there any deep ruts in the road?"

"I can't see any."

"Then we must turn back."

We turned, and now we faced the wind which hit and stung our faces like a whip. Indeed, it seemed that my face was being scorched by a flame.

"When you see some ruts, tell me," Vitalis said, "for then our road should be to the left with a clump of thorn-trees showing where we must turn off."

We went on struggling against the wind for a quarter of an hour, and in the sad silence of the night the noise of our footsteps echoed on the frozen ground. Although I could hardly put one foot in front of the other it was I who dragged Vitalis. Anxiously I

122

kept looking to the left, and in the darkness I suddenly saw a little red light.

"Look," I said, pointing.

"Where?"

Vitalis looked, and although the light was only a short distance away he couldn't see it. It was then that I realized that his sight was failing.

"The light you're talking about is either a lamp burning on some workman's table or else it's near the bed of someone who is sick. We can't knock on a door here. In the country it's different and even at this time of night you can ask for shelter. But Paris is different. Come along."

A few yards further on I thought I could make out the turning by some thorn-trees and I let go of Vitalis's hand to go ahead faster. There were deep ruts crossing the road, too, and I told him so.

"Give me your hand, we are saved," Vitalis said. "In five minutes we will be there."

We tramped on, and those five minutes seemed ages.

"We must have passed the entrance to the quarry without seeing it. I think we'd better go back." Once again we turned back and somehow or other in the darkness we came upon a wall. Vitalis told me to look for a way through it and I felt along it — there was no opening, no gate.

"There is no way through," I told him.

Our situation was desperate. There was no doubt that Vitalis was ill and almost delirious. Perhaps there was no such thing as a quarry here. He stood for a moment as though in a dream, and Capi started to bark impatiently.

"What do you think, shall we go on?" I asked.

"We had better go in the direction of Paris. If we come across a policeman we can ask him to take us to the nearest police station. I don't like doing that but we can't die of cold here Remi."

We turned back the same way we had come. We had walked for hours, a long, long time, and so very slowly, and I had no idea of the time. The sky was still very dark with no moon, and the few stars seemed to me to be smaller than usual. The wind was now blowing harder and the houses we passed were closed tight for the night. I felt that if the people who were sleeping there, warm under their blankets, could know how cold we were outside they would have opened their doors to us.

Vitalis walked slower and slower now and when I tried to speak to him he signed to me to be quiet. We were getting nearer to the city, but when Vitalis stood still I knew that he had nearly reached the end of his strength.

"Do you want me to knock at one of the doors?" I asked at last.

"No, they wouldn't let us in. The people who live here are market-gardeners. The won't answer the door at this time of night. Let's go on."

But he had more will than strength, and after a while he had to stop again.

"I must rest for a minute or two," he said in a weak voice. "I just can't go on."

Near us was a gate leading into a big garden. Winds had blown into the street a good deal of straw that had been covering a manure heap.

"I'll sit down here," he said.

"But you've always told me that once we sat down we would get too cold to get up again."

He didn't answer. All he did was to sign to me to pile up the straw against the door. When I had done this he fell rather than sat down on it. His teeth chattered and the whole of his body shook as he managed to say: "Bring more straw, as much as you can, and we'll shelter from the wind."

From the wind, yes, but not from the cold; so I gathered up all the straw I could find and sat beside him.

"Come closer to me," he said, "and lift Capi onto your lap. You'll get some warmth from him."

Vitalis was certainly ill, but I was not sure that he knew how ill he was. As I crept closer to him he bent over and kissed me. It was only the second time he had done this and, alas, it was to be the last.

124

Scarcely had I snuggled up against him than my eyes started to close. Try as I would to keep them open I couldn't. I pinched my arms hard but there was no feeling. Capi was already asleep stretched out over my legs and part of my chest. The wind was blowing wisps of straw onto us, just like dried leaves falling from a tree. There was not a soul about and around us was complete silence.

This silence frightened me. But what could I be afraid of? I didn't know, but it seemed to me that something dreadful was going to happen. My thoughts went to Chavanon and Mother Barberin. Must I die without seeing her again, and our little cottage with my little garden? All of a sudden it seemed to me as if I was back in my garden; the sun was shining and it was warm, the jonquils were in flower and the birds were singing in the trees and on the hedgerows. Yes, and Mother Barberin was hanging out the clothes she had just washed in the stream where it rippled over the pebbles.

And then I had left Chavanon and had rejoined 'Le Cygne', with Arthur asleep on his wooden board and Mrs Milligan sitting beside him. My eyes stayed shut, my heart seemed to beat more slowly, and I remembered nothing more.

CHAPTER TWELVE

When I woke up I was in a bed and the flames from a big fire lit up the room. I had never seen the room before and I didn't recognise the people who were standing near me. As well as three or four children there was a man wearing a grey smock and yellow-painted clogs. One of the children I noticed particularly was a little girl of about six years old who was gazing at me in astonishment — her eyes had so much expression that they seemed to speak. I lifted myself up on an elbow and they all came closer.

"Where is Vitalis?"

"He's asking about his father," a girl who seemed to be the eldest of the children said.

"He's not my father, he's my master," I replied. "Where is he? Where's Capi?"

If Vitalis had been my father I am sure that they would have broken the news to me gently, but as he was only my master they thought they could tell me at once everything that had happened. At about two in the morning the man in the grey smock, who was a gardener, had found us lying under the straw. He and one of his sons had been starting off for the market. Vitalis was already dead, and I would have died too but for Capi keeping me warm. They had carried us into the house and I had been put into one of the children's warm beds.

And so my poor master was dead.

"What about Capi?" I managed to ask again.

"Capi?"

"Yes, our dog."

"We don't know. He disappeared."

"He followed the body when it was taken away," a boy said. "Didn't you see him, Benjamin?"

"Yes, I did," the other boy answered. "He walked behind the two men carrying the stretcher. He kept his head down, but every now and then he would jump onto the body and when he was pushed off he howled most terribly."

Poor Capi. I remembered how many times as an actor he had followed Zerbino's mock funeral. Even the most serious children could not help laughing at the grief he showed, and the more of an act he put on the more they had laughed.

The gardener and his children left the room then and not knowing what to do I got out of bed and put on my clothes. My harp was at the foot of the bed so I strapped it over my shoulder and, after trying out my legs to see if they were still shaking and weak, went into the room where they all were. There was a smell of soup and it reminded me that I had not eaten anything for hours. I felt faint and staggered a little before I dropped into a chair beside the fire.

"You're not feeling well are you," the gardener said.

I replied that I was still very tired and asked him if I could stay by his fire a while to warm myself. But it wasn't the warmth I wanted so much as food, and I felt worse as I watched the family eating their soup. If I had dared I would have asked for a bowl, but Vitalis had taught me never to beg. I couldn't tell them I was ravenous. Don't ask me why for I don't quite know, unless it was that I could not ask for anything that I could not pay for.

The little girl with the eyes that seemed almost to speak, and whose name I gathered was Lise, was sitting opposite me. All of a

127

sudden she got up from the table, took hold of her bowl which was still full, brought it over to me and put it on my knees. Feebly, for I seemed no longer able to speak, I nodded my head to thank her; but even if I had been able to speak, her father did not give me time to say anything.

"Eat it up," he said. "Whatever Lise gives is always given with a kind heart, and there is more if you want it."

I can tell you that that bowl of soup was quickly swallowed and Lise, when I put the empty bowl down, gave a little sigh of happiness. She picked it up, held it out to her father to be filled again, and handed it back to me with such a lovely smile that despite the fact that I was still hungry I sat staring at her without thinking of taking it from her. But soon the second bowlful disappeared as quickly as the first, and there was no longer a smile on Lise's lips — she had burst out laughing.

"Well," said her father, "you've an appetite and no mistake."

I was ashamed when he said this and after a moment or two I thought it better to confess the truth rather than be thought a glutton, so I told them that I had had no supper the night before.

"What about lunch?"

"No lunch either."

"And your master?"

"He was the same as me."

"Then he died as much from starvation as from the cold."

The hot soup had brought back some of my strength, and I stood up to leave.

"Where are you going?" the father asked. "Have you friends or relatives in Paris?"

"No."

"Where do you live?"

"We hadn't any home. We only arrived in the city yesterday."

"What are you going to do then?"

"Play my harp and earn a little money."

"In Paris? You had better go back to your parents in the country. Where do they live?"

"I haven't any parents. My master bought me from my foster-

128

parents. You have been very kind to me and I thank you with all my heart. If you would like me to then I will come back next Sunday and play my harp to you."

As I was saying this I had started walking towards the door, but I had taken only a few steps when Lise took my hand and pointed to the harp.

"Would you like me to play something now?" And I smiled at her. She nodded and clapped her hands.

Although I must admit that I didn't feel like playing I chose my prettiest waltz for the little girl. At first she listened with her eyes fixed on me, then she began to keep time with her feet, and very soon she was dancing around the kitchen while her brothers and sister watched her. Her father, too, never took his eyes off her. When the waltz was ended she came and curtsied to me. Now I felt that I could have played for the rest of the day to please her, but her father thought she had danced enough, so instead I sang the Neapolitan song that Vitalis had taught me. Lise stood in front of me moving her lips as if she was copying the words. Then, suddenly, she turned round and in tears clung to her father's knees.

"I think we've had enough music," he said.

"Isn't that silly," the brother named Benjamin said. "First she dances then she cries."

"She's not silly," the elder sister retorted, bending affectionately over Lise. "She hears and is trying so hard..."

While Lise stayed by her father I picked up my harp and again made for the door.

"Where are you going?" he asked, and then went on: "Would you like to stay here with us and work in the garden? You will have to get up early and work hard all day, but you can be quite certain that you won't have to go through what you did last night. You'll have your bed and your food, and you'll know that you have earned them both. If you are a good boy, and I'm sure you are, you will be one of the family."

Lise turned towards me and smiled at me through her tears. I could hardly believe my ears, and just stared at the gardener.

Then Lise came and took my hand.

"Well, what do you say?" her father asked.

A family! I would have a family and at last I would not be alone. The man who had been so kind to me was dead, and good dear Capi, my companion and friend, was lost. I had thought that everything was finished for me but now here was this friendly man offering to take me into his family. Life could begin for me again. What meant most to me, more than the food, more than anything, was the family life I would have with these boys as my brothers and pretty Lise as my sister. In my childhood dreams I had more than once imagined that I might somehow find my father and mother, but I had never dreamed that I would have brothers and sisters. And this was what was being offered to me.

"There's his answer," the father said with a laugh, and turning to me: "I can see by your face how pleased you are. Put your harp over there against the wall and when you get tired of us all you can take it and go on your way again. But you must copy the swallows and choose the right time of year for your flight. Don't start off in the depths of winter."

There were five people in my new family — the father whose name was Pierre Acquin, two boys named Alexis and Benjamin, Etiennette the elder of the two girls, and Lise who was the youngest of them all. I should tell you now that Lise was dumb. She had not been born that way, but when she was about four she had lost her power of speech because of some illness which, luckily, had not affected her in any other way; quite the contrary, for she was very intelligent and understood everything that was going on about her. From the day of her mother's death Etiennette had taken her place and had left school to stay at home to do the cooking and sewing and all the other work in the house.

It was not five minutes after I had put my harp where I had been told to before I was telling them all of what had happened the night before, and of how we had hoped to sleep in the quarry. While I was speaking of all this I heard scratching on the door that opened into the garden, and then a plaintive little bark.

"That must be Capi," I cried, and I jumped up. But by then

Lise had opened the door. Capi sprang upon me, and when I hugged him he licked my face and made funny little noises of joy, his whole body trembling.

"But what about Capi?" I asked, and I was told that, of course, he could stay too. As though he understood what had been said he jumped to the ground, put a paw to his chest, and bowed. That made the children laugh, especially Lise. To amuse them more I wanted Capi to perform some of his tricks, but he didn't want to. Instead he jumped onto my knees and then sprang down again, pulling at my coat-sleeve.

"He wants to go out to lead you to your master," someone said.

Here I should tell you that the police who had taken Vitalis away had told the gardener that they wanted to talk to me when I was feeling stronger. Nobody knew when they would come, and I was very anxious, for perhaps Vitalis was not dead as everybody thought. When Monsieur Acquin saw how restless I was he offered to take me to the police station. When we went there I was asked a great many questions and I only answered these after I was told that Vitalis was, indeed, dead. Then I told them what I knew, which was very little, for all I could say was that I had no parents and that Vitalis had bought me from Barberin. The police superintendent then asked what I was going to do now, and when Monsieur Acquin answered that he was going to look after me if he was allowed to the superintendent was pleased.

The conversation then came back to Vitalis. It is not easy for anyone to hide very much from a police officer for he can quickly trap people into telling him what they might want to hide. This was true with me, for the superintendent soon learned all he wanted to know.

"I think that the only thing to do is to take Remi to this man Garofoli," he said to one of his men. "Once in the street he has mentioned he will soon recognise the house he has told us about. You can go up with him and question this fellow."

The three of us set off and, as the superintendent had said, we soon found the street and the house. We climbed to the fourth floor. There was no sign of Mattia. He had probably been taken off to the hospital, but Garofoli was there and when he saw a policeman and recognised me he went pale and looked very scared indeed. However, his composure came back when he knew that the only questions he would be asked were about Vitalis.

"So the old man's dead?" he said.

"You knew him did you? Well then, tell us all you can about him."

"There's not a great deal I can tell you. His name was not Vitalis but Carlo Balzini, and if you had lived in Italy thirty-five or forty years ago that name would tell you all you want to know. He was the greatest singer of his day and he sang all over Europe. The time came when somehow or other he lost his beautiful voice, and as he was no longer one of the greatest of singers he decided to hide himself from the world and everyone who had known him in his triumphs. He had to live somehow but he was never successful in anything he tried, and in the end he took up the training of dogs. In all his misery and poverty he was still very proud. He would have died of shame if the people who had applauded him when he was most famous had ever learned of what had happened to him. It was quite by chance that I learned of his secret."

Poor Carlo Balzini; poor dear Vitalis.

Vitalis had to be buried the following day and Monsieur Acquin promised to take me to the funeral. But I could not go, for during that night I developed a very high temperature and my chest seemed to burn just as Joli-Coeur's had done after he had spent so long in the tree.

A doctor was called in and he said that I had pneumonia. He wanted me to go into hospital but the family would not hear of such a thing. It was while I was so ill that I learned to appreciate Etiennette's goodness for she spent a lot of her time looking after me, and when she simply had to go and do her housework Lise took her place. I can remember clearly now that often in my delirium I would see the little girl sitting at the foot of my bed looking anxiously at me with her big eyes; I imagined she was my guardian angel and whispered to her all of my hopes and desires. It was from then that I began to regard Lise as someone quite different from other people I had met.

I was ill for a very long time. During the nights when I was nearly suffocating the two brothers would take it in turn to sit beside me. At last I was allowed out of bed and it was Lise who took me for walks down by the river. Of course during our walks she could not talk but, strange to say, we had no need for words for we understood each other well. And then at last came the day when I was well enough to work with the others in the garden.

I had been impatient to start, for I wanted to repay my good friends for all the kindness they had shown me. As I was still not very strong I was given light tasks. Every morning after the frost had gone it was part of my duties to raise the glass frames and at night, before it got cold again, to close them. This wasn't difficult, but it kept me busy for there were several hundred of these frames. Then during the rest of the day I had to shade with very light straw-coverings a lot of the flowers that were to go to Les Halles in Paris to be sold there.

Weeks, months, passed and I was very happy. Indeed, sometimes I thought that I was too happy, that it was too good to be true. I should tell you that Monsieur Acquin was regarded as one of the best flower growers near Paris. For many weeks we had all been working very hard, not even having a day off on Sundays. But one Sunday near the end of summer it was decided that we should all go and have an early supper with one of Monsieur Acquin's friends who was a gardener too. Capi was to be one of the party. We were to work until four o'clock and then the gates were to be locked and off we would go. After supper at six we would come home at once so as not to be late in bed, for on Monday morning we had to be up early again for work. A little before four we were all ready.

"Come on all of you, let's get on our way," Monsieur Acquin called out and, "Come Capi."

I took Lise's hand and began running with her to join the others and Capi jumped about barking. We all wore our best clothes and were looking forward to a good supper. People turned round to watch us as we passed; I can't now remember anything much of how we were all dressed except that Lise in her straw hat, blue dress and matching shoes was the prettiest sight one could ever see.

Time passed quickly and we had just finished eating supper out of doors when someone said how overcast it was getting. Clouds were, certainly, gathering rapidly.

"Children, we must hurry home," said Monsieur Acquin. "There's going to be a thunderstorm."

"What, leave already!"

"Yes, if the wind gets up the glass frames will be lifted and smashed."

We all knew how costly these frames were and what their loss would mean.

"I'll hurry on ahead with the boys," Monsieur Acquin went on. "Remi, you follow with Etiennette and Lise."

No one was laughing or joking now as the sky became even darker for the storm was coming up very quickly indeed. Dust whirled about us, and we had to turn our backs to the wind and cover our eyes with our hands to stop being blinded by it. There was a flash of lightning followed by a heavy peal of thunder. Etiennette and I had taken Lise by the hands and tried to pull her along faster. Would the others get home before the storm broke, we were wondering, and fasten down the frames securely before the wind lifted and broke them?

The thunder came closer and louder and the clouds were so heavy that it seemed almost like night. Then the wind dropped all of a sudden and there was a hailstorm. The hailstones hit our faces, so we had to run and take shelter in a big gateway. In no time the road was white just as if it was winter after snow had fallen. The hailstones were as big as pigeons' eggs and when they hit the ground they made a deafening noise, and every now and again we could hear the breaking of glass. With the hailstones as they slid from the roofs fell all sorts of things, pieces of tile, plaster and broken slate.

"Oh, what about our glass frames!" Etiennette cried, and I was thinking the same. "Even if they get home before the hail they'll never have time to cover all the glass with straw. Every frame will

134

be smashed.'

I knew what a disaster it would be if five to six hundred frames were broken, as well as the value of the flowers. Now we could hardly hear each other's voices and we just watched hopelessly the hailstones falling, like people watching their house burning. The storm stopped as suddenly as it had started and I suppose it had lasted about six minutes. The clouds swept towards Paris and we were able to leave our shelter. The hailstones were lying thick on the ground, and as Lise could not walk on them in her thin shoes I lifted her onto my shoulder. Her face, so bright when we set off for the party, was now grief-stricken and the tears were rolling down her cheeks.

It did not take us much longer to reach home; the gate was open and when we went quickly into the garden what a sight greeted us — frames were smashed to pieces, and flowers, pieces of glass and hailstones were all piled together. We looked everywhere for Monsieur Acquin and at last found him in the big conservatory of which every pane was broken. He was sitting on a wooden stool in the middle of all the debris that covered the ground. The two boys were standing silently near him.

"Oh, my children," he said in a shocked voice when we joined him. He took Lise in his arms and was too grief-stricken to say any more. What could he say? It was a disaster, and worse was to come. It was later that Etiennette told me that ten years before their father had decided to buy the ground and to build their house himself. The man who had sold him the land had also lent him the money to buy everything that was needed for him to establish his nursery. Monsieur Acquin was to pay back what he had been lent in annual payments over fifteen years, and if he was late in any payment he would lose everything, the ground, the house, the equipment and, of course, the payments he had made over the past ten years.

It was not long before we had no doubt as to what would happen, for the day after the next payment was due a man dressed all in black came to the house and delivered a piece of paper with a stamp stuck on it. I was told he was a bailiff. He came so often that

135

he soon began to know us all by our Christian names. He always handed us his piece of paper with a smile, almost as if he was a friend of ours. Monsieur Acquin was not often at home, and he never told us where he went, but thinking back I think he was probably seeing friends who might be able to help him, or he might even perhaps have been answering a lot of questions in front of a judge. I remembered so clearly then what had happened to Vitalis in Toulouse.

Autumn had come and gone. We had not been able to repair the conservatory or to renew the glass frames so we had grown vegetables and hardier flowers that did not need any shelter. These didn't make as much money, but at least it was something and we were all kept quite busy.

One evening Monsieur Acquin returned home even more depressed than usual. "I can't do anything more," he said, "everything is finished."

When I heard this I wanted to leave the room, for I felt that if things were so serious he would not want me to hear what he had to say to his own children, but he made a sign to me to stay.

"You are one of the family, Remi," he went on, "and although you are not very old you know everything that has happened." He paused. "I must tell you that I have to go away."

There was a silence and then everyone tried to speak at once. Lise threw her arms around her father's neck, and he held her very close to him.

"I know it's hard to leave you but I have been ordered by the court to pay all I owe. I have no money and so everything here must be sold, and if that's not enough I have to go to prison for five years. My lawyer has told me that it used to be much worse for a man like me. So I have decided that the best thing to be done is for Remi to write to my sister Catherine and explain things to her and ask her to come here. Your aunt has plenty of common-sense and will decide what must be done for the best."

This was the first time I had ever written a letter and it was a very painful one. But Aunt Catherine did not come as soon as we had hoped. A few days after I had written to her Monsieur Acquin was just leaving the house to call on a friend when he met the police coming to arrest him. He came back, very pale, to say goodbye to us all.

"Don't be so down-hearted, my friend," one of the policemen said to him, "going to prison for debt is not as dreadful as you seem to think and you'll find you're among good company."

I went to call the two boys who were busy in the garden. The parting was soon over. I had been standing a little apart from the rest but Monsieur Acquin came over and kissed me as affectionately as he had the other children. Then he was taken away and we all stood forlorn, none of us able to say a word.

About an hour later Aunt Catherine arrived. She told us that the responsibility of looking after four destitute children, the eldest of whom was not yet sixteen and the youngest a little dumb girl, was too much for her. She had once been a nurse in a lawyer's family and when she received my letter she had gone at once to this man for advice; it was he who had decided our fate. We were then told what had been arranged — the two boys and Etiennette were to go to stay with uncles and an aunt, and I listened waiting until it came to my turn.

When she had finished speaking, and I had not been mentioned, I said: "But what is going to happen to me?"

"You don't belong to the family."

"I'll work for you. Ask the others if I can work or not. I like work."

"He *is* one of the family, Auntie, he *is* one of the family," the others called out, and Lise went over to her aunt and her expression said more to her than words could do.

"Poor Lise," she said, "I know you'd like him to come and live with us, but we can't always have everything we want. You're my niece and if your uncle is not very pleased when I bring you home all I need to say is that you're a relation and I'm going to have you with us. It will be the same with the other uncle and aunt. They will take in relations, but not a stranger."

I knew there was nothing I could say, for what she had said was only too true. I was not one of the family and I could neither claim nor ask anything. And yet I loved them all, and they loved me. After being told how we would all be split up next day we were sent off to bed. Scarcely were we upstairs than they all crowded around me, and then I knew that in spite of their sadness at being parted from one another it was of me that they were thinking, pitying me because I would be alone again. Suddenly I had an idea.

"Listen," I said, "even if your uncles and aunts don't want me I know that *you* think of me as one of you."

"Yes, of course," they all cried.

Lise took hold of my hand and waited for me to go on. Etiennette interrupted by saying that there might be a job for me with a neighbour and that she would go over and speak to him before they left next day.

"I don't want a job here for that would mean that I wouldn't see you all again. What I am going to do when you all go is to put on my sheepskin and take my harp and visit you all wherever you are going to live. I will be able to bring you all news of each other. I haven't forgotten my songs or my dance music, and I'm sure I'll manage somehow."

There were smiles all round, and I was glad that my idea pleased them. After we had talked for quite a time Etiennette made us all go to bed. But no one slept very much, least of all me. Departure time had been fixed for eight in the morning and a cab had been ordered to take them all first to the prison to say another goodbye to their father and then to the different stations where they were to catch their trains. Just before they left Etiennette took me into the garden.

"I want to give you a keepsake, Remi," she said. "Have this little box, my godfather gave it to me. In it you'll find thread, needles and a pair of scissors. When you're tramping along the roads you'll need them, for I won't be there to put a patch on your clothes or to sew on a button for you. And when you are doing your mending think of us all."

While Etiennette was talking to me Alexis was nearby, and when she went back to the house he came over.

138

"Remi, I have two five-franc pieces and I want you to have one."

Now, of all of us he was the only one who showed any interest in money, and we used to make fun of him for the way he saved every sou and was always counting his little hoard. I wanted to refuse but he pushed a shiny coin into my hand. Benjamin, too, had not forgotten me and gave me his knife, but he asked for a sou in return for, as he said, 'a knife cuts friendship'.

The moment had now come for us to say our goodbyes but as the cab drew up at the house Lise made a sign to me to follow her into the garden, even though her aunt tried to call her back. She took no notice but ran quickly down the path, stopped at a big rosebush, and cut off a stem with two roses on it. She divided the stem in two, gave me half and kept the other half. Her aunt again called to her, for everybody's luggage was now in the cab.

I went to get my harp and to call Capi. When he saw me in my sheepskin he jumped about and barked with joy. He loved the freedom he had on the roads far more than being allowed to roam wherever he wanted to in the garden. By now everyone was in the cab and I went over to put Lise onto her aunt's knees. I stood beside the cab in a sort of daze; then the aunt gently pushed me away and closed the door. They were off. Through a mist I saw Lise leaning out of the window waving to me, and then the cab turned a sharp bend and all I could see was a cloud of dust.

With my harp beside me and with Capi stretched at my feet I stayed staring absentmindedly down the road. A neighbour who had been asked to lock up the house and to take care of the keys called out to me: "How long are you going to stay there?"

"I'm going now."

"Where to?"

"I'll follow my nose."

"If you'd like to stay," he said, probably out of pity, "you can with me. I won't pay you anything because you'll not be much use to me. Later on I might."

I thanked him politely but said no.

139

"Just as you like. I was only thinking of your own good. Good luck."

He went away. The house was locked up and everyone was gone.

"Come, Capi."

I turned away from the home where I had lived for two years and where I had hoped always to go on living. The sun was well up, the sky was clear, the weather warm, and everything was very different from that terrible night when Vitalis and I had fallen exhausted and frozen by the gate.

So these two years had been only a brief stop after all, and I must go on my way again. But my stay had done me good — I had become bigger and stronger and, better still, I had made dear friends. I was no longer alone in the world.

CHAPTER THIRTEEN

I was my own master and now I could go anywhere I wanted. But before I set off I wanted to see the man who had been so kind to me. I did not dare to walk across Paris with Capi running behind me. I was afraid that a policeman might stop me and ask questions and my greatest fear was of the police, for I had not forgotten Toulouse. So I tied a piece of cord to his collar which I didn't like doing one bit for I knew that it would hurt his self-respect, but it had to be done. I had to tug him along to the prison in Clichy where Monsieur Acquin was serving his sentence.

For some minutes when we reached there I was filled with fear at the sight of the enormous doors, thinking that perhaps once they had closed behind me I might never get out again. After a long wait and a lot of questions I was at last allowed to see my friend. When I went into the room where visitors were allowed to see prisoners I saw that there were no bars on the windows, as I had imagined there would be, and that Monsieur Acquin when he came in was not handcuffed.

"Hello, Remi, I was expecting you. The children told me that you are going on your travels again. I hope you've not forgotten that it wasn't so very long ago that you nearly died of cold and hunger."

"No, I've not forgotten and I don't think I ever will."

"You weren't alone then, you had someone to look after you. Remi, I don't think it is wise for you to go tramping across France by yourself."

"Then you don't want me to bring news of your children to you?" I asked. "I have Capi," I ended up.

141

"They told me you were going to see them all. I agree that Capi is a fine dog, but he's only a dog, and I am not thinking just of us when I ask you to give up this wandering life." He looked at me for quite a long time and then suddenly took hold of my hands. "You are a good-hearted boy, Remi, and I won't say another word. The good God will take care of you."

The time soon came for me to say goodbye and as I was leaving he felt in a pocket and pulled out a large silver watch.

"Here, Remi, take this. I want you to have it. It isn't of much value, if it had been I would have sold it, and it doesn't keep very good time either. When anything goes wrong with it just give it a good shake. It's all I have."

I wanted to refuse such a lovely present, but he pushed it into my hands.

"I don't need to know the time here," he said sadly. "Time passes so slowly I would die counting the hours. Goodbye, Remi, and good luck."

I was very unhappy when I left him and hung about the prison doors for a long time. I might perhaps have stayed there until night if my hand had not just then touched something hard and round in my pocket. I had forgotten — it was my watch, and my sadness left me. I pulled it out to see the time. Twelve o'clock, but it was of no importance what time it was. In my pleasure at holding and looking at the watch I hadn't noticed that Capi was almost as pleased as myself. He pulled at the legs of my trousers and barked several times, and went on barking.

"What is it, Capi?"

He looked at me, waited a few moments, and then came and stood against me with his paws on the pocket in which I had put back the watch. I took it out again and he looked at it for some time as though trying to remember. Then with much tailwagging he barked twelve times. He hadn't forgotten. We could earn money with my present, and that was something I hadn't thought of. I took one last look at the prison and we went on our way.

What I needed most was a map of France and I walked towards the river, for I knew that I would find one in the bookstalls on the quays. I did at last get a map that was so yellow with age that the man let me have it for fifteen sous. I was now able to leave Paris and I decided to do so at once. I had two roads to choose between and chose the one going to Fontainebleau. As I walked along the Rue Mouffetard memories of Garofoli, Mattia, Ricardo, the soup-pot with its padlock, the whip, and Vitalis who had died because he would not leave me with the 'padrone', rushed back.

As I passed a church I saw a young boy leaning against the wall and I thought I recognised him. Surely it could only be Mattia, with that big head, and those soft eyes with their resigned look. If it was he hadn't grown a bit. I went nearer to have a better look, and sure enough it was Mattia. When he saw me he smiled.

"I remember you," he said. "You came to Garofoli's a long time ago with an old man with a white beard, didn't you? That was just before I went into hospital."

"Is Garofoli still your master?"

He looked carefully about him before he answered, and then lowering his head; "Garofoli is in prison. They arrested him because he beat Orlando to death."

I was shocked at what he told me but I was glad to know that Garofoli had gone to prison, and for the first time I thought that prisons, which always filled me with so much dread, had their uses after all.

"What about the other boys?"

"I don't know. I wasn't there when Garofoli was taken away. When I came out of the hospital he wanted to get rid of me so he sold me for two years to a circus and was paid in advance. The circus wanted a child for the trick where a body is supposed to be cut in half, but my head was too big to fit in the box. So when I was thrown out of the circus there was nothing I could do but go back to Garofoli's. The place was all shut up and a neighbour told me what had happened. Now I don't know where to go. I have no money and I haven't had anything to eat since yesterday morning."

I wasn't rich but I had enough money to buy something for Mattia. I knew how grateful I would have been if someone had given me even a crust when I had left Toulouse famished, just as Mattia was now.

"Wait here until I come back," I told him. I ran to a bakery at the corner of the street and soon I came back with a small loaf which he gobbled up. "Now," I said, "what would you like to do?"

"I don't know. I had been thinking of selling my violin when you came along. I would have sold it long ago if I hadn't hated parting with it. It's all I have, and when I'm feeling depressed I find a place where I can be alone and play it to myself."

"Why haven't you played it in the streets?"

"I used to, but nobody threw me any money."

I knew all too well what it was to play and never be given even a sou.

"Where are you going and what are you going to do?" he asked.

I don't know why, but on the spur of the moment I told him that I was the head of a troupe. It was true enough, but my 'troupe' was made up only of Capi.

"Can I join your troupe?" Mattia asked shyly.

I smiled and pointed to Capi. "He's all my troupe."

"What does that matter? I'll make two. I can play the violin, sing, walk the tight-rope," Mattia went on excitedly. "I'll do anything you wish. I don't want to be paid, only to be given enough to eat. And if I perform badly you can beat me, but don't hit me on the head because it still hurts from the blows Garofoli gave me."

Mattia's little speech rather upset me, for how could I refuse to take him with me. Coming with me there was always the chance that we would both go hungry, and I told him so, but he wouldn't listen.

"No, no," he said, "when there are two of us each helps the other, and we won't starve."

I no longer hesitated and he at once grasped my hand and actually kissed it in gratitude. I put my harp back over my shoulder and in a quarter of an hour we had left Paris behind us.

My choice of roads was made because I wanted to see Mother

Barberin. Often I had wanted to write to her and tell her how much she was in my thoughts, but my dread of the horrible Barberin always stopped me, for if he found out where I was writing from he might easily come for me and then sell me to another man. He might have been in his rights to do this and so I preferred that Mother Barberin should think that I might be dead, even if I ran the risk of seeming to her to be a coward.

But if I couldn't write I could always go and see her. It could be easily enough arranged, for I would ask Mattia to go on ahead to find out if she was alone, and he could tell her that I was not far away and only waiting to know if it was safe for me to come and visit her. If Barberin was at home, or in the village, Mattia could ask her to come to some place where we could meet. I tramped along wrapped in my thoughts, working out my plan. Mattia also seemed to be deep in his own thoughts.

When we stopped for a rest I thought that I would show him everything in my knapsack, and opening it I spread out my possessions on the grass. I had three linen shirts, three pairs of socks, five handkerchiefs, all of them in good repair, and one slightly used pair of shoes. Mattia was dumbfounded.

"What have you got?" I asked.

"Only my violin."

"All right then, we're friends and we'll go shares. You can have two of the shirts, two pairs of socks and three handkerchiefs. But it's only fair that we go shares in everything so you'll carry my knapsack for one hour and I'll do it for the next, and so on."

Mattia didn't want to take the clothes, but I told him that he had to or I would be angry. When I emptied my knapsack I had put Etiennette's small case to one side as well as a little box in which I kept Lise's rose. Mattia wanted to open the box but I wouldn't let him; I put it back in the knapsack.

"If you want to please me," I said, "you'll never touch this box, it was a present to me," and Mattia solemnly promised he would never touch it.

After I had started wearing my sheepskin again there was one thing I was worried about and that was my trousers. They had

145

been given to me by Monsieur Acquin and at the time I had been very proud of them, but it seemed to me to be wrong for a 'strolling player' like me to wear long trousers — these were all right for a gardener but I was no longer a gardener. So I got out my pair of scissors and started to shorten them. I did not consider I was spoiling them by doing this, quite the contrary, and one day I would buy some coloured ribbons to criss-cross over my stockings.

"While I'm doing this," I said to Mattia, "let me hear you play the violin."

He was only too happy to do this and at first I hardly listened, but soon I stopped snipping away with the scissors and became all ears, for Mattia played nearly as well as Vitalis.

"Who taught you the violin?" I asked, clapping my hands.

"No one."

"Has anyone taught you to read music, then?"

"No, I play by ear."

I wanted to show Mattia that I was a musician too so I took hold of my harp, struck a chord, and sang the famous 'canzonetta'. Then, as it should be between two musicians, he said how good I was and both of us were pleased with ourselves.

We had to get on our way, so I buckled up my knapsack. It was Mattia's turn to carry it and he hoisted it onto his shoulders. At the first village we came to we decided we must give a performance and it was to be called: 'First Appearance of Remi's Company'.

"Teach me that song of yours," Mattia said, "and we'll sing it together. I'll soon be able to accompany you on the violin. I think that would be a good idea, don't you?"

I agreed, and if there had been an audience it would have to have had a heart of marble not to have been generous when Capi took his bowl around.

Before we reached a village after our rest we had to pass a big gate leading to a farm, and when we looked through it we saw a lot of people dressed in their Sunday best. Some were carrying bouquets tied with satin ribbons, and it was clear that there had been a wedding. I thought that perhaps they might like some music to dance to so I opened the gate and, followed by Mattia and Capi, I walked up to a big, good-natured looking man with a ruddy face. When I had spoken to him he didn't answer me but, turning to the guests, he put two fingers in his mouth and gave such a high-pitched whistle that it scared Capi. Then he called out:

"How would you like some music? The musicians have arrived! Take your places for the quadrille." And he nodded to us to follow him.

The dancers soon formed into groups in the centre of the paved yard, while Mattia and I climbed onto a waggon.

"Do you know the music for a quadrille?" I whispered in Italian.

"Yes."

He played a few notes and by great good luck I knew the tune. We were saved. Although we had never played together before we didn't do too badly, but I think I should add that the people we were playing to hadn't much ear for music.

"Can either of you play the cornet?" the man who had welcomed us in asked.

"I can, but I haven't one with me," Mattia answered.

"I'll go and find one. A violin is too squeaky."

It turned out that Mattia could play almost anything. The music went on long into the night. I didn't mind, but poor Mattia was not strong and every now and then when I looked at him I saw that he was very tired; and yet he went on blowing with all his might. I was not the only one to notice how tired he looked, for the bride did too.

"That will be enough," she called out. "The boy playing the cornet is tired out. Hands into your pockets, please, for the musicians."

I threw my cap to Capi who caught it in his jaws, and they all clapped their hands and were delighted at the grace with which Capi bowed to them. Everyone was very generous, and the husband, who was the last to give, dropped a five-franc piece into the cap. What marvellous luck! But that was not all. We were invited to have something to eat, and they even gave us a place in

147

the barn where we could sleep. The next morning when we left this hospitable farm we had as much as twenty-eight francs.

We were indeed wealthy. When we reached Corbeil we could easily afford to buy some things that I felt were absolutely necessary. First of all, a cornet, which might cost three francs at some secondhand dealer's; then some red ribbons to decorate our stockings; and, finally, another knapsack for it would be much easier for each of us to carry a small one all the time than a heavy one taking it in turns.

We felt so rich that I decided we should set out for Mother Barberin's. There was plenty of money for me to buy a present for her. More than anything else there was something I wanted to give her to make her happy, not only now but in her old age, and that was a cow to take the place of poor Roussette. How happy she would be if I gave her a cow. Before arriving at Chavanon I would buy one, and Mattia would lead it by a rope into her yard. All going well Barberin would not be at home.

I could picture the scene. Mattia would say to her: "Here is a cow that I've brought you," and she would reply with a sigh: "A cow! You've made a mistake, my boy." "Oh no, I haven't. You are Mother Barberin aren't you? Well, just as in a fairy tale, the prince has sent you this present." "What prince?" Then I would appear from nowhere and throw myself into her arms, and after we had hugged each other we would make pancakes and apple fritters and only the three of us would eat them. Her husband wouldn't, and that would repay him for that Shrove Tuesday when he had come home and seized our frying-pan and put our butter in his soup.

What a beautiful dream! But I had first to buy the cow.

How much would one cost? I hadn't the faintest idea. A great deal probably, but I didn't want a very big cow because the bigger the cow the higher the price. Then, of course, the bigger the cow the more it would eat, and I did not want my present to be an embarrassment to Mother Barberin. But the first thing to do was to find out the price of cows, or rather of a cow of the kind I wanted. Luckily that would not be too hard for we often met drovers and cattle-dealers at the villages where we stopped. I asked the first drover that I met one day at an inn.

He burst out laughing and banged the table with his fist. Then he called out to the innkeeper's wife. "Listen to what this little musician wants to know. How much does a cow cost, not a very big one, but a healthy one that will give plenty of milk."

Everybody else laughed, but that didn't worry me. "Yes, she must give good milk and not eat too much," I said.

"And she mustn't mind being led by a halter too, I suppose?"

When all the jokes had ended he was quite willing to talk to me and to take matters seriously. He told me he had just the very animal, a nice cow which gave delicious milk and hardly ate a thing. If I could pay one hundred and fifty francs the cow was mine. Although I had trouble at first in getting the drover to talk, once he started it was difficult to stop him. At last we were able to go to bed and I dreamt of what he had told me.

We had nothing like a hundred and fifty francs, but perhaps if our luck held we could, if we saved every sou, get together that large amount. It would take time, and we would have to give all the performances we possibly could on our way to see Alexis at a town named Varses. Then on our way back we would have the money to go to Chavanon and act out the fairy tale 'The Prince's Cow'.

In the morning I told Mattia of my plan and he was pleased with it.

It was a long way to Varses and it took us nearly three months, but when we were getting near the town I had in my leather purse one hundred and twenty-eight francs, only twenty-two short of the amount needed to buy Mother Barberin's cow. Mattia was just as happy as I was, and I knew that without him and Capi we would never have collected anything like that sum. Between Varses and Chavanon we must surely earn the difference.

It was three in the afternoon when we saw Varses not so very far away. The sun was shining in a blue sky but as we came nearer to the town everything became dark because of the heavy pall of smoke which hung over it. I had been told that Alexis's Uncle worked in a coal-mine which was called 'Truyère', but I did not know whether he lived in the town or outside it. I asked someone where the mine was and was told to follow the left bank of the river to the small valley that had given the mine its name. At the mine we were told where Uncle Gaspard's house was in a winding street not far from the river and quite close to the mine itself.

When we came to the house we saw a woman with her arms akimbo leaning against the door talking to one of the neighbours. She told me when I asked her if Alexis lived there that he stopped work at six and would not be home until sometime after that. She looked me over and then saw Capi.

"Are you Remi by any chance? Alexis has talked about you and has been expecting you. Who's that boy?" And she pointed at Mattia.

"He's my friend."

This woman was Alexis's aunt. I felt sure that she would ask us in to rest for we were dusty and felt very tired, but she only repeated that work at the mine stopped at six. I thanked her and we went back to the town to find something to eat. I was ashamed at our reception for I felt sure that Mattia would wonder about it and why we should have tramped so many miles for only this. It seemed to me Mattia would not have much of an opinion of my friends, and that when the time came for me to tell him about Lise he would not listen to me with very much interest.

The welcome we had been given did not encourage us to return to the house, so at a little before six we all went to the pithead to wait for Alexis. We had been told where the miners would come to the surface and a little after six we saw in the darkness of the shaft leading out of the mine tiny lights which slowly became bigger and bigger. The miners, holding their lamps, walked slowly and clumsily as if their knees were cramped. Their faces were blacker than any chimney-sweep's, and their clothes and helmets were coated with coal-dust. Each of them went into the lamplighter's hut and hung up his lamp on a nail there.

Although I was keeping a very good look-out I did not see Alexis until he rushed up to me. It was hard to recognise, black from

150

head to foot, the companion who had raced along the paths in the garden with me in his open shirt with sleeves turned up at the elbow and showing his pale skin.

"It's Remi," he said excitedly, and turned to a man of about forty who was walking behind him and who had the same kind, open face as Monsieur Acquin. This was not so very surprising for they were brothers and I knew at once that this could only be Uncle Gaspard.

"We've been expecting you for a long time," he said with a smile.

"The road is long from Paris to Varses," I replied, and smiled back at him.

"And your legs are short," he retorted.

Capi, happy at seeing Alexis, tugged at a leg of his trousers with all his strength. While this was going on I told Uncle Gaspard that Mattia was not only my friend but my partner, and that he played the cornet better than anyone else.

"And I think that must be Monsieur Capi," Uncle Gaspard said. "It is Sunday tomorrow and you can entertain us. Alexis has told me how clever that dog of yours is, as well as being a bit of a comedian."

Ill at ease as I had felt with the aunt it was so very different with Uncle Gaspard, who then said:

"Now, I'm sure that you two boys have a lot to say to each other, and while you're having your talk I'm going to learn something from this young man who plays the cornet so well."

Alexis wanted to hear all about my journey, while I wished to hear about his work. We were so busy asking questions of each other that neither of us waited for any reply. When we reached the house Uncle Gaspard invited us in for supper, and no invitation gave me so much pleasure after the welcome we had had from the aunt, for I was wondering as we were walking along the road if we would have to say goodbye at the door.

"Here are Remi and his friend," Uncle Gaspard called out as we all went in.

We sat down and supper didn't take long for the aunt liked to exchange gossip with the neighbours and had had only the time to fry some pork sausages. Uncle Gaspard was an easy-going man who asked merely for peace and quietness and ate what was put in front of him without a word of complaint.

He told me that I was to sleep in Alexis's room and said to Mattia that he would make up a bed for him in the kitchen. Alexis and I spent a good part of the night talking and everything he told me was of tremendous interest. I had always wanted to go down a mine, but when I spoke about this to Uncle Gaspard next morning before he left the house he told me that I couldn't do this as only workers in the mine were allowed past the pithead.

I had no intention of staying long in Varses, but on the day that we were to leave a large lump of coal fell on Alexis's hand almost crushing a finger, and he was told to stay in his bed for several days. Uncle Gaspard was desperate; he had nobody now to push the coal-skip he had to fill and he was afraid that he, too, would have to stay at home, a thing he could not afford to do.

"Why can't I take Alexis's place?" I asked when he returned later after having had no luck in finding anyone.

"I was frightened that the skip might be too heavy for you," he said, "but if you're willing to try, all the better. It is very hard to find a boy for only a few days."

"And while you're down the mine I'll go off with Capi and earn the rest of the money to pay for the cow," Mattia called out.

The few months we had spent together in the open air had completely changed Mattia. He was no longer the poor sickly boy I had come across near the church, and even less was he the puny creature I had first met in Garofoli's attic when he was looking after the soup. Mattia never had headaches now, for the sun and the fresh air had restored his health and on our tramps he was always laughing and in good spirits. I would have been very lonely without him.

So it was agreed that while I worked in the mine beside Uncle Gaspard, Mattia and Capi would entertain passers-by in Varses to increase our little fortune. I explained what we had decided to Capi and he understood and barked his approval.

152

Next day I put on the working clothes Uncle Gaspard gave me at the pithead and following close behind him I went down the mine. He warned me to be careful as we walked along the tunnel that led to the pit, and I was very careful indeed. When we had gone what seemed to be a long way I looked back over my shoulder and the glimmer of light at the entrance looked just like a tiny moon in a dark sky. Soon a black pit was in front of us, and far down below I could make out the lamps of other miners swaying in the darkness.

At last we reached the face where Uncle Gaspard worked. The skips were pushed by boys, with the exception of a man who was called 'Professor'. He was quite old, and when he was younger he had worked as a carpenter in the mine, but because of an accident which had crushed his hand he had had to give up this kind of work.

I was soon to find out how very dangerous it could be to work in a coal-mine, for only a few days after I had started I was pushing my skip when I heard a loud roaring noise which seemed to be coming from all directions. I was terrified and wondered if there had been an explosion; all of a sudden what seemed to be hundreds of rats raced past fleeing for safety like a regiment of cavalry, and almost immediately there was the sound of rushing water. Leaving my skip I ran back to where Uncle Gaspard was working.

"The mine's flooding!" I had to shout as loud as I could to make my voice heard. "Listen!"

The way I shouted made him stop work and then he shouted back: "Run for your life!" and then warned the Professor.

The old man joined us in the tunnel where the water was now starting to rise rapidly. There was no time for any politeness and when we reached the ladder Uncle Gaspard climbed up first, I followed, and then came the Professor. Before we even reached the top water had risen so fast that our lamps were put out. We clung to the rungs and some of the men who were lower down were washed away. When we came to the mine level above us water was starting to seep through here too and came to our knees. Just

154

then some other miners whose lamps were still alight came running towards us. The water was now rushing through the whole mine in a torrent and big pieces of wood used for pit-props were being whirled about like matchsticks.

"We must head for the old workings," the professor said. "We should find safety there."

These old workings had long been abandoned and he was the only person who knew the best route to them. Usually no one took any notice of him when he spoke except to poke fun at him, but now even the bravest man among us was in mortal fear and everyone was only too ready to listen to him. He took the lead, dragging me along with him with the water up to my waist. At last we came to an airshaft, but two miners refused to go in saying that it was a blind-alley, and went along another tunnel that branches off it — we never saw them again.

Then there was the most deafening noise followed by a further rush of water, the splintering of wood, and explosions caused by the compressed air. We were all terror-stricken.

"It's the end of the world!" someone shouted.

But the Professor said quite calmly: "We are going to have to stay here, how long for we don't know so we must scoop a hollow in this shale to make ourselves as comfortable as we can."

We took his advice, but working with our hands and lamphooks was difficult and was made even worse by the fact that the airshaft sloped here and was very slippery. We knew, too, that if we made a single false move we would slide to our deaths. At last we made a fairly deep hollow and were able to rest. I now knew that there were seven in our little band.

The terrible noise continued and I cannot possibly describe it. We stared at each other in fear for an explanation of it all. One said that there had been an earthquake, another that it was a flood coming through from some other old workings, and yet another that it was the mine's evil spirit taking its revenge on those who had disturbed it. I suggested that the river bed had somehow become worn through and that the river was flowing into the mine.

155

The Professor shrugged his shoulders and said nothing, looking from one to another in the half-darkness as though he could have argued all day if he could only have been sitting quietly in the shade of a mulberry tree munching an onion. At last he said: "That's stupid about the evil spirit of the mine. We know that the mine is flooded and that's all we do know."

Now that our sodden clothes were starting to dry and the water had stopped rising no one wanted to listen to him, his authority in a moment of great danger had gone now that that danger seemed to have receded.

But he went on: "At any rate we shan't be drowned for we are in a pocket of air here and because of it the water has stopped rising. This shaft has no outlet for the air we are breathing to escape and is doing for us what the diving-bell does for the diver. But the foul air is what we have to fear."

I started thinking of the hundred and fifty men, perhaps more, who had been working in our shift in the mine, and wondered how many of them had been lucky enough to escape through tunnels, or like ourselves had found places of refuge somewhere or other. There was complete silence everywhere now; below us the water was still, with not even a ripple or a gurgle. The mine must have been completely flooded and the silence was more terrifying than the dreadful uproar when the water first rushed in. We were in a tomb buried deep underground, and even the Professor seemed in the depths of despair.

By now the air was becoming difficult to breathe, and I was starting to feel suffocated and my ears were buzzing. I was afraid, terribly afraid, of everything — the water, the darkness, and what would happen to me. I wondered whether I would ever see Lise again, and Arthur and his mother too, and Mattia. Would anyone be able to explain to Lise that I was dead and that I could not bring news of her brothers and sister to her? And, as always, my thoughts flew to Mother Barberin. No on had spoken for a very long time, when Uncle Gaspard broke the silence.

"I don't think anyone is trying to rescue us," he said, "I can't hear a sound."

"You don't know what you're saying," the Professor replied curtly. "You must know that in any disaster like this miners never desert their mates, and that twenty men, a hundred, would sooner die than leave a single comrade helpless. That's true isn't it?"

"Yes, that's true," Uncle Gaspard admitted.

"I'm certain that they're trying their hardest to reach us. They may be either tunnelling down to us here or else starting to pump away all the water."

There now started a sort of vague discussion as to how long a rescue operation would take to reach us, and it ended up by the men agreeing that it would probably take about a week. A week! Somewhere I had read of miners being trapped for much longer than that, but it was not in real life. All the same I was too stunned to pay any further heed to what was being said by the others.

Silence fell again for everyone had his own thoughts, and how long this continued I cannot remember. It seemed hours, and then someone called out: "I can hear pumps working." We all somehow got to our feet for we knew now that we were going to be saved. But before we saw the sun again we were to pass through long and cruel days of suffering and to wonder whether we would, indeed, ever see daylight again. We all developed a raging thirst but the problem was how anyone could get down to the water, for one false step could make the shale we had piled up give way even under one man's weight, and whoever it was would not escape being drowned.

"Remi is the lightest one here. Here's my boot. He can go and get water for us," someone said.

A boot was handed to me and I was all ready to slide down when the Professor told me to take hold of his arm so that he could steady me. When I said that I could swim if I fell in he told me to do as I was told. I don't know whether in trying to help me the old man either miscalculated his step or else the shale gave way under him, but he slithered and fell head first into that awful black water. We had no light and luckily I was already prepared to get into the water, so I slid down on my back after him.

I had learned to swim and dive during my wanderings with

157

Vitalis, but how could I find my way about in this big black hole? I had not thought of that when I let myself slide, my only thought was that our Professor might drown. I was still wondering what to do when he grabbed my shoulder and I was dragged below the surface. I managed to strike out with one foot and could come up again for breath with his hand still gripping my shoulder.

"Hold on to me," I shouted, "and keep your head up and we'll be safe." Safe! I had no idea in which direction I should swim, but then I heard Uncle Gaspard's voice to my left.

"Remi, we are over here."

As a matter of fact I was still close to the bank, and was able to clutch at a lump of coal that was sticking out near me and to keep the old man's head clear of the water. It was just as well that I did this for he had swallowed a lot, but when my companions took hold of him and pulled him to safety he soon came round. I clambered up after him.

It was not long after this incident that everyone became more depressed and despairing. Speaking for myself I became very drowsy, but our refuge was no place for sleeping for if I had dropped off I could easily have rolled into the water. The Professor knew this and he put his arm about me, and whenever I moved a little in my half-sleep he changed the position of his arm which had become stiff and sat motionless again. I somehow knew that he would not let go of me.

By now we had lost all idea of time. It could have been two days or six since we had heard the sounds of pumps working, and there was no talk any more of when we might be rescued. You may not believe it but we were driven to gnawing pieces of rotten wood that were lying about. Vitalis had often told me tales of men who had been shipwrecked, and once described how a crew shipwrecked on a desert island had eaten the ship's boy! When I saw how near starvation we all were I wondered if that would be my fate. I knew that Uncle Gaspard and the Professor would never eat me but I was not so very sure about the others.

Once when I had been drowsing I had been startled to hear the old man speaking in a whisper, as though he were dreaming, about clouds, the sky, and the wind, and then of what he would like to have to eat. He was delirious. My own thoughts were becoming vague and wild. For hours and what seemed days we all lay huddled together chattering foolishly and in low voices to each other.

It was some time after this that somehow or other my brain cleared and I managed to slip away from the others to the water's edge and saw, to my astonishment, that its level had dropped a lot. I scrambled back and told whoever was ready to listen that I could now swim to the ladders and tell our rescuers where we were.

I did not wait for an answer, but said goodbye to Uncle Gaspard, took off my clothes and went into the water. Then I called: "Keep shouting to me and your voice will be a guide."

I wondered for a moment if the space over my head was high enough for me to swim freely, but after a few strokes I found that I had no need to worry if I swam carefully. I had been told by the old man that several tunnels met not so far away and so I had to be very careful, for if I made a mistake I would lose my way. The roof and walls were not enough to guide me, but below the water there was a certain guide — the rails for the skips. If I followed them they would lead me to the ladders. So every now and then I put my feet down and felt for the rails. With these to guide me I was not completely lost. As Uncle Gaspard's voice became less distinct the noise of pumps grew louder.

Swimming along the centre of the tunnel I went some little distance further and then felt again for the rails, but there were none. I must have made a mistake somewhere, probably by turning off into another tunnel. I was now very confused and did not know which way to turn in the black, cold water. Then all of a sudden I heard the sound of voices and I knew which way to go. I swam back a few yards, and turned to the right and then to the left, but could only touch walls. Where were the rails? I felt quite sure that I must be in the right tunnel and that the only reason could be that the rails had been washed away in the flood. This meant that it was impossible for me to carry out my plan, so I swam as quickly as I could back to our place of refuge guided by

159

my companions' voices. As I came nearer to them they sounded much more cheerful, and when I was quite close the Professor shouted to me:

"Hurry, the pumping has nearly finished and they have started digging towards us. They can hear our voices and we can hear theirs."

I clambered out of the water and listened. There was, indeed, the noise of picks and the sound of men's voices although they were not very clear. After the first feeling of joy I realised that I was nearly frozen and as there were no warm clothes to change into they buried me with only my head and chest showing in coal-dust and shale, and Uncle Gaspard and the old man huddled up against me to warm me. We knew now that the rescue-party must soon reach us, but these last hours of imprisonment were the hardest to bear and, strangely, the nearer the time of our deliverance came somehow or other the weaker we grew. I was lying shaking, but I wasn't cold.

Before we all knew it there was a rush of air and twisting my head around I saw a bright light coming wobbling towards us. An engineer was leading several men, and almost before I knew it he had lifted me into his arms. I was just aware of being carried away wrapped up in a blanket. I closed my eyes and when I opened them again it was daylight. We were in the open air. At the same moment something jumped on me. It was Capi. With a bound he had sprung upon me as I lay in the engineer's arms and was licking my face. Then my hand was held and I heard a voice saying my name. It was Mattia and I smiled at him before I looked about me.

Lots of people stood in two straight rows leaving a passage down the middle. It was a silent crowd for it had been told to stay quiet so as not to excite us, but the expression on everyone's face spoke louder than any words. I don't remember how many arms were stretched out to carry me, but the engineer would not give me up and carried me to the mine buildings where beds had been made ready for us all.

Two days later I was walking down the road where Uncle Gaspard lived, with Mattia, Alexis and Capi. Some of the folk who saw me came up to me with tears in their eyes to shake hands but there were others who looked away, and they were the mourners who were asking themselves bitterly why a child should have been saved when their husbands and brothers were dead, buried under rubble or drifting about in those black waters.

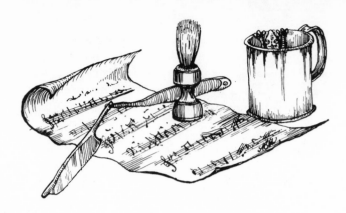

CHAPTER FOURTEEN

I had made friends in the mine, and Uncle Gaspard and the Professor in particular had, I think, grown fond of me. Although the engineer had not shared our imprisonment he had become attached to me in the way one is, I suppose, to a child whom one has snatched from almost certain death. He invited me to his house and I had to tell his daughter all that had happened to us after the flooding. He told me that if I wanted it he could get me a job in the mine's offices, while Uncle Gaspard said that he would find me permanent work down the mine — he was going back to work there again with all that indifference to danger that men showed who are used to facing it every day. It seemed that everyone wanted me to stay in Varses.

A mine was very interesting and I was glad that I had seen one, but I had not the slightest wish to stay and work in one. I preferred to have the sky over my head, even a sky full of snow. Open-air life suited me better, and I told them this. They were all rather surprised, even the Professor.

While they were trying to persuade me to stay Mattia was gloomy and seemed to be wrapped in his own thoughts. When I asked him what was wrong he always replied that there was nothing the matter. It was not until I told him that we would be starting off on our tramps in a few days' time that he owned up why he had been so preoccupied.

"I thought that you would be wanting to stay here," he said, "and I would have to go my own way."

I gave him a good thump on the back to teach him to have more confidence in me. But even so Mattia was now quite able to look after himself, and while I was working in the mine he had earned eighteen francs. So what with we already had there was a total of a hundred and forty-six francs. With four more we could buy the prince's cow!

And so, with Capi rolling about on the road with happiness, we set out from Varses. It was Mattia's idea that we should earn as much more money as we could before buying the cow for, as he pointed out, the more money we had the better the cow, and the better the cow the more pleased Mother Barberin would be.

While tramping from Paris to Varses I had started giving Mattia reading as well as elementary music lessons, and I continued these lessons now. Either I was not a very good teacher, which was quite possible, or Mattia was a poor pupil, and that may have been possible too. At any rate the reading lessons weren't a success; often I got angry and shutting the book with a bang I told him he was a thickhead.

"That's true," he said, "my skull is only thin when it's hit. Garofoli found that one out."

I laughed, and we went on with the lessons. From the start he made amazing progress with music and finally he so astonished me with his questions that I had to admit that I could not answer many of them. I felt humiliated and he didn't spare me.

"I'd like to go and have one lesson, just one, from a real musician," he said, "and then I'd be able to ask him all the questions I want answered."

"Then why didn't you go to your real musician while I was down the mine?"

"Because I didn't want to use your money for what he would charge."

"But my money is yours too. You have earned it even more than I have. You can take as many lessons as you like, and I'll take some with you."

163

The musician, the *real* musician, that we wanted would not be found in a village but only in some large town, and when we looked at our map we saw that the nearest was Mendes. It was already late evening when we reached it and as we were tired we decided that our lesson could wait another day. All the same we asked the innkeeper's wife where we would find a good music-master. She said that she was very surprised that we should ask such a question, for surely we must have heard of Monsieur Espinassous.

"We've come from a distance," I answered.

"Then you must have come from a very great distance."

"From Italy," Mattia said.

Then she admitted that she was no longer astonished, and as we had come from so far away we might not have heard of Monsieur Espinassous.

I was afraid that such a celebrated musician might not be very willing to give only one lesson to two boys like us, so I asked whether he would be too busy for us to call on him next day.

"Certainly he is a busy man but he always welcomes anyone who has money in their pocket, that's natural."

We understood that, of course, and before going to sleep we talked about all the questions we intended asking this famous man. Mattia was excited at our luck in finding just the kind of musician we were looking for.

Next morning we set out to find Monsieur Espinassous, Mattia with his violin and me with my harp. Capi wanted to come with us but we tied him up in the stables because we thought it would not be good manners to call on this celebrated man with a dog. When we reached the house where we had been told the musician lived we thought we must have made a mistake for near the front door were two small engraved copper-plates which could never, by any stretch of the imagination, lead anyone to believe that a music-master lived there. The place seemed to be a barber's shop, and we stopped a man who was passing to ask if he could tell us the way to Monsieur Espinassous's house.

"But that's it," he said, and pointed to the door.

After all, why shouldn't a musician live with a barber? We went in. The shop was divided into two, with on the right barbers' chairs and shelves on which were brushes, combs and jars of haircream, and on the left, on a bench and hanging on the walls, violins, cornets and trombones. A dapper little man who fluttered about like a bird and who was shaving a customer replied in a deep voice to Mattia's enquiry that he was, indeed, Monsieur Espinassous.

I glanced at Mattia as if to say that this barber-musician could not be the man we were looking for and that it would be a waste of good money to come and ask him a lot of questions, but Mattia took no notice and sat down deliberately in a vacant chair.

"I'd like you to cut my hair after you have finished shaving the gentleman," he said.

"Of course, and I'll give you a shave too if you want me to."

While I looked on with astonishment Mattia thanked him and looked at me out of the corner of his eye as if to tell me to wait before getting annoyed with him. When the customer had been shaved and left Monsieur Espinassous, with a towel over his arm, got ready to cut Mattia's hair.

"Monsieur," Mattia said when the towel had been tied round his neck, "my friend and I have had an argument. We don't know very much about music but we have been told that you are a very well-known musician so we thought that you might give us your opinion and so settle the matter once and for all."

"What is it all about, young man?"

Now I knew what was in Mattia's mind. He had wanted first of all to see if this barber-musician would answer our questions, and if he would his idea was to get a music lesson for the price of a haircut. All the time this was being carried out he never stopped asking questions, to the great amusement of the barber who readily and with obvious pleasure answered every one put to him. As we were leaving he asked Mattia if he would like to play something on his violin, and he played a Strauss waltz.

"And you told me you knew so very little about music!" Monsieur Espinassous exclaimed.

Then Mattia took down a clarionette from among the instruments hanging on the wall, and played it, and finished up by playing a cornet. Monsieur Espinassous was in raptures and said that if he stayed with him he would train him to be a great musician. In the mornings he would have to learn how to shave the customers and the rest of the day would be spent in studying music. "Please don't think that because I am a barber I don't know music. I have to earn more money somehow."

I looked at Mattia and wondered what he would reply. Was I to lose my friend and companion? "Do what you think best, Mattia," I said, and as I spoke I must admit that my voice shook.

"I could never leave my friend," Mattia answered, "but thank you all the same."

Monsieur Espinassous insisted and told Mattia that later on he would find some way of sending him to the Conservatoire in Paris, but Mattia couldn't be shaken. In the end Monsiuer Espinassous said that he would give him a book so that he could learn what he didn't know from that, and handed him a copy of *The Theory of Music*. It was old and rather battered but that didn't matter, and Monsieur Espinassous wrote in it: 'For a young boy who when he becomes famous may remember the barber of Mendes'.

I don't know whether there were other music-masters in that town, but that was the only one we were told about and we never forgot him.

As we were leaving Mendes we heard that there was going to be a big cattle-market at Ussel so, as it was not so very far from Chavanon, we decided to go there and buy Mother Barberin's cow. We gave performances everywhere we could along the route and by the time we arrived in Ussel, after paying all our expenses, we had two hundred and forty francs. We had economised in every possible way for Mattia was just as keen on buying the cow as I was, our only difference of opinion being on what its colour should be, for he thought a white one would be best and I wanted her to be russet in memory of poor Roussette. We both agreed, however, that she must be a very gentle beast and give plenty of milk.

Neither of us knew how to recognise a good cow when we saw one so we decided to ask a vet to help us. It would cost money but that couldn't be helped, all the more so as we had been hearing stories of how many people had been cheated and we did not want to run any risks. There was one story of a man buying an animal very cheaply and finding after he had driven her home that her tail was not her own but an imitation one, and another was of a cow which looked very healthy with a big udder but which gave only a couple of tumblers-full of milk a day. Mattia said that as far as an imitation tail was concerned there was no need to worry for he would pull every cow's tail in sight before we even talked to the dealer. When I told him that if he did that and they were real tails he would be kicked all over his body his keenness cooled off.

It was a long time since I had been in Ussel and that was when Vitalis had bought for me, among other things, a pair of boots with nails. Out of the six in our party then there were now only Capi and me left. After we had left our knapsacks and instruments in the same inn where I had stayed with Vitalis we went to look for a vet. We found one fairly easily, and he was most amused when we described to him the kind of cow we wanted and asked if he would come with us and buy it for us.

"But what on earth do you two boys want with a cow, and have you enough money to buy one?" he asked.

I explained to him that the cow was to be a present and showed him the money we had saved and which I had wrapped up in a handkerchief. He was a most friendly man and agreed to go to the market with us, and we were to meet him at seven o'clock next morning. When we asked him how much he would charge for his advice he said that after knowing why we wanted the cow he would be only too pleased to help for nothing, and promised he would look out for a good cow with its own tail.

Very early the next day the town, so quiet at night, was full of noise and bustle and from our room in the inn we could hear the waggons rattling over the paving-stones, horses neighing, cows bellowing, sheep bleating, and the farmers shouting and joking with each other. We hurried downstairs for we wanted to inspect

167

the cows and make our choice before the the vet arrived. And what lovely cows they were, of all colours and sizes, some fat and some not so fat, and some even with their calves. There were pigs there, too, some with their small fat piglets making an awful din with their squealing. But we had eyes only for the cows which were standing quietly and chewing the cud. After half an hour we had found several that we liked, this one for size, that one for something else, three because they were red, and two because they were white, which of course started an argument between us. As he had promised he would the vet arrived at seven and we showed him the cows we liked.

"I think this ought to be a good one," Mattia said, pointing to a white animal.

"I think that is a better one," I said showing him a red one.

The vet did not look very long at either of the cows and went on to a third. It was rather a small beast with slender legs, a russet coat, lovely brown ears and and a white muzzle.

"This is just what you want," the vet said, and he asked the farmer who was holding the cow by a halter how much he wanted for it.

"Three hundred francs."

We didn't know what to think for that was more than we could ever pay. I made a sign to the vet that we should try some other farmer but he signed back to me that he would try to drive a bargain. Then a discussion started. The vet went up from one hundred and fifty to one hundred and seventy francs, and the farmer came down to two hundred and eighty. At this point our friend began to examine the cow carefully — she had weak legs, he said, her neck was too short, her horns were too long and her udder was too small. The farmer answered that as we knew so much about cows he would let us have her for two hundred and fifty francs, especially as he was sure that she would be well looked after. Mattia and I were scared when he said that for we imagined that, after all, his cow could only be of little use to the farmer and he wanted to be rid of her.

"Let's go and see some others," I said, but when he heard this the farmer lowered his price to two hundred and ten francs, and said that that was the lowest price he would take. The vet gave me a nudge to tell me that he had only been joking in what he had said about the cow and that it was, indeed, an excellent animal. But all the same two hundred and ten francs was a lot of money to Mattia and me.

While this had been going on Mattia had gone behind the cow and had pulled a long hair from the end of her tail. The animal had given him a good kick and that decided me. "All right then, two hundred and ten francs," I said, and thinking the sale had been made I held out a hand to take the halter."

"Haven't you brought one with you?" the farmer asked. "I'm selling the cow, not the halter."

A new argument started and finally it was agreed that the price for the halter should be all of three francs. The cow was handed over and we shook hands. Now we had a cow to feed as well as ourselves and we did not have a lot of money left. After thanking the vet for his kindness and help we walked back to the inn leading the cow and tied her up in the stable.

As it was a busy market-day Mattia agreed with me that it would be best for each of us to go his own way and see what we could make. By the evening Mattia had collected nearly five francs, while I had brought back three. With this we were rich again. We persuaded a scullery-maid to milk our cow and we had the milk for supper. Never had we tasted anything so good. We were so delighted with the milk's richness that we went into the stable to stroke our cow on its muzzle; she was pleased at this and licked our faces with her rough tongue.

Next morning we were up at daybreak to start on our way to Chavanon. I was most grateful to Mattia for without him I could never have collected enough to buy the present for Mother Barberin so soon. I wanted him to have the pleasure of leading the cow, and he was very proud indeed to have her plodding beside him on the halter while I walked behind. She ambled along slowly, swaying a little, but holding herself like a beast that was only too well aware of how valuable she was to us. I didn't want

We ran after her yelling at her to stop. But the louder we yelled the faster she trotted.

her to get too tired so I decided that we should all rest at the spot where I had slept in a barn with Vitalis on some bracken, and Capi, on seeing how unhappy I was, had come and snuggled beside me. We could then leave the following morning to arrive in good time at Mother Barberin's cottage.

Before reaching the barn we came to a pleasant shady place and throwing down our knapsacks we decided to have a rest, pulling our cow into a shallow ditch close by. At first I thought I would keep hold of her rope, but she seemed very quiet and quite accustomed to grazing quietly, so after a while I twisted the rope about her horns and sat down near her to have something to eat. Of course we had both finished eating before she had, so after admiring her for some time and not knowing how to fill in the time we began to play a game together. When we had finished our game she was still eating and when I went to her she pulled at some grass as much as to tell us that she was still hungry.

"We'll have to wait until she has finished," Mattia said.

"But don't you know that a cow will go on grazing all day?" I replied.

We started to gather up our knapsacks and instruments.

"I'll tell you what I'll do," Mattia said, for he was as eager as I was to get on our way, "I'll play her a tune on my cornet. There was a cow in the circus I told you about that loved music."

He started by blowing a fanfare. At the very first note the cow lifted her head and then before I could grab hold of the rope she had gone off at quite a trot. We ran after her yelling at her to stop. But the louder we yelled the faster she trotted. I shouted to Capi to stop her — a cattle-drover's dog would have headed her off, but not Capi. He jumped at her legs and this made her trot even faster. As fast as she could she went to the village we had passed through not so long ago, and as the road was straight we could see in the distance several people blocking her way and trying to catch hold of her.

We slowed down to a walk for now we knew that we wouldn't lose her, and all that we would have to do would be to claim her from the good folk who had stopped her. When we arrived on the

171

scene quite a crowd had gathered, but instead of giving her up to us at once as we thought they would we were asked as to how and where we had got the cow. They all kept on saying that we had stolen her and that she was trying to get back to her owner, and they also said that we ought to be locked up in prison until the truth could be discovered. At the very mention of the word 'prison' I went pale and as I was out of breath, too, from all the running I started to stammer.

Just then a policeman arrived on the scene and there was a lot more talk which did not make things any clearer. It finished up by the policeman saying that he would put the cow in the public pound, and lock us up until we could prove that the cow was ours. The whole village seemed to be in the procession which followed us to the town hall under which were the cells. The crowd pushed at us and shouted that we were thieves. If the policeman had not protected us we could have been badly hurt.

The janitor at the town hall was also the village gaoler and did not want to put us in a cell, and I thought what a kind man he was. But the policeman insisted that we must be locked up and, finally, the gaoler going ahead of us turned the big key in a double-locked door. It was then that I saw why he had made difficulties — his onion crop had been put to dry in the cell and it was strewn about all over the floor. He gathered the onions into a heap in a corner, and then we were searched and our money, knives and matches were taken from us. After that we were locked in.

"I wish you would give me a good thump for being so stupid," Mattia said miserably when the door was slammed.

"I was just as big a fool for letting you play the cornet to a cow," I replied.

"I feel awful about it," he said broken-heartedly. "Our poor cow, the prince's cow."

I tried to cheer him up by saying that things were not as bad as they seemed. We could prove that we had bought the cow by asking our friend the vet to say so.

"But what if they say we stole the money to buy it? We can't prove that we earned it."

172

That was true. We continued to talk together for some time and we were both very melancholy, for one of the things that worried us was whether our cow was being fed. A good deal later the cell-door was thrown open and an old man with white hair came in.

"Now, you rascals, answer this gentleman," the gaoler who had come in with him said.

"I'll question this one," said the gentleman who, somehow, I could tell was a magistrate, and he pointed at me. "You take charge of the other, and I'll talk to him later."

After Mattia had left the magistrate looked at me for what seemed a long time. Eventually he said that I had been accused of stealing a cow. I answered that we had bought the cow at a fair in Ussel and told him the name of the vet who had helped us to choose her.

"That will be checked," he replied. "And now tell me why you bought the cow."

I told him that it was going to be a present for the woman who had been a mother to me.

"And what is her name?"

"Madame Barberin, and she lives at Chavanon."

"If that is the wife of a stone-cutter who had a bad accident in Paris years ago I know her, and she is well. What you have said will be checked."

I had to tell him that if he asked Mother Barberin questions our cow would not then be a surprise for her, and to give her a surprise was our main wish. During the course of the questioning I learned from the magistrate that Barberin had gone back to Paris a short time ago, and this of course delighted me. Then came the question that Mattia had feared.

"But where did you get the money to buy the cow?"

I explained that from Paris to Varses and from Varses to Ussel we had collected it sou by sou by giving performances.

"And what were you doing in Varses?"

I then told him that I had been visiting a friend and had been in the mine disaster there.

"Are you Remi, then?" he asked. "The policeman said that you

173

have nothing to show who you are. You must tell me about this disaster and what you did in it."

The softer voice in which he was now speaking cheered me up. I told him of my experience in the mine and I thought when I had finished that from the way he looked at me he would give us our freedom at once. Instead, without a word, he left the cell and some time later returned with Mattia.

"I am now going to Ussel to see the vet you have both told me about," he said. "If what you have told me is true, as I hope it is, you will be set free tomorrow."

"What about our cow?" Mattia asked.

"She will be given back to you."

"I didn't mean that. Who is going to feed and milk her?"

"You needn't worry about that."

Mattia was reassured. "Then if our cow is milked can we have some to drink?"

"Yes."

As soon as we were alone I told Mattia the wonderful news that had made me almost forget that we were still locked up. "Mother Barberin is alive, and Barberin has gone to Paris," I cried.

"So the prince's cow will make her triumphal entry," he said, and started to sing and dance with joy.

Carried away by his excitement I joined in and Capi, who until then had been lying looking sad and nervous near the door, jumped up and took his place between us and stood on his hind paws. We went into such a wild dance that the gaoler rushed in to see what was going on, probably afraid for his onions. He told us to stop, but he spoke very differently from the way he had before the magistrate's visit, and somehow I felt that our plight was no longer serious. I had further proof of this when our gaoler returned later carrying a big bowl of milk. He brought, too, a large chunk of white bread and some cold veal which he said the magistrate had sent us. Most decidedly prisons were not so bad after all with dinner and lodging for nothing.

We slept well enough on our hard prison beds, and next morning the magistrate came to see us, bringing with him our

174

friend the vet who had travelled from Ussel especially to see that we were freed. Before we left the magistrate handed us a piece of paper with an official stamp on it.

"You are two silly boys to go tramping through the country without anything to show who you are," he said. "I asked the mayor to give me this for you, and it is all you will need if you run into any other kind of difficulty. Now, goodbye, and good luck."

He shook hands with us, and so did the vet. We had come to the village as miserably as anyone could, but we left in triumph. Leading our cow by her halter, and with our heads high, we exchanged looks with the villagers who were watching us from their doorsteps.

There was still quite a fair distance to go before we reached Chavanon and I didn't want to tire our cow. I thought that it would be a good idea, and Mattia agreed, to buy on our way the things needed for making pancakes, and so we went into the shop where Zerbino had stolen the bread and bought a pound of butter and two pounds of flour. We didn't buy any eggs because of the risk of them being broken, and if Mother Barberin hadn't any in the cottage she could easily borrow them from a neighbour.

When we reached the spot where I had asked Vitalis to let me rest and have my last look at the cottage I told Mattia to take hold of the halter. I jumped up onto the bank. Nothing had changed, a little puff of smoke was even coming out of the chimney to float across the valley. I jumped down again and hugged Mattia. Capi sprang at me, and I held them both tight.

"Come on, let's get there as quickly as we can," I said.

"What a pity our cow doesn't like music," Mattia sighed. "If she did what a triumphal entry we would make."

We reached a turn in the road and saw Mother Barberin come out of her cottage and walk in the direction of the village. I knew that she never locked the door so I decided to go straight in after we had tied up the cow in the shed. There was wood lying about in it so we stacked it all in a corner and put our cow where Roussette used to stand. When we were in the house I told Mattia that I would sit in my old place beside the fire where I had always sat on winter nights, and that he and Capi were to hide behind the bed.

175

From where I sat I could watch the gate. I looked around the room and saw that here again nothing had changed, everything was where it always had been. Even the pane of glass I had broken still had the piece of paper pasted over it, now yellowed by smoke and age.

Suddenly I saw a white bonnet, and the gate creaked. Soon the door was given a gentle push and Mother Barberin came in and stared at me.

"Who is there?" she asked.

I looked at her without answering and she gazed back at me. Her hands started trembling. "Good heavens! Is it possible, is it Remi!" she murmured.

I jumped up and ran to her. "Mother!"

All she could say was 'My Remi!' and went on gazing at me. Some minutes passed before either of us could speak again, and at last she said:

"It's so long since I have seen you that it was hard to recognise you. How you've grown."

A muffled noise from behind the bed reminded me where Mattia and Capi were hiding, and I called to them to come out.

"This is Mattia, my brother."

"So you have found your parents," she cried.

"No, he's my companion, but just like a brother. And this is my other companion, Capi," I added after she had welcomed Mattia. "Capi, come and salute your master's mother."

Capi stood on his hind legs, put a paw to his chest and bowed very gravely. His performance wiped away Mother Barberin's tears and she burst out laughing. Mattia signed to me that it was time to spring our surprise.

"Let us all go and see if the pear tree is still bent by the wind. I have told Mattia about it. And we can see how the garden is looking too," I said.

"I have kept your piece of the garden just as it always was, for I somehow felt that one day you would come back."

"What about my Jerusalem artichokes? Did you enjoy eating them?"

"Yes, that was a lovely surprise. You always liked giving me surprises, didn't you."

The moment had come. "Is the shed just the same as when Roussette was with us?" I asked.

"Oh no, I keep my firewood there now."

By now we had reached the shed and I pushed open the door. As I did this our cow, who was either hungry or wanted to be milked, gave a loud moo.

"A cow! What is a cow doing here in my shed!" Mother Barberin cried out.

Mattia and I couldn't help laughing at the way she said this.

"She's a surprise," I said, "and a much better one than the Jerusalem artichokes. It's a present for you. I didn't want to come back empty-handed after all you have done for me. She will take the place of Roussette. Mattia and I bought her with the money we saved up."

She kissed us both before she went into the shed to examine her cow, and as she looked her over she gave little cries of joy. "I think she will give even more milk than Roussette," she said at last, and all the time the cow went on mooing.

"I am sure that she is asking to be milked," Mattia said, and I ran back to the cottage to get the pail that had not been used for so many years. While I was there I put the butter and flour on the table. The pail was soon three-quarters full of lovely frothy milk and Mother Barberin was delighted, and she was even more so when we all went back to the cottage and she saw what I had put on the table for making our pancakes.

"You must have known that Barberin is in Paris then," she said.

After I had explained to her how I had heard the news she went on the say that she would tell me later why he had gone there.

"Yes, let's have our pancakes first," I said. "I have never forgotten the night he came in and took the pan so that onions could be fried for his soup. Have you any eggs?"

"No, I don't keep chickens now."

"We didn't bring eggs with us in case they got broken, so I'll go and buy some from a neighbour and while I am away Mattia can chop some wood for tomorrow."

I came back with a dozen eggs as well as some lard, and before long Mattia and I were cramming pancakes down our throats. As soon as we had finished one we held out our plates for another, and Mattia declared that never in his life had he tasted anything so good, not even the first milk we had from the cow. Capi, of course, had to have his share and when Mother Barberin looked shocked at a dog being given pancakes I told her that as well as being chief actor in our company he was a genius and that he must be treated with respect and given every consideration.

Later, while Mattia was getting more wood ready for the morning, she told me why Barberin had gone back to Paris.

"Your family is looking for you," she said. "That's why he has gone to Paris, for he wants to find you."

"My family!" I exclaimed, "So I have a family of my own after all."

Then I became scared. I did not believe that I had a family or, that if I had, this family of mine would be looking for me. All Barberin was trying to do was to find me so that he could sell me again. I told Mother Barberin this, but she said no, my family was indeed trying to find me. She went on to say that about a month before, while she was doing some cooking, a man with a foreign accent had come to the door. He had asked Barberin what had become of the boy he had taken to the police many years ago in Paris, and Barberin had asked him what business that was of his.

"You know how easy it is to hear everything from this room, and when I knew that they were talking about you of course I listened harder. I moved a little nearer to the door but unluckily I trod on a twig of wood that snapped.

"Oh, so we're not alone," the man said.

"Don't worry, that's only my wife."

"The man then said that they could talk better further from the house. They went away and it was nearly four hours before Barberin came home alone. I wanted to make him tell me everything they had been talking about, but the only thing he would tell me was that this man who was looking for you was not your father, and that he had been given a hundred francs. I think that since then he must have been given more money. At any rate he said one day that he must go to Paris to find a musician named Vitalis who would tell him where he could find another man whose name was Garofoli. The names meant nothing to me."

"Have you had a letter from Barberin since he left here?" I asked, and she told me that she hadn't.

Mattia was passing by the door just then. I called out to him and when he came in I repeated to him all that Mother Barberin had just told me.

CHAPTER FIFTEEN

I did not sleep very much that night in spite of being in my old familiar bed.

I had hoped to spend several days with Mother Barberin but she told me that I must set out for Paris at once and find Barberin, and through him find my parents. In my heart I knew she was right, but I wanted first to see Lise. Mattia and I agreed that this could quite easily be done on our way to Paris, for Uncle Gaspard had told me that the uncle with whom she was staying was a lock-keeper on the Midi Canal, and he lived in a cottage near its banks. On our journey north it would however be impossible for me to see Etiennette where she was staying for that would mean us walking a long distance out of our way.

Mother Barberin and I spent the last day talking together, and I told her that when I was rich she would have everything that she wanted, but she simply said that the cow we had given her when I was poor would always mean more to her than anything I could give her when I had lots of money.

Before we left the next morning I wrote a letter to Etiennette explaining why I could not come and see her. We said goodbye to Mother Barberin and started on our long walk. For a long time Mattia was deep in thought and said very little, but I felt that I knew what was worrying him — I had parents who were rich. I told him that my father and mother would certainly think of him as one of our family, and that he would stay with the best masters

180

that could be found. But all he did was sadly shake his head.

In the meantime I was not yet rich, and so we had to play in the villages we passed through to get enough money to buy our food and to pay for our lodgings. I wanted, too, to make some money to buy a present for Lise, and after much thought I decided that it should be a doll. That would certainly not cost as much as a cow. We had reached Chatillon and in a shop-window there I saw a lovely doll which I somehow knew she would like, so I went in and bought it.

From there on we followed the banks of the canal and I often thought of Mrs Milligan and Arthur and their beautiful barge and wondered if we would ever see it. We never did. Autumn was coming now and with it shorter days, and one evening we saw, not so very far away, the cottage where Lise must be staying with Aunt Catherine and her uncle.

The cottage was in a field not so very far from the canal bank and the trees near it seemed to be floating in the early evening mist. When we were closer we could see the window lit up by the flames from a big fire inside. My heart started to race. The front door and the window were shut, but there were no curtains pulled and Lise was sitting beside her aunt eating her supper. I whispered to Mattia and Capi to keep quiet behind me, and then, taking my harp from my shoulder I got ready to play it.

"Good," Mattia whispered back to me, "what a marvellous idea, a serenade from the two of us."

"No, I am going to play alone."

I played the first notes of my Neapolitan song. I didn't sing for I was not wanting Lise to recognise my voice, but as I played I watched her. Soon she lifted her head and from where I was I could see her radiant smile. Then I started to sing and she jumped from her chair, ran to the door, and I was soon hugging her. Her aunt soon came to the door and when she remembered who I was shook hands with me and asked us in, and then set two more places at the table.

"We've another friend with us," I said to her, and asked whether another place could be set. As I asked this I took the doll from the knapsack and put it on the chair beside Lise, and I will never forget the expression on her face as I did this.

If we had not been in such a hurry to get to Paris I would have wanted to stay longer beside Lise for we had so much to tell each other; I could do the talking but, of course, she could only use signs to me. By these I was told how kind her uncle and aunt had been to her, that there were five children in the family, and that she had been taken for lovely trips in the barges when she was not at school. In my turn I told her of my work in the mine with Uncle Gaspard and how I had been rescued after its flooding. I mentioned, too, that my family was looking for me, and that was why I was in such a hurry to get to Paris, and also why it had been impossible for me to go and see Etiennnette.

The three of us were able to go for long walks and we always took Capi and the doll with us. In the evenings when it was not too cold and damp we sat in front of the house, and inside before the fire if the mist had come down. I played my harp and Mattia either his violin or cornet. Lise liked the harp best which made me happy and proud, and when the time came to go to bed I always played and sang to her my Neapolitan song.

But Mattia and I had to get on our way. I told Lise that I hoped I would be able to come back and see her again soon after I was reunited with my family, and my final words to her were: "I will come and fetch you in a carriage drawn by four horses." She believed me and moved an arm as if she were cracking a whip to urge on the horses, for like me she could see in her mind's eye the carriage and four shiny, black horses.

If it had not been for Mattia I would not have stopped the rest of our way to Paris except to buy what was necessary in the way of food, for there was now no cow nor doll to buy. I didn't even want to be bothered taking my harp along with me.

"I think we should give some performances and collect all the money we can," Mattia said. "We don't know if we will ever find Barberin, and anyone would think that you had forgotten the night when you nearly died of hunger."

"Oh no I haven't, and I never will."

"And I haven't forgotten, either, how hungry I was when you happened to meet me near that church. I can't bear the thought of being hungry again in Paris."

"We will eat all the better when we get to my parents!"

"All the same, I think we should work just as if we were going to buy another cow."

This was good advice, but I must admit that I didn't seem to be able to put my whole heart into playing and singing as I had done when we were saving up for our cow or Lise's doll.

"How lazy you will be when you have all this money," Mattia said more than once.

The nearer we came to Paris the happier I was, and the sadder Mattia grew. I kept on telling him that we would not be separated, and at last he told me that his worry and great dread was of a chance meeting with Garofoli, for he knew that if this happened Garofoli would take him in his charge again.

"You know how afraid you are of Barberin," he said, "and so you can imagine how much more afraid I am of Garofoli. If he's out of prison, and he must be by now, he'll find me somehow. And then he will part us. He can't force you to go with him, much as he would like to, but remember he's my uncle and not yours and can do anything he wants with me."

I must admit that I hadn't given much thought to Garofoli but what Mattia had said seemed possible, and in the end it was agreed that I should go to the various addresses I had written down where Barberin might be found. Then I would go to Garofoli's place, and after that we would meet again at about seven o'clock outside the main doors of Notre Dame.

For the first time in six months we separated. I went from one place to another; at one lodging-house I was told that Barberin had lived there about five years ago but had not been back since. The owner told me that he would like to catch the rogue for he owed him a week's rent. I was beginning to grow despondent, for by now there was only one place left for me to make enquiries and that was at a restaurant. The waiter said that he had not seen Barberin for a very long time, but a man who was having a meal called out that he knew Barberin had been staying for the last three weeks at a hotel not far away called the Cantal.

Before going there I decided to visit Garofoli's old place to see if I could find out anything about him so that I could bring back some sort of news to Mattia. When I reached the yard I saw, as on my first visit, the same old man hanging rags on the wall.

"Is Garofoli back?" I asked.

The man stared at me and gave a hacking cough, but did not answer. I could see that this rag-and-bone man would tell me nothing unless I let him know that I knew all about Garofoli, so I said: "You don't mean to say that he's still in prison? I thought he'd been let out months ago."

"No, he's got another three months to serve."

So Mattia could breathe again. I didn't stay any longer and hurried off rejoicing to the Hotel du Cantal to find when I reached it that, despite its name, it was nothing better than a cheap lodging-house. There was an old woman sitting inside the door and when I opened it she picked up an ear-trumpet.

"I want to see a man named Barberin," I said almost in a shout. "He comes from Chavanon. I have been told he is staying here."

She threw up her hands so abruptly that the cat sleeping on her knees jumped down frightened and ran away.

"Hélas!" she cried, and then she quickly added: "Are you the boy he was looking for?"

My heart leapt. "He has told you all about me then. Where is he?"

"He's dead. He died a week ago."

I put down my harp, and wondered how I would find my parents now.

"You must be the boy he was looking for, I'm sure you are."

"Yes, I am the boy. Did he ever say anything about my parents?"

Again she threw up her hands. Just then someone who looked like a servant joined us and the old woman turned and said: "Now here's a fine thing. This is the boy that man Barberin talked so much about."

"But did he mention my family?"

"Oh, yes, indeed, many, many times. A very rich family."

"But can you tell me where they live and what's their name?"

"Barberin wouldn't tell us anything. He was that mysterious about everything. He wanted all the reward for himself. We knew nothing about him, and it was only when a letter was found in his pocket at the hospital that it was known he came from Chavanon. If that hadn't turned up we couldn't have let Madame Barberin know that he had died."

"So she has been told that he is dead."

"Of course."

I stood for some time unable to speak. After all, there was nothing I could say, for I could learn nothing more there. At last I turned slowly towards the door.

"Where are you going?"

"To meet my friend."

"Does he live here in Paris?"

"We both arrived here this morning."

"Well, if you haven't anywhere to stay why don't you both come here? You will be well looked after and I'm not telling any lies when I say that everyone here is honest. If your parents get tired of waiting to hear from Barberin they may come here, and then they'll find you. I'm saying this in your own interests. How old is your friend?"

"He's a little younger than me."

"Just think! Two boys in the streets of Paris. We're very respectable here you know. You could finish up in a much worse place."

I was not sure about this, for the Hotel du Cantal was one of the dirtiest and poorest so-called hotels I had ever seen, and I had seen and been in some pretty awful ones. But what the old woman had said was worth thinking about and, besides, we couldn't afford to be particular. My family in its mansion was still to be found. Mattia had been right to want to get together as much money as we could on our way to Paris, and I could not help wondering what we would have done if we hadn't had the seventeen francs we had collected.

"How much will you charge for a room for my friend and me?"

"Ten sous a night. That's not dear."

"All right then, we'll come back tonight."

"Come back early. Paris can be dangerous after dark," she called after me as I went out.

There was still some time to fill in before I met Mattia again so I walked to the Jardin des Plantes and sat down there wrapped in thought. It seemed so extraordinary that Barberin should have died just at the one time I had ever wanted his help. Engrossed as I was I noticed a small child following his parents and pulling a little cart. An idea came to me and I took my harp and softly played a dance tune. The child tapped his feet to the tune, and when it was ended the father offered me a coin which I did not take, telling him how glad I was that I had given his child pleasure. I hoisted the harp back on my shoulder and as I turned to walk away I saw that the two grown-ups were watching me as I went.

By now it was early evening and as I walked to meet Mattia the street-lamps were already being lit. I was tired and feeling utterly alone when I saw Notre Dame as I crossed the road near the Hotel Dieu. And then I heard a bark, and before I knew it Capi had sprung at me and was licking both my hands. I patted him and kissed his cold nose.

Mattia did not take long to appear and I told him that Barberin had died and that there now seemed little hope of my ever finding my parents. He told me to cheer up, for if they had traced Barberin they would wonder why he had not kept in touch with them and so would make enquiries at this Hotel du Cantal I had told him about. On our way back to the hotel I told him that Garofoli was still in prison and would be there for another three months, and he did a little dance in the street. Our room was a very small one in the attic and our only light came from a smoky old candle.

Next morning I wrote to Mother Barberin, for I knew that she would be upset, and at the same time I asked her whether she had had any news from Barberin before he died. The village priest wrote back for her saying that Barberin had written while he was in hospital and had told her that should anything happen to him she was somehow to contact the lawyers who had sought him out to look for me. Their name and address in Lincoln's Inn Fields in London was given in the letter.

As soon as I had finished reading the letter to Mattia he said that he thought we should go at once to London because as the lawyers were English it seemed to show that my parents were English too.

"I would rather be the same as Lise and the others. But," I added, "if I'm English then I'll be the same as Arthur and Mrs Milligan."

"I'd much rather you were Italian," was Mattia's only comment.

It did not take us very long to pack our knapsacks and we walked out of the hotel, to the great dismay of the old woman. It took us a week to tramp to Boulogne, and when we arrived there we had just thirty-two francs to pay for our tickets on a cargo boat sailing to London next day. The Channel crossing was very rough and I could not help thinking of the days on 'Le Cygne' when we all glided along the canals. Mattia declared that he would never travel by sea again, and when at last we were steaming up the Thames and I begged him to get out of his bunk and watch with me everything we passed he begged me to leave him alone.

At last our boat was at the quay; we had arrived in London. I had learned a little English from Vitalis, and Mattia had picked up quite a lot from an Englishman who had been working at the circus. So when we left the boat he went up to a man and asked him the best and quickest way to walk to Lincoln's Inn Fields. As we followed his directions we often thought we would get lost in the maze of streets, but finally we reached the Temple Bar and from there found Lincoln's Inn Fields easily enough.

My heart was thumping when we stood at the door of the lawyer's office, and as Mattia stretched out his hand to ring the bell I had to tell him to wait a few moments until my heart quietened down again. Mattia gave one of the clerks in a large

When we were in the street the clerk hailed a cab
that was not very far away.

room my name and told him the reason why I had come, and we were at once shown into another room lined with books where two men were standing talking. Luckily one of them could speak French and asked me all sorts of questions, going into every detail in my life. My answers must have convinced him that I was the boy he was looking for, for he then said that my parents were living in London and that he would send me to join them at once. He pressed a button and when a clerk came in he gave him an address and told him to look after us.

"Oh, I had nearly forgotten to tell you," the lawyer said as we were leaving, "your father is Mr John Driscoll."

The lawyer had an ugly face, but in spite of that I think I would have hugged him if he had given me the chance. However he pointed at the door and we both went out after the clerk.

When we were in the street the clerk hailed a cab that was not very far away and told us to jump in. The driver sat on a box behind a hood which sheltered us, and I learned later that this curious-looking vehicle was called a hansom cab. There was quite a long discussion between the clerk and the driver and we heard the name Bethnal Green mentioned several times. This could only be the part of London where my parents lived. Mattia and I knew that the word 'green' could mean a park and this fitted in with my idea of my parents' house, which would be a mansion surrounded by trees.

We drove for what seemed a long time through the busy London streets, and Mattia and I were huddled in a corner of the cab with Capi between my legs. There were a lot of people about and every now and again the driver stopped as if he had lost the way. Finally he stopped altogether and there was a lot of talk through the judas window of the cab between him and the clerk. From what Mattia could make out the driver was saying it was no use, he was lost, and was asking the clerk the way he should go next. The clerk replied that he had never been in what he called 'this thieves' kitchen' before. We both understood the meaning of the word 'thieves'. In the end the clerk gave some coins to the driver and then told us to get out. The man grumbled at his fare but he turned his horse and drove away.

We were standing in a muddy street in front of what is known in England as a gin-palace. Our guide looked about him with disgust and then went inside with us at his heels. Although we were in a very poor part of London I had never seen such luxury. There were gilt-framed mirrors everywhere and the counter shone like polished silver. Yet the people who filled the place were dirty and in rags. Our guide went up to the counter and ordered a drink which he swallowed at a gulp, and then he asked the man who had served him where the address was that he wanted.

He must have been given the information he had asked for as he hurried out again with us following close behind. The streets we walked through were now much narrower, and across the alleys were stretched lines on which tattered and not very clean clothes were hanging. The women who were gossiping in the doorways all seemed to be pale and thin with matted hair hanging down to their shoulders. The children were nearly naked and what clothes they did wear were nothing but rags. In the middle of the alleys was stagnant water, and there was a dreadful smell.

Our guide stopped, for he now had most certainly lost his way. But just then a policeman strolled along and after the clerk had spoken to him the policeman told him he would lead the way. We all went down more narrow alleys and at last we stopped in a square in the centre of which there was a pool filled with green and slimy water.

"This is Red Lion Court," the policeman said.

I wondered why we could be coming here for I felt that it was impossible that my parents lived in a neighbourhood like this. The policeman banged on a door, and Mattia took my hand and gave it a squeeze and I pressed his hand back. When the door was opened all we saw was a big room with a lamp hanging from the ceiling and a fire burning in the grate.

Sitting motionless in front of the fire in a cane chair was an old man with a white beard, and on his head was a black skull-cap. At a table sat a hard-faced man of about forty and a woman some six years younger who at one time could have been quite pretty.

There were also two boys and two girls between the ages of eleven and three who were all fair-haired like the woman. I could not hear what the clerk was saying, but I did catch the name Driscoll which, so the lawyer had said, was my father's name. The clerk left.

"Which of you is Remi?" the hard-faced man asked.

"I am," and I took a step forward.

"Then come and kiss your father."

I suppose I should have been overcome with happiness and have leapt into his arms, but I felt quite the reverse. However I went and kissed him.

"Now," he said, "you must meet your grandfather, your mother, and brothers and sisters."

I went over to my mother and put my arms around her. She let me give her a kiss but did not return it. All she did was to say two or three words which I couldn't understand.

"Go and shake your grandfather's hand, but do it gently for it's paralysed," my father then said.

I also shook hands with my brothers and sisters. I wanted to take the younger one in my arms, but she was too occupied with Capi and pushed me away. As I went from one to the other I was angry with myself for not feeling any pleasure at having at last found my family. I had longed for this moment and yet all I could do was to stare curiously at all these people, unable to find a single word to say to any of them. I wondered if there was something wrong with me — if I had found my parents in a palace instead of a hovel like this would I have had more affection for them?

I felt ashamed of myself and on an impulse went to my mother again and kissed her this time on her lips. It was clear that she did not understand what made me do this, for instead of returning my kiss she looked at me with no interest, shrugged her shoulders, and then said something to the two men which made them laugh. Her indifference and my father's laugh particularly hurt me.

"Who's he?" my father asked, pointing at Mattia.

I told him that Mattia was my closest friend.

"Good. Would he like to stay and see the country?"

191

I was about to answer for Mattia but he spoke first. "Yes, I would like to do that."

My father then asked why Barberin had not come with us, and I told him that he was dead. He seemed pleased to hear this piece of news and repeated it to my mother, who appeared to be just as pleased. I remember that at the time this surprised me a little.

"You are probably curious to know why we have waited thirteen years to search for you," my father said, "and then all of a sudden to have the idea to look up this man Barberin who found you in Paris."

I told him that I was both surprised and curious, and that I would like to know why.

"Come nearer the fire, then, and I'll tell you all about it."

When we had come in I had put my harp against the wall, and I now set my knapsack down near it and sat down on the chair he pointed to. My trousers were covered with mud and were wet and as I stretched out my legs before the fire to dry them my grandfather spat to one side of me like a cat that is angry, but never spoke. I quickly pulled back my legs.

"Don't take any notice of him," my father said. "He doesn't like anyone else sitting in front of his fire."

All the same I still kept my legs under my chair.

"I must tell you that you are my oldest son," my father went on. "You were born a year after your mother and I were married. Before I married her there was a young girl who thought she was going to marry me, and to have her revenge she stole you when you were six months old. We had you searched for everywhere, but it was impossible to believe that you would be taken all the way to Paris and then abandoned in a street there. We believed that you could only be dead, but three months ago, when she was dying, the person who stole you confessed what she had done. I went at once to Paris and the police told me that you had been adopted by a stone-cutter who was now living in Chavanon.

"I traced him there and he gave me the story that he had lent you to a musician named Vitalis and that you and he were tramping through France. I had to come back to London, but before I left I gave Barberin some money and told him to search for you, and that when he had any news of you he was to write to my lawyers. I did not give him my address because we are only in London in the winter and spend the rest of the year travelling in England and Scotland. We are hawkers and we have our own caravans. And that is the story of how you have been found and come back to us after thirteen years. You may feel a little shy with us at first but you'll soon feel one of the family. It won't be long before you become used to our ways."

Yes, of course, I thought, I would soon feel one of the family for after all I was now one of them. The fine baby-clothes I had been found in must have belonged to someone else, that was clear. But what did it all matter for after all affection was worth much more than all the money in the world. While my father had been talking the table had been laid, and a large joint of roast beef with baked potatoes around it put in the centre.

"Are you two hungry?" my father asked. Mattia smiled, showing his white teeth. "Good, come to the table."

Before sitting down himself he gave my grandfather's cane chair a good push up to the table. Then, sitting down with his back to the fire, he started carving the joint and gave each of us a thick slice and some potatoes. Although I had not been taught many table-manners I could not help noticing how my brothers and sisters behaved, for more often than not they took the food with their fingers, sticking them into the gravy and then licking them without my father and mother paying the slightest attention. As for my grandfather he was concerned only with what had been placed in front of him, and the hand that he was able to use went ceaselessly from the plate to his mouth. When he let a piece of meat or potato slip from his shaky hand my brothers laughed and imitated him.

When we had finished I expected that we would all spend the evening together, but my father said that he was expecting some friends and that it was time for us to go to bed. He took a candle and led us both out to a coach-house along a passage. In it were two large caravans. He opened the door of one and we saw two

193

small beds, one above the other.

"There are your bunks," he said, "sleep well." Such was my welcome.

When we went out my father left the candle with us but locked the caravan door from the outside. As we usually did we got into bed as quickly as we could and did not talk much. In any case Mattia did not seem to want to talk any more than I did. After I had blown out the candle I found it impossible to go to sleep, and as I turned over and over in my narrow bed I thought of everything that had happened that day. I could hear Mattia in the bed above me being restless too, for he could not settle down to sleep either.

Sleep just would not come, and I was filled with a vague fear which I could not understand. It was not of sleeping in a caravan in this London slum, for I had spent many a night during my vagabond life less well protected than I was now. The hours passed one after another; a clock striking somewhere near told me how late it was. Then suddenly I heard a noise at the coach-house door which opened onto Red Lion Court. At regular intervals there were a number of knocks which were followed by a light which reflected into our caravan. Capi, who was asleep by my bed, woke up with a growl. I saw then that this light came through a little window against which our beds had been placed and which I had not noticed when going to bed because there was a curtain hanging in front of it. The top of the window was close to Mattia's bed and the bottom part close to mine. I was afraid that Capi might wake up the whole house so I put my hand over his mouth, and then peered outside.

I saw my father come into the coach-house and quickly and quietly open the door leading to the Court. After that two men with heavy bundles on their shoulders came in and he closed the door again. Then he put a finger to his lips and with the other hand, in which he held a lantern, he pointed to the caravan where we were supposed to be asleep. I felt like calling out something but I was afraid of waking Mattia who, I thought, was by now fast asleep. So I kept still and watched.

194

After he had helped the men take their packs off their shoulders my father went out, but came back soon with my mother. While he was away the men had emptied their bundles, and on the ground was all sorts of clothing — hats, underwear, trousers, stockings and gloves. I thought at the time that these men must be merchants who had come to sell their goods to my parents. My father examined everything carefully by the light of his lantern and then passed each article to my mother who cut off all the labels with a little pair of scissors and put them in her pocket. That she should do this seemed a little odd to me, as did the hour of the night for bringing the goods to the coach-house.

While my mother continued with her snipping my father was speaking in a whisper to the men. If my knowledge of English had been a little better perhaps I might have been able to catch some of what he was saying, but all I could pick up was the word 'police' which was said many times and, I suppose, for that reason made me more interested than ever.

When all they had been doing was completed my parents and the men went into the house, and once again all was dark. I supposed that they had gone to settle the bill. I wanted to convince myself that what had gone on was quite normal, but all the same I could not believe that this was so. I asked myself why these men who had come to see my parents hadn't used the door in Red Lion Court, and why all the talk of police was in whispers as though they were afraid of being heard outside. Again, why did my mother snip off the labels after the goods had been examined?

These thoughts would not leave my mind. In a while the light shone again into our caravan and, in spite of myself, I looked out, to see that my parents were alone. As my mother tied up the goods my father swept a far corner of the coach-house. In the cleared space was a trap-door which he lifted. By now my mother had finished what she was doing and my father took the bundles and lowered them to the cellar underneath, my mother holding the lantern for him to see properly. Then he shut the trap-door and brushed back over it the dry sand he had swept away. They both strewed whisps of straw on the sand so that the spot would look the same as the rest of the floor. That done, they went out.

At the moment when they gently closed the door behind them I thought that Mattia had moved in his bed and I wondered if he, too, had seen what was going on. I didn't dare ask him, for I was scared and in a cold sweat. It was only when a rooster crowed at daybreak that I at last fell asleep. The sound of a key being turned in the door of our caravan woke me up, and thinking it was my father who had come to tell us that it was time to get up I closed my eyes so as not to see him.

"It was one of your brothers," Mattia called out. "He has gone now."

As we got dressed Mattia did not ask me had I slept well, and neither did I have anything to say to him. Once I caught him looking at me but I averted my eyes. When we entered the kitchen neither of my parents was there. My grandfather was sitting in front of the fire as though he had not moved since the night before, and my eldest sister, whose name was Annie, was wiping the table clean. Allan, the elder brother, was sweeping the floor. I went over to them to say good morning but they continued what they were doing and took no notice of me. I stepped towards my grandfather but he would not let me come near him and, as on the previous evening, he spat to one side of me, and I stopped short.

"Please ask him," I said to Mattia, "when I can see my mother and father."

Hearing Mattia speaking English my grandfather seemed to be in a better mood and for quite a long time went on mumbling something.

"What did he say?" I asked when he had stopped.

"He said that your father has gone out for the day and that your mother is asleep. If we want to we can go for a walk."

"Was that all?"

Mattia seemed a little embarrassed and said that he wasn't quite sure that he had properly understood the rest.

"Tell me what you think you could understand."

"It sounded to me as if he was saying that if we found any bargains during our walk we were not to miss them, and he ended
196

by saying that we should remember that all of us here were able to live because of stupid people. That is all of what he said that I could make out."

My grandfather must have guessed what we were talking about for with the hand that was not paralysed he made a movement as if he were slipping something into his pocket and at the same time gave us a knowing sort of look.

"Let's get away from here," I said.

We wandered about for two or three hours but did not dare to go very far for we were frightened of getting lost. We could see that Bethnal Green was a pretty dreadful place even on a clear day, and Mattia and I hardly spoke to each other as we looked about us. When we were back at Red Lion Court my mother was still in her room, and I could see her through the open door bowed over a table. I thought she was ill and ran to comfort her. She lifted her head and looked at me, but didn't see me. I drew back and her head fell forward on her arms spread on the table.

"Gin," was all my grandfather said, and grinned at us.

I stood stockstill, unable to move. I don't know how long I stood like that, but anyhow Mattia and I went out again and for what seemed hours we walked without knowing where we were going. At last Mattia asked me: "Would you like to find somewhere we can sit down, Remi?"

"I suppose so. Somewhere we can talk. There's something I want to say to you."

By then we had reached a wider street than any of the others we had pushed our way along, and at the end of it we saw some trees. We hurried towards them and found it was a public park with benches. When we had sat down I said: "Mattia, we must separate. You must go back to France."

"Leave you? Never."

"Mattia, you *must* go back to France. Did you sleep at all last night?"

"Not much."

"Did you see anything?"

"Yes, everything."

"And you understood what was going on?"

"Of course. All those clothes were stolen, and I can tell you that your father was angry because the men knocked at the coach-house door instead of coming to the house. They told him that the police were watching them and they couldn't."

"Surely you can understand now why you must leave."

"If I must go back to France then you must too," Mattia said. "It's no use one of us staying alone here."

"But look, if Garofoli had come across you in Paris and made you go back to him you know that you would not have wanted me to stay with you. I am simply telling you what you would have said yourself."

Mattia didn't answer.

"You must go back to Paris," I insisted. "Go and see Lise, and then go to Mother Barberin and tell them both that my parents are not as rich as I believed they were. That is all you need to say."

"It's not because they have no money that you want me to go. I know why. After what we both saw last night you are afraid for me. Well, if that is so I'm afraid for you. Let's both leave."

"That's impossible. They are my parents and it's my family so I must stay."

"Your family! Your father a thief and your mother a drunkard. Anyway, and I *am* going to say this, you don't look like either of them, and their children are all fair while you are dark. And how did they find the money to seek you out? For these reasons alone I am certain that your name is not Driscoll. You know what you should do? Write at once to Mother Barberin and ask her to tell you just what the clothes were like that you were wearing when you were found. Then ask that man you call your father to describe how this baby he was talking about was dressed when it was stolen. Until we know that I am staying here with you."

We did not return to Red Lion Court until dusk was falling and nothing was said to us by either of my parents. After we had all had something to eat my father pulled two chairs in front of the fire, which brought a growl from the old man, and then asked how we had made enough money to live on in France. I told him our story.

"Not only did we earn enough to live on, but we collected enough to buy a cow," Mattia said proudly, and then told of how we had worked to get our cow.

"You both must be very clever," my father said, "and now we would like to hear you play."

I took my harp and played something that I cannot remember now, but it was certainly not my Neapolitan song. Then Mattia played his violin and cornet, but it was the cornet which brought the most applause from the children, who had been standing in a circle around us.

"What about Capi? He must have been able to earn his keep."

As you know, I was very proud of Capi's talents and so I asked him to perform some of his tricks, which he did to everybody's delight.

"That dog's worth a fortune," my father said, and I assured him that Capi could learn practically anything.

My father thought for a moment or two and then he asked Mattia whether he would like to stay and live with all of them.

"I want to stay with Remi," was all he said.

"Well, I think that this is what we should do," my father went on. "We are not rich and we all have to work for a living. In the summer we travel about England and the children here go knocking on doors and selling our goods. In the winter we can't do that. While we are in London, you Remi, and you Mattia, can go and play music in the streets and as Christmas is getting near you both should make quite a bit of money. We can't afford to waste time so your two brothers, Allan and Ned here, must take Capi with them and he can show off all his tricks."

"Capi won't perform well with anyone but me," I said quickly, for I could not bear being parted from him.

"He'll easily learn to work with the two boys, and we'll make more money this way."

"But we will get lots more if Capi is with us," I insisted.

"That's enough," my father answered. "I'm the boss here, remember that, and I don't want any arguments."

I couldn't say anything more. When we were sent to bed Mattia took longer than me undressing and he came over when I was in bed to whisper: "Now remember, tomorrow you are to write to Mother Barberin," and then he got into his own bed.

But next morning I had to give a lesson to Capi. I lifted him up and while I kissed him gently on his nose I explained to him what he had to do. I then put him on his leash and he went obediently with the two boys, but he looked very forlorn. Mattia and I were taken by my father across to a part of London where there were big houses, splendid streets with wide footpaths, and carriages with windows that shone like glass, drawn by magnificent horses and driven by coachmen with powdered hair.

It was late when we got back to Red Lion Court, and how delighted I was to see Capi again. He was spattered with mud but frisky, and after I had cleaned and brushed him I wrapped my sheepskin about him and put him into my bed to sleep.

For several days Mattia and I went our way and Capi and the two boys went theirs. Then one evening my father told me that in the morning we could take Capi with us as he wanted everyone else to do something or other at home. Naturally we were very pleased to hear this and we intended to do our utmost to bring back as much money as we could so that he would let us have the dog always, for we simply had to get Capi back. I gave him an extra good brushing before we left after breakfast.

Our route took us along Holborn and Oxford Street, but unluckily for us the heavy fog which had been hanging over London for the previous two days did not lift. It was so dense that we could hardly see a few steps ahead of us, and those who stopped to listen to our music could not see Capi so our collections did not bring in nearly as much as we were hoping. But we were to be grateful in the end that there was such a heavy fog.

We were still in Holborn, a very busy street, when I suddenly noticed that Capi was not beside us; this was unusual for he always stayed as close to us as he could. I stood at the entrance to an alleyway and whistled to him. I was beginning to think that someone had stolen him when he came running up wagging his tail, and with a pair of woollen stockings between his jaws. He put his front paws on me and offered the stockings to me, and seemed as proud of himself as if he had just done one of his most difficult tricks. It had all happened in a matter of a very few minutes and I was dumbfounded. Then Mattia grabbed the stockings with one hand and with the other dragged me down the alleyway.

"Walk fast, but don't run," he said in a low voice.

When we were able to stop he told me that a man who had rushed past him on the pavement was crying: "Wait until I catch that thief!"

The thief was Capi, and if it hadn't been for the fog we could both have been arrested. For a moment I stood almost choking. My good and honest Capi had been trained to be a thief.

"We're going back to the house," I said. "Hold Capi tight on his leash."

We walked quickly to see when we arived the whole family seated around the table folding all sorts of clothes into piles. I threw the stockings on the floor. "You've made a thief of my dog," I shouted. I was trembling with anger. "You said he would be taken out to amuse people. Capi is not going to be a thief again, any more than I ever will be."

My father glared at me and I thought he was going to hit me, but I did not lower my eyes. At last he said: "Oh, all right then, I suppose that from now you may as well take your dog with you."

From that day on my parents and brothers and sisters showed how much they disliked me, and my grandfather always spat angrily if I went anywhere near him. Indeed, the only time that my father spoke to me was when he demanded to know every evening how much money we had collected and told me to hand it over to him. Although I had not wished to listen to what Mattia had said I gradually began to wonder whether I really did belong to this family. I had done nothing to deserve the way I was treated and Mattia saw how very upset I was.

At last I did write to Mother Barberin. It would have been silly to ask her to send her letter to me at Red Lion Court so I said in my letter that her reply should be addressed to me at the 'poste-restante' in Smithfield. When her reply, which had been written for her by the priest at Chavanon came, Mattia and I went into the nearest quiet side street and read it. It read:

'My little Remi,

I was surprised, and very sorry, to read what you told me in your letter. From what Barberin said to me after he had found you in the clothes you were wearing I believed that you belonged to a very rich family.

I can remember so clearly what clothes you wore, indeed, I kept all of them carefully for the day when your parents would come to claim you. I should tell you that you were not dressed like French babies. You were wearing a lace bonnet, a vest made of fine wool, a white linen dress with over it another made of silk, white woollen bootees tied with silk ribbons, and a long white cashmere coat which was beautifully embroidered and lined with silk.

None of your clothes had any markings except the vest and the dress, but the markings on these had been carefully cut out. That is all I can tell you.

Don't worry, Remi, that you can't give me all the things that you promised. Your cow you bought with your savings is worth all the presents in the world to me. She is well and gives me a lot of lovely creamy milk, so I am very well off now and I never look at her without thinking of you and your friend Mattia.

Let me have news from you sometimes and I hope that now you have found your family they will love you as you deserve to be loved. My affectionate kisses.

Your foster-mother,
Widow Barberin.'

Poor Mother Barberin, I thought, imagining that everyone must love me because she did.

"She is a good lady," Mattia said. "And she even thought of me! Now that we know all about your clothes let's go and see what your Mr Driscoll has to say."

"He might have forgotten all about them and what they looked like."

"Don't be silly. Does one ever forget the clothes one's own child was wearing when it was stolen? Why, it's only through the clothes that a child can be identified."

"Let's wait until we hear what he has to say before we start thinking anything."

It was not easy for me to ask my father what I was wearing on the day I disappeared. I suppose that if one evening I had asked him the question casually it would have been easy enough, but I was bound to be nervous and start stammering. Then one day when heavy sleet had driven us home earlier than usual I took up my courage in both hands and spoke to him. At first my father stared hard at me, and I looked back at him far more bravely than I had ever imagined I could. He soon smiled — there was something hard and cruel in his smile, but still it was a smile.

"We have kept a description of what you were wearing on the day that you were stolen," he said, and he went to a drawer and pulled out a large sheet of paper which he read out. What he read was exactly the same as Mother Barberin had written in her letter.

My father went on to say: "Two of your garments were marked 'F.D.' which stands for 'Francis Driscoll', your real name, but these were cut off by the woman who stole you, for she hoped that by her doing this you would never be traced. And I will now show you your birth and baptism certificates."

Again he looked in the drawer and when he had found them he handed them to me along with the list of clothes.

"If you don't mind," I said, and I had to try hard to speak, "I would like Mattia to read them both to me."

Mattia did as well as he could and it seemed from the certificates that I was born on a Thursday, the 2nd of August, the son of John and Margaret Driscoll.

There were no further proofs I could ask for. But Mattia wasn't at all happy, and when we had gone to our caravan that night he said to me: "That's all very fine, Remi, but what I would like to know is how these hawkers had enough money to buy a child such fine clothes. You know as well as I do, and you have seen for yourself, that these people have no money."

"Perhaps because they are hawkers they can get things cheaper," I replied.

Mattia whistled softly and then shook his head. "Do you know what I think? You are not their child. Driscoll is the one that stole you."

Before I could answer he climbed up to his bed.

CHAPTER SIXTEEN

I suppose that if I had been Mattia I would perhaps have had his imagination. To me it had been proved beyond any doubt that Mr Driscoll was my father. Mattia might have his doubts but I hadn't and when he tried to convince me otherwise I told him to be quiet. But he was pig-headed and I could not always get the better of his obstinacy.

"Why are the rest of the family fair and you dark? How could these poor people dress you in silk?" were two questions he kept repeating, but I could only reply:

"Very well, why did they search for me if I was not their child, and why did they give money to Barberin?"

Mattia had no answer, and yet he would not be convinced.

"I think that we should both go back to France," he then urged.

"That's impossible."

"And all because you think it's your duty to stay here with your so-called family."

These and other exchanges between us made me all the more unhappy, and yet in spite of my wish not to have any doubts I wondered who would ever have believed, when I talked so much of my family, that I should be in such despair now that I had one. How could I find out the truth? In the meantime I had to sing, play my harp, and smile to passers-by. Sundays were better because we did not have to go out and earn money and, with Capi trotting beside us, we could both wander about the streets of Bethnal Green.

One Sunday, however, my father told me to stay at home because he wanted me for something, and he sent Mattia off on his own. All the others had gone out except my grandfather who was still somewhere in the house. I had been sitting with my father for about an hour when there was a knock on the door and a man who was unlike any of the others who usually called on him came in. He was about fifty and was very well-dressed, but what struck me most about him was that when he smiled in a way he thought looked pleasant he drew back his lips to show teeth which were very white and pointed like a dog's. He spoke to my father in English and all the time turned to stare at me, but after a while he started talking in very good French.

"And this is the young boy you spoke to me about?" he said, pointing at me. "He looks very strong and healthy."

"Answer the gentleman," my father said, as if his visitor had spoken to me.

"Yes, I feel fine," I replied, rather surprised and not quite knowing how to answer.

"You have never been sick have you?"

"I had pneumonia once."

"When was that?"

"About three years ago. I had slept out in the cold all night. My master who was with me was frozen to death, but I caught pneumonia. I sometimes get tired but that's only when I have walked a lot, and I don't get ill."

He came over to me and felt my arms, then he put a hand over my heart, then on my back and told me to take deep breaths. He also told me to cough. When this was all finished he looked at me for what seemed a long time and it was then that I thought he wanted to bite me, for I saw his teeth gleaming behind his lips. He repeated in English to my father his conversation with me, and after a few minutes they left the house together, not by the door on to Red Lion Court but through to the coach-house.

After they had gone I started to wonder what it all meant and whether I would be separated from Mattia and Capi. There was one thing I was quite certain about and that was that I wouldn't be a servant to anyone, let alone this man whom I already disliked. After a time my father came back and told me that I could go out for a walk if I wanted to, and as it was raining I went to the caravan to get my sheepskin coat. To my great surprise Mattia was lying on top of his bed, and when he saw me come in he put a finger to his lips.

"Go and open the coach-house door," he whispered. "I'll tiptoe out behind you. They mustn't know I was here."

It was only when we were in the street and well away from the house that Mattia would speak in his normal voice. As we continued walking he said: "Do you know who that man was with your father? I will tell you. It was Mr James Milligan, your friend Arthur's uncle."

I stopped and stared at him, but he took me by the arm and pulled me along.

"I didn't want to go out by myself," he went on. "The shops are closed on Sundays and there's no one about so I decided to lie on my bed and have a sleep. But I didn't drop off; later, your father and this man came into the coach-house and I overheard all they said. At first I didn't take much notice but when I heard the visitor say that you were lucky to be alive, for nine out of ten would have died from pneumonia, I pricked up my ears. Then your father asked him about his nephew and was told how much better he had been since three months ago when the doctors said he would not live. Apparently everything was due to Mrs Milligan's nursing.

"You can imagine how hard I listened when I heard her name mentioned. You father also said that if Arthur was so much better everything that this visitor of his had done had been wasted. The man answered that that might be so, but he wouldn't say any more than that it would be a miracle if his nephew lived many more years, and that on the day he did die he would inherit all the money. Before they parted the man said that he knew he could rely on your father to attend to matters — nothing more was said and I wondered what that could have meant."

My first idea on hearing all this was to go to my father and ask him for Mrs Milligan's address so that I could find out more about Arthur and his mother. But then I realised how stupid this would be, for it would mean that my father would know that their conversation had been overheard. The man would almost certainly be coming to the house again and next time Mattia, whom he didn't know, could follow him.

It was not so long after this that while we were playing our music in Oxford Street I noticed a man in our audience trying to attract Mattia's attention. When we were getting ready to move on this man came over and joined us and he greeted Mattia as if he were an old friend. Mattia recognised him at once as the clown, Bob, from the circus in Paris, who had taught him the English he knew. As you will see he was to be of great help to me when I was in serious trouble.

I should tell you that James Milligan did not, however, come back to Red Lion Court, or if he did we must have missed him. Time passed slowly but at last the day arrived when it was decided that the family would leave London to travel in the country. The caravans had been gaudily repainted and were loaded with hats, shawls, handkerchiefs, stockings, underwear, buttons, thread, ear-rings, soap, powders, everything that one could imagine. Horses were bought, how and from where they came I did not know but we both saw them arrive. All was made ready, but until the last minute we did not know whether we were to stay with the old grandfather or go with the family. The evening before the departure my father told us that as we earned quite a lot in London with our music we were to come with them and to continue to play and collect more money.

"I think we should go back to France while we have the chance," Mattia said to me later.

"Why can't we travel through England while we have the chance?"

"Because I have the feeling that we are heading for trouble."

I told him that I had to stay, and so we set out traipsing behind the caravans. When we arrived at any large village the caravans stopped on the green, one of the sides was lowered, and the goods were displayed for everyone to see.

"Look at the prices! Look at the prices!" my father shouted. "You won't find anything like these clothes anywhere at these prices. I'm not selling them, I'm giving them away. Look at the prices!"

"They must be stolen," I overheard people saying, and if they had looked at me and seen my blushes they would have known that they had guessed right. And if they did not notice my face Mattia did, for he said to me one night: "How much longer do you think you are going to stay?"

Again he urged that we should return to France, that he felt that something was going to happen to me, and happen soon. He thought that it wouldn't be long before the police would become suspicious of Driscoll because of his very cheap prices, and then the cat would be out of the bag.

"If you are determined to keep your eyes shut I will keep mine wide open," he said. "We will be arrested even though we have done nothing, but how can we prove that? Aren't we eating food that is paid for by the money he gets from the sale of his stolen goods?"

I had never thought of that and it was like a blow.

"But we earn our food," I stammered, trying to defend myself.

"That's true, but we're living with thieves. And if we are sent to prison we can't try and find your family, or even warn Mrs Milligan about the danger to Arthur. I am going to say it again, let's go while we can."

"Mattia, please give me a few more days to think things over."

"Well hurry up with your thinking. That giant in the fable smelt flesh and I smell danger."

Several weeks had passed now since we had left London and we had reached a town where a horse-race meeting was soon to be held. My father had parked his caravans quite close to the race-course which was some distance from the town. As Mattia and I had nothing to do with the selling of the clothes we wandered over

209

to it. There was a sort of fair there with stalls selling trinkets and all manner of things, as well as side-shows.

As we were passing close to an open-air fire over which a kettle was hanging we saw Mattia's friend Bob. He was delighted to see us again and told us that he had come to the race-meeting with two of his friends and was going to do some circus tricks and give an exhibition of weight-lifting. Some musicians who had said they would play to attract a crowd before the performances had not turned up, and Bob asked us if we would help him out. Whatever was collected would be shared out between the five of us, and Capi would get something too for he would also be doing some of his tricks. We agreed and promised to be there the next day at the time he wanted us.

When we got back to the caravans I told my father what we were going to do and he said that he would be wanting Capi, and so we could not take him with us. I wondered if they were going to use him for stealing again and he must have guessed my thoughts.

"Capi has very good hearing," he said, "and must stay beside the caravans, for with all these people milling about we could easily be robbed. You two go alone and play for your friend Bob. If you come back late, which will be likely, you will find us at the 'Big Oak Inn', you know where that is. We will be on our way again tomorrow."

This inn, which was kept by a sinister-looking couple, was on a straight road about three miles from the town in open country, and we had stayed there the previous night. For me the annoying thing was that it would be a long walk after a tiring day, but when my father spoke like that I had to obey. Next morning, after I had fed Capi and given him a drink, I tied him to the wheels of a caravan and hurried off with Mattia to the racecourse.

As soon as we reached there we had to start playing and we went on until after midnight, for when dusk came the performances continued in a big tent. My fingers ached as if they had been pricked by a thousand pins and Mattia had blown his cornet for so long that he could hardly breathe. Just as Bob was doing his last turn a big bar of iron he was lifting slipped and fell on

210

one of Mattia's feet. I thought his foot was broken but luckily there were only severe bruises which, all the same, made it impossible for him to walk. It was decided that he should spend the night with Bob and that I should go back alone to the 'Big Oak Inn', for I had to know where the Driscolls were going in the morning. I left my harp with Mattia and set out. I was very tired when I reached the inn and was amazed to find that the gaudy-coloured caravans had gone. All I could see in the darkness besides two or three miserable carts covered with tarpaulins was a big structure with wooden shutters from which as I drew near I heard the roars of animals belonging to some circus or other.

I went over to the inn and knocked on the door. When the landlord opened it and saw by the light of a lantern who I was, instead of letting me in he told me to hurry off after my parents who had gone to a town called Lewes, and then he slammed the door in my face without saying another word.

In the time I had been in England I had learned enough English to be able to understand him, but I had not the slightest idea of where Lewes was, and in any case I could not go there and leave Mattia behind even if I knew the direction. I wearily walked back to the racecourse and about an hour and a half later was sleeping in Bob's wagon on a heap of straw beside Mattia. When I got up in the morning I saw Bob crouching beside a fire waiting for his kettle to boil and I was standing near him when a policeman came up leading Capi on a leash. As soon as Capi was near me he gave a tug at the leash and, escaping, bounded towards me and jumped into my arms.

"Is this your dog?" the policeman asked me.

"Yes."

"Then come along, you're under arrest," and he took hold of my arm.

"What's this all about?" Bob demanded, jumping up.

"Are you his brother?"

"No, his friend."

"I'll tell you why I am here. Last night a man and a boy climbed a ladder and broke into St George's Church in the town.

This dog was to give the alarm if they were disturbed. They were caught in the act and in their hurry to get away they left the dog still tied up. I knew that, having the dog, I would be sure to find the thieves. Here's the boy and now we have to find the man."

I was speechless. Mattia, who had heard the voices, came out of the wagon and hobbled over to me. Bob was explaining to the policeman that I could not have been the culprit because I had been with him until one o'clock and had then gone to the 'Big Oak Inn', spoken to the landlord, and come back at once.

"It was a quarter past one that the church was broken into," the policeman said, "and if the boy left here before that he could have met the other thief and reached the church."

"It takes more than a quarter of an hour to get from here to the town," Bob said.

"Not if you run. And what proof can you give me that he left here at one o'clock?"

"I can prove it."

The policeman gave a shrug. "I am taking the boy with me. He can tell his story to the magistrate."

As I was being led away Mattia came over to me and whispered to me to keep my courage up. "Take care of Capi," I managed to say in French, but the policeman could understand and said that he would keep the dog since, having found me, it would help him to find my so-called companion.

It was the second time that I'd been arrested, and held tight by the policeman I had to pass through an interested crowd of people who had quickly collected. But they did not jeer at me like the peasants in France, for most of them were gypsies or tramps and they had no great love for the police. In this gaol where I was locked up there were no onions strewn about the floor of my cell, and the window had bars which put any thought of escape out of my head. There was only a bench and a hammock and I dropped onto the bench and sat there for a long time feeling very sorry for myself. When at last I got up I went to the window and saw that the bars were of iron and crossed to form a lattice. The walls were more than three feet thick and the ground outside was paved with

212

large stones, while the cell door was iron-plated.

I wondered how long I would have to stay there. How could I prove my innocence in spite of Capi being at the church? Certainly Mattia and Bob might be able to help me. When a gaoler, who did not seem a bad sort of man, came in to bring me some food I asked him how long it would be before I was brought before the magistrate and he told me that it would certainly be next day. I had heard stories of prisoners finding messages from their friends in the food that was brought to them, so I crumbled my bread, but found nothing. There were some potatoes too, so I mashed them but didn't find the tiniest note. It goes without saying that I spent a sleepless night.

Next morning the gaoler came in with a jug of water and a basin. He told me to wash if I wanted to for I was to appear before the magistrate very soon, and looking clean never went against anyone. I washed and paced my cell until the gaoler came back and told me to follow him. We walked along a lot of passages before we came to a small door which he opened and told me to go through. The room I entered was stuffy even though it was fairly large with a high ceiling and big windows. There was a confused murmur of voices and my head was throbbing as I looked about me. The magistrate was seated above three court officials and where I was told to stand there was a man wearing a robe and a wig, which surprised me, for I had not known I was to have a lawyer to defend me.

Among the people in court I saw Bob and his two friends, the landlord of the 'Big Oak Inn', and some other men I had never seen before. Then I noticed the policeman who had arrested me, and not far from him was standing Mattia looking very embarrassed. The crime was described — a robbery had taken place in Saint George's Church; the thieves, a man and a boy, had climbed a ladder and broken a window to get in; they had a dog with them to give warning if they were disturbed; at a quarter past one someone passing had seen a light in the church and had at once awakened the sexton who had taken several men with him to the church; the dog had barked and the thieves had escaped and

213

left the dog tied up when they ran away.

It was then stated that the dog's intelligence was remarkable, for it had led the policeman to the racecourse where it had recognised its master, who was none other than one of the accused standing in the dock. As for the other thief the police were on his trail and it was hoped to make an arrest shortly.

I was next asked a lot of questions which I answered as best I could, and my friends tried to give me an alibi, but the man who was prosecuting said that I had had more than enough time to meet my accomplice at the church and, after the alarm had been raised to run to the 'Big Oak Inn'. But I declared that I was innocent, and my lawyer did his best for me. In the end, and after a long time, the magistrate said that I was to be taken to the county gaol and brought before the next Assizes.

The Assizes! I fell back onto the chair that was in the dock. Why, why hadn't I listened to Mattia's good advice. Apparently the magistrate wished to await the arrest of the man who was thought to be my accomplice and we could be tried together. I would have the shame of appearing beside him in the prisoner's dock of the next Assizes.

That evening when it was getting nearly dark I heard the sound of a cornet being played, and from the clearness of the notes I knew it could only be Mattia wanting to tell me that he was near and thinking of me. It sounded as if he was in the street on the other side of the wall opposite my barred window. Then I heard footsteps and people's voices and it seemed likely that Mattia and Bob were giving a performance. A little later I heard called out distinctly in French: "Tomorrow at daybreak", followed by a loud blast on the cornet.

No great intelligence was needed to understand that these words in French were not meant for English listeners, but I was not too sure of their meaning. Pretty obviously I had to be on the alert early next morning, and as soon as it was really dark I climbed into my hammock. However, although I felt very tired it was some time before I dropped off to a restless sleep. When I awoke it was still night with the stars shining, and everything was silent. A clock struck three, so I stayed awake and counted the hours and half hours, leaning against the wall and with my eyes fixed on the window.

When dawn came roosters started crowing. On tiptoe I managed to open the window so that I would be able to answer whatever Mattia might have to say to me. There were still the iron bars and that high wall and I could not possibly escape, and yet, silly as the thought was, I expected to gain my freedom. The morning air was very cold but even so I stayed by the window and listened without knowing what I would hear. A big white cloud appeared in the sky and by then I could see things outside more clearly. I held my breath and my heart started thumping.

In a few minutes I seemed to hear a scratching on the wall, but I had heard no sound of footsteps. I listened more carefully as the scratching went on, and then I saw Bob's head appear. When he saw my face pressed against the bars he whispered very softly: "Keep quiet," and signed to me to move away from the window. I did as I was told and as I did so he put a child's pea-shooter to his mouth and blew. A small white ball was blown into my cell and fell near my hammock. Bob's head disappeared and, again, all was quiet.

I pounced on the ball which was made of tissue paper. The light inside the cell was to dim for me to see the message it was certain to contain, so I carefully closed the window and lay down again in my hammock. Then, after what seemed hours, I unrolled the tiny ball and could just read the message:

> 'Tomorrow afternoon you will be taken by train
> to the county gaol. A policeman will be in the
> compartment with you. Stay close to the door
> you entered by. At the end of 45 minutes (count
> them carefully) the train will slow down as it
> comes near a station. As it does, open the door
> and jump out. Climb the slope and we will be
> waiting behind it with a gig and a fast horse.
> Two days later we will be in France. Jump as far
> as you can and land on your feet.'

I was to be saved and would not have to appear at the Assizes after all. I could not believe it was true, and it was all because of Mattia and Bob. I read the note again. 'At the end of 45 minutes... jump... land on your feet.' It was a very risky thing to jump from a moving train, but even if I was killed it would be better than going to prison as a thief. And what about Capi? I read the note a third time, then chewed it to a pulp and swallowed it. Now I could sleep in peace.

Time passed quickly enough and the next day in the afternoon a policeman came for me and told me to follow him. He was a big man of about fifty and did not look to me as if he would be very quick on his feet. I did as I had been told and sat near the door when the two of us got into the train. We were the only people in the compartment, and the policeman sat near me. As soon as the train left the station he asked me whether I knew any English.

"Yes, a little. I can follow it if it's not spoken too quickly."

"Well then," he said, "I would like to give you some advice. Don't try to be clever. Just tell me how it all happened and I'll give you five shillings. If you have a little money on you things will be easier for you in prison."

I nearly said that I had nothing to tell him but I felt that that might only annoy him, so I didn't answer. After a while I got up to lean against the door. The window was open and the fresh air was blowing in. My guardian was finding it too draughty and moved over to a seat with its back to the engine. I felt for the handle and gently turned it, all the time holding the door with my other hand.

The minutes passed, and then the engine gave a whistle and started to slow down. The moment had come. Quickly I pushed the door open, turned, and jumped as far as I could. Luckily I was able to land with arms outstretched at the bottom of a slope, but even so I fell so heavily that I rolled over unconscious. When I came to I thought I was still on the train for I was sure that something was moving under me. I looked about and saw that I was lying on some straw in a cart of some kind. A soft, warm tongue was licking me and I moved to make out an ugly dog, with blobs on its coat that made it look something like a Dalmatian, stretched out close to me. Mattia was kneeling beside me.

"You're safe now," he said, and gave the dog a push.

"Where am I?"

"In a gig. Bob's driving."

Bob called out from his seat above to ask if I could move my legs and arms, and I moved all four of them to show that nothing was broken.

"What happened?" I asked Mattia.

"You jumped from the train as you were told to, but you landed badly and then rolled into a ditch. When you didn't come over to us I held the horse and Bob went for you and carried you back to the gig. We thought you were dead."

"What about the policeman?"

"The train didn't stop."

I looked again at the dog that was gazing at me with eyes like Capi's. But Capi didn't have spots.

"Where's Capi?"

Before Mattia could reply the funny-looking dog had jumped on me and was licking me and making odd noises.

"That's Capi, we dyed him."

"Dyed him? Why?"

But Bob interrupted our talk by stopping the gig and telling Mattia to hold the horse while he altered the appearance of the gig completely, and inside it he arranged things so that Mattia, Capi and me could not be seen from the outside. When all this had been done I asked Mattia, who was now crouching beside me, where we were going.

"To Littlehampton," he answered. "Bob has a brother living there who goes to Normandy in his own boat to bring back butter and eggs. We owe everything to Bob. There was very little I could do by myself, and it was his idea that you should escape from the train."

"What about Capi? How did you manage to take him from under the noses of the police?"

"The police weren't very clever to let us take Capi away from them, but Bob knows all the tricks of getting a dog to follow him.

217

And it was Bob who decided to dye him so that the police wouldn't recognise him again."

"How's your foot now?"

"Better, or almost. I haven't had time to think about it."

We started off again and travelled quickly, for we had quite a distance to go and we were sure too that as soon as the train stopped the police would be hunting for me. Every now and then we passed other vehicles; the villages we drove through were all very quiet and as night was now starting to fall there were lights in a few windows. Mattia and I kept well under cover as for some time a very cold wind had been blowing, and when we licked our lips they were salty. Soon we saw a light flashing at regular intervals — it was a lighthouse, and we had arrived at Littlehampton.

Bob stopped the horse, jumped down, and told us to wait where we were. He said he was going to see his brother and ask him if it would be safe to take us onto his boat. Bob seemed to be away for a very long time, and we kept absolutely quiet. We could hear the waves breaking on the shore fairly close to us, and we were both trembling.

"It's cold," Mattia whispered.

I wondered whether it really was the cold that made us tremble, for whenever a cow or a sheep in the field on one side of the road stumbled on a stone or scraped against the fence we trembled even more. At last we heard footsteps. Bob was not alone for he had brought with him a man wearing, from what I could make out, a sailor's thick jersey and an oilskin hat.

"This is my brother," Bob said. "He'll take you on his boat. We will have to separate now, and no one knows that you're here."

I wanted to thank Bob but he cut me short and shook hands with me. "We'll meet again someday," he said, "and I'm only too glad to have helped one of Mattia's friends."

With the wind in our faces we followed Bob's brother down some narrow and silent streets to the wharf where, without saying a word, he pointed to his boat. In a few minutes we were on board and were told to go below into a little cabin.

"I'm sailing in two hours," he then said. "You sit down, and don't make a sound."

He locked us in and went away, but we were not trembling now as we sat in the darkness side by side.

After Bob's brother had left us we listened to the noise of the wind and the waves slapping against the hull, and a good while later we heard footsteps on the deck which almost touched our heads, the creaking of pulleys, and then the sound of an anchor being hauled up. A sail was hoisted, and suddenly the boat gave a lurch and then began to roll. In a few minutes it was pitching about in heavy seas.

Mattia was again very seasick, but all he said when I comforted him was that nothing mattered now that we were on our way back to France. During the day I spent my time between our cabin and the deck. At last I saw the French coast a blur in the distance, and late that afternoon we arrived at Harfleur. I rushed down to the cabin to tell Mattia the good news. Bob's brother told us that if we wanted to we could sleep on his boat that night.

"If ever you want to go back to England," he said the next morning as we wished him goodbye and thanked him, "remember that I am here every Tuesday to collect my cargo."

It was very kind of him but Mattia and I had our good reasons for not wanting to return there, for a long time at any rate. We landed with our instruments and the clothes that we were wearing — our knapsacks and extra clothing were with the Driscolls. With the money that we had received as our share for playing those long hours for Bob we had altogether forty francs; Mattia, who had kept the money for us both, had wanted to pay Bob something towards the hire of the gig before we left him, but he would not hear of it, and neither would his brother take anything.

The first thing we did when we were ashore was to buy more clothes, new knapsacks, and a map of France. While we were studying the map Mattia said that he thought we should follow canals leading to the south, for he felt that Arthur having been so ill, it was pretty certain that he would be taken sailing on 'Le Cygne' during the summer months for the warmth and to help him regain his strength.

"But what about Lise and all the others?" I asked.

"Perhaps we'll be able to see them while we are looking for Mrs Milligan. And as we go along the Canal du Midi we can stop and see Lise."

We sat for quite a long time on a grassy slope beside the road and finally decided that first of all we would head towards the nearest river, the Seine, and ask barge owners and fishermen along its banks if they had seen 'Le Cygne'. It would be easily remembered because of the verandah giving it a different appearance from any other barge.

Before we started the long journey that was ahead of us I bought a cake of good soap to wash the dye out of Capi's thick coat. To me, Capi with blobs all over him was not Capi. At the first stream we came to we washed him thoroughly, each of us taking it in turn to scrub him, but Bob's dye was of very good quality and many shampoos were needed before we could completely clean off all the stains. Each day we had to give him his bath, and happily Normandy is a country of streams.

One morning we arrived at the top of a wooded hill and Mattia saw the Seine away ahead of us winding in a big curve. When we reached it we began to question people as to whether they had seen 'Le Cygne', a beautiful barge with a verandah. No one had, and at Rouen we had no better luck. Time, however, meant little to us, and it took two months to reach Charenton where we received for the first time the news that a barge like 'Le Cygne' had passed that way up-river some weeks before.

Even though so much time had passed we were not discouraged; if the barge was being pulled by the legs of two fine horses we had our own legs, and we would catch up with it one day. The main thing, the marvellous thing, was that 'Le Cygne' had been found. We had no need to stop now and question people, we had only to follow the canal. We continued on our way and were now getting nearer to where Lise lived, and I could not help wondering if she had seen the barge as it passed through the locks near her new home.

We never seemed tired at night, no matter how far we had tramped, and we were always up early next morning. To save as much money as we could we ate only bread and hard-boiled eggs, sometimes buying a little butter if the bread was a bit stale, and although we were among vineyards and could have bought cheap wine there we drank water. Mattia, however, talked a lot of the good things he would like to eat during our long walks.

"I hope Mrs Milligan still has the cook who made those tarts you have told me about," he said one day. "Apricot tarts must taste good. I have eaten apple-turnovers, and seen apricot tarts, but never had the chance of eating them. What are those little white things they stick all over the fruit?"

"Almonds."

"Oh!" And Mattia opened his mouth as though he was swallowing a tart, whole.

At every lock we came to we had more news of 'Le Cygne'. Everyone we spoke to had seen the lovely barge, and they mentioned the kind English lady and the boy lying on a camp-bed in the shade of the verandah.

At last we saw the woods where we had played the last autumn with Lise, and we quickened our steps. When we came in sight of the cottage we started running and Capi, who seemed to know where he was, went racing ahead of us as if to let Lise know we would be there soon. A man we didn't know was opening the lock-gate on the canal. When we got to the cottage a woman we had never seen came to the door.

"Is Madame Suriot at home?" I asked.

For a moment or two she looked at us both as though we had asked her a silly question.

"She doesn't live here now," she answered at last. "She has gone to Egypt."

Mattia and I stared at each other in dismay. We did not know where Egypt was but we thought, in a vague sort of way, that it must be far away, very far away, somewhere beyond the seas.

"What about Lise? Is she still here?"

"Lise! Oh no, she went away with an English lady on a barge."

Lise on 'Le Cygne'! We thought we were dreaming when we heard this, but the woman brought us back to earth by asking me if I was Remi. I said that I was and she went on to say that Monsieur Suriot, Lise's uncle, had been drowned when he fell into the lock.

"He got jammed under a coal-barge. Madame Suriot was at her wit's end to know what to do after his death, and then a lady whose children she had looked after when they were young and who was going to Egypt offered to take her with her as a companion. She didn't know what to do with Lise, and while she was wondering this barge with the English lady and her sick son came along the canal. Somehow they got into conversation. The lady said that she was looking for a child who would keep her boy company and it was agreed that she would take Lise with her. The lady also said that she knew of doctors who could cure Lise, and she was sure that one day she would be able to speak again. Before they left Lise wanted her Aunt Catherine to explain to me what to tell you if ever you came here to see her. That's all."

I was so astonished that I couldn't say a word, but Mattia never got tongue-tied like me.

"Can you tell us where the English lady went?" he asked.

"Across France to Switzerland. Lise was going to write to me so that I could also give Remi her address, but so far I haven't had a letter from her."

CHAPTER SEVENTEEN

After we had thanked the woman we decided to go on our way at once, and Mattia said to me as we were leaving the cottage: "What marvellous luck. It's not only Arthur and Mrs Milligan but Lise we are going to find, and then who knows where fortune will lead us."

On we went in search of 'Le Cygne', stopping only to eat and sleep and earn a few sous.

"To get to Switzerland one can go through Northern Italy," Mattia said, "and if in our search for Mrs Milligan we pass anywhere near Lucca that would be fine for I would be able to see Christina again."

At Lyons we were told that boats could not go up the river Rhone as far as Lake Geneva; we had somehow always thought that Mrs Milligan would sail in her barge into Switzerland. Imagine our surprise when we reached the next town where the river shallowed to see 'Le Cygne' moored by the bank. Everything was shut up and locked and there were no longer flowers decorating the verandah. We stood near the barge looking at each other and feeling sad.

A man who was keeping watch on the barge in case anyone tried to break into it came across to us and asked what we wanted. We told him that we were trying to find the English lady-owner of 'Le Cygne' and he said she and her boy and the little girl had left in a carriage for Switzerland. The servants had followed with the heavy baggage. We breathed again.

"Do you know where she was going to stay in Switzerland?" Mattia asked.

"She has taken a house on the shore of Lake Geneva at a place called Vevey. I don't know anything more than that she and the children are going to spend the summer there."

And so we started off for Vevey, knowing that they were not getting any further away from us, and that in the end if we searched long enough we would be able to find them. About a week later we reached Vevey with just three sous in our pockets and the soles of our boots worn through. We were to discover that Vevey was by no means a little village but a town, and we knew it would be silly to go to every house asking for an English lady with a sick son and a girl who couldn't speak, especially since there were so many English people living there in the summer that it was almost like a British colony.

We decided that the best thing to do would be to ask at houses where there was a chance that they would be living. We thought that that would not be too difficult, and we agreed we would only play our music in streets in which there was the possibility of either Lise or Arthur hearing us. We had no luck — shutters stayed closed when we played and the few questions we asked were a waste of time.

Then we went from the lake up to the foothills of the mountains behind it, and down again, questioning whenever we could people who might give us some information. One man told us to go to a chalet some distance up one of the mountains, while another said he was certain that Mrs Milligan lived on the shores of the lake. Indeed, there were English ladies living in the chalet on the mountain and in the big house by the lake, but not our Mrs Milligan.

Several days later, in the afternoon, we were playing in the road in front of a house which stood well back in a garden with a big iron gate set in a stone wall. I was singing quite loud and had just finished the first verse of my Neapolitan song and was starting the second when we heard from behind the wall a weak and unfamiliar voice repeating the words as I sang.

Mattia, eyebrows raised, said: "Arthur?"

"Nonsense," was my answer, "it can't be. I've never heard

224

that voice before."

Capi, however, started to bark and jump against the wall.

"Who's singing?" I called out, for I was very curious.

"Is that you Remi?" we heard spoken slowly and hesitatingly.

Mattia and I just stood and stared stupidly at each other, and then I saw a white handkerchief being waved at a corner of the wall not far away from where a hedge started. We both ran there, and it was not until we arrived that we could see who was doing the waving. It was none other than Lise. At last we had found her and there would be, not far away, Mrs Milligan and Arthur. But who had been doing the singing? That was the first question we asked when we could find our tongues.

"Me," Lise said.

Lisa was able to sing and talk! She had been cured.

"Where are Mrs Milligan and Arthur?" was my next question.

Lise moved her lips, but in her excitement she could not form the words she was wanting to say, so impatiently, she went back to making signs with her hands. Then I noticed Arthur at the end of the garden near some trees, stretched out in a long garden chair. Behind him was standing his mother and, I could not believe my eyes, on one side was. . . Mr James Milligan! Instantly I dropped behind the hedge and pulled Mattia down with me, forgetting that the man did not know him.

Lise must have wondered what was going on so I whispered to her that Mr Milligan must not know I was here. "Don't mention that you have seen me. Come here at nine tomorrow by yourself, and I want to talk to Mrs Milligan later. Now please go back to the others."

She hesitated for a moment or two and then did what I asked. After she had left us and we had gone behind the wall to hide Mattia said:

"You know, we shouldn't wait until tomorrow if you are going to see Mrs Milligan. Between now and then this man Milligan may do any sort of harm to Arthur. He doesn't know who I am and I'm going now to Mrs Milligan to talk to her."

There was sense in what Mattia said, so I agreed, telling him

225

that I would wait for him a little distance away under some chestnut trees, for it would be a good place to conceal myself if Mr Milligan should leave the garden to go into the house. I waited for Mattia for what seemed ages and nearly a dozen times I wondered if I was wise in letting him leave me. At last I saw him coming back with Mrs Milligan. I ran to her and took the hand she held out to me and kissed it. She stooped down, put her arms about me, and kissed me on the forehead.

"Remi," she murmured, and with her lovely white fingers she pushed back the hair from my forehead and gazed at me for a long time. "Yes, it's you."

I was too happy to say anything.

"Mattia and I have had a long talk," she went on in her normal voice, "but I want you to tell me yourself how you came to meet these Driscoll people, and also of your meeting with my husband's brother."

I told her everything that had happened as quickly as I could, and she interrupted me only when she told me that I must be quite certain of a number of things I had said to her. I had never been listened to with such attention, and as I talked her eyes never left mine. When I had finished she was silent for quite a little time, still looking at me, and at last she said:

"All that you have told me is very serious, but we must do what we have to very carefully. In a couple of hours you and Mattia are to go to the Hotel des Alpes where you will stay. I will ask someone from the hotel to come and take you there. Now I must go."

She hugged me again, shook hands with Mattia, and walked quickly away.

"What did you tell Mrs Milligan?" I asked Mattia after she had left us.

"Everything that you have just told her, and a lot more besides. She's a marvellous lady."

"Did you see Arthur?"

"Only from a distance, but enough to see why you liked him."

I went on asking Mattia questions, but he answered me only

226

with grunts. Although we were in our tattered musicians' clothes we were taken care of when we arrived at the hotel by a servant dressed in black and with a white tie, who took us up to our room. It was a beautiful one with two white beds placed side by side. The windows opened onto a balcony with a view of the lake. The servant asked us what we would like for dinner which, if we wished, would be served on the balcony.

"Have you any tarts?" Mattia asked.

"Yes, three kinds, rhubarb, strawberry and gooseberry."

"Lovely. We will have them."

"All three?"

"Certainly."

"And what else would you like?"

When each course was mentioned Mattia opened his eyes wider, but he wouldn't let himself be put out. "Whatever you think is best," he replied with all the coolness and aplomb in the world, and the servant gravely left us.

"I think we are going to eat better here than with the Driscolls, don't you?" Mattia said when we were alone.

On the following day Mrs Milligan came to see us, bringing with her a tailor and a shirtmaker who measured us. She told us that Lise had been trying her very best to get over her difficulty in talking and the doctor, indeed, had promised that one of these days she would be quite cured. Mrs Milligan spent all of an hour with us and when she left she kissed me and shook hands warmly with Mattia. She continued coming for the next few days, and then on the fifth day the servant that I had seen on 'Le Cygne' arrived instead and told us that a carriage was waiting outside the hotel to take us both to Mrs Milligan's house. Mattia sat down in the carriage as though he had been used to riding in one all his life, and Capi jumped in and made himself at home on the cushions.

The distance from the hotel was not very far and as we were driven I was rather like someone in a dream. When we reached the house we were shown into a drawing-room. Mrs Milligan was there, Arthur was on a sofa, and Lise was sitting near him. Arthur held out both hands to me and I rushed over to him, and then I kissed Lise.

"At last the day has come," Mrs Milligan said after she had kissed me, "when you belong to me and to Arthur."

As I looked at her trying to make out what she meant she went to a door and opened it. And who should I see but Mother Barberin holding a parcel in her arms. She came in, undid the parcel, and put on a table two baby's dresses, one made of silk and the other of linen, a lace bonnet, a long white coat, a woollen vest, and two white woollen bootees. I was soon hugging her. It was then that Mrs Milligan spoke to a servant. I heard the name Milligan mentioned and looked quickly at her, and I know that I had turned pale.

"You have nothing to fear," Mrs Milligan said gently. "Quite the contrary. Come to me and put your hand in mine."

James Milligan came into the room, smiling and showing his very white and pointed teeth, and when he saw me the smile turned into his rather frightening grimace. But Mrs Milligan did not give him time to say anything.

"I have asked you to come in," she said, and her voice trembled, "so that I may introduce you to my elder son, whom I have at last found." She pressed my hand. "Here he is, but I know that you've already met him at the house of the man who stole him. You made an excuse for going to that house — your poor excuse was to enquire after Remi's health."

"I don't know what you are talking about," Milligan interjected.

"The man who stole Remi is in gaol for robbing a church and has made a full confession admitting that he stole my baby, took it to Paris and abandoned it there. He imagined that by cutting off some of the markings on the clothing the baby would never be traced. Here are the clothes that my child was wearing, and which have been kept all these years by Madame Barberin who brought up my son. Would you like to read the confession and to look at the clothes?"

James Milligan stood stock-still for quite a time looking at me

228

with hatred, then he turned on his heels and when he reached the
door called out over his shoulder: "We shall see what a law-court
thinks of all this."

Quietly my mother replied: "*You* may take the matter to court.
I will not, because you are my husband's brother."

The door slammed. Then for the first time in my life I kissed my
mother on her lips.

"Would you like me to tell you how well I have kept your
secret?" Mattia asked me.

My mother interrupted. "I told Mattia not to mention
anything to you. I somehow could not believe that you must be
my son and of course I had to have proof. One way of getting this
was to ask Madame Barberin to come here and bring your baby-
clothes with her. It would have been dreadful for us here if, after
all, there had been a mistake. Now we have all the proof we need
and we shall never be parted again." Then turning to Lise and
Mattia, "These dear friends of yours who you loved when you
were poor will both be part of our family."

The years have passed, and I now live in my ancestors' house,
Milligan Park. It is, strangely, about sixty miles from the very spot
where I jumped from the train to escape from the policeman, and
I live here with my wife, my mother, and my brother. The little
wanderer who so often slept out of doors under the stars, or in a

229

barn sheltering from the rain and wind, has become the heir to an old and historic castle.

I should tell you that we are about to christen our first child, a boy, and he will be named Mattia; under my roof will be reunited to take part in the celebration all those who were my friends in my poorer days. For the last six months I have been writing the history of my castle and today I have received copies from the printer, and I will give these to my guests as a little memento of the occasion.

This reunion is to be a surprise for my wife, and she will see her father, and brothers and sister, as well as her aunt. Only my mother and brother are in the secret. But one person will be missing, and that will be my dear master Vitalis who is buried in Paris. At my request my mother has had his burial-place removed to the Père Lachaise cemetery, with a bronze bust, the bust of Balzani, upon it; a copy of this bust is in front of me as I write and often when I am at my desk I look up and meet Vitalis's eyes. I will always remember his kindness and tenderness to me.

I can now see my mother coming down the staircase leaning on my brother's arm; now it is the son who supports the mother, for Arthur has grown into a big and strong young man. A few steps behind them comes an old woman in her peasant's clothes with a baby in a white silk robe in her arms — it is Mother Barberin carrying my son Mattia.

Arthur has brought me a copy of *The Times* and has asked me to look at a report in it from Vienna which states that Mattia, the famous violinist, has completed his recitals in Austria and is returning to England to keep an urgent engagement. I have no need to read all the report, for Mattia has become famous and is known as the 'Chopin of the violin'. It amuses me to remember that when the three of us were being taught together Mattia was not very good at Latin or Greek, but at music it was very different and Espinassous, the barber-musician in Mendes, was right in what he said.

Now I have been shown a telegram which reads:
'Delayed by rough sea. Seasick again. Bringing

And she, looking beautiful, is now coming down the staircase.

Christina from Paris. Arriving four o'clock.
Mattia.'

The mention of Christina has made me look at Arthur, for I know that he is very fond of her. I know, too, that my mother is not happy at the thought that he may one day wish to marry her. But she did not oppose my marriage to Lise and she, looking beautiful, is now coming down the staircase. It is nearly four o'clock and I can hear the sound of wheels on the drive. One by one our guests are arriving and Lise and I will go and stand at the door to welcome them.

The first arrivals are Monsieur Acquin, Aunt Catherine, Etiennette, and a young man who has just returned from a scientific expedition to the West Indies, the well-known botanist Benjamin Acquin. The next to arrive are an old man with a much younger companion, and when they leave here they are both going to Wales on a tour of the coalmines there; they are the old Professor and Alexis, and Alexis now has a highly-paid job in the mine at Truyère. I can hear the sound of more wheels on the drive and a dog-cart has stopped; in it are Bob and his brother.

After the christening Mattia takes me aside. "I have an idea. Hundreds of times we played to people who did not care and did not know what they heard. Let's now play for those we love, and who know and understand music."

"It was not only people who had no ear for what *you* played. Do you remember how you scared our cow?"

Mattia's only reply is to ask me if I am going to sing my Neapolitan song.

"Yes, of course," I answer, "for it was that song that helped to give Lise back her power of speech."

Mattia has taken from a velvet-lined case an old and beautiful violin, and I uncover my harp, the wood-frame of which has been washed so often by rain that the varnish has gone and the grain can be clearly seen. Our guests form a circle about us and a white poodle joins them — Capi, who is deaf now but who is still blessed with good eyesight. Seeing me uncover the harp he has left the cushion on which he usually lies and has come over, limping rather, for the 'performance'. In his jaws he is holding a saucer for he wants to make his usual rounds of the 'distinguished audience'. He finds he hasn't the strength to walk on his two hind paws, so with a paw on his heart he gravely salutes everyone.

I sing my song now and we both accompany it, and Capi gets up as best he can to make his round. Everyone drops a coin in the saucer and Capi delightedly brings it over to me. It is the best collection he has ever made for in his saucer are all gold and silver coins, a magnificent hundred and seventy francs. I kiss him on his cold nose as I have done in other days, and the thought of my penniless childhood suddenly gives me an inspiration. I announce to our guests that the money so generously given will go to a fund for homeless boys who play music on the streets of Paris, and that my mother and I will soon start a home where they may sleep in comfort.

Mattia says that he wishes to be allowed to help, and the money from his first concert in London will be given to Capi's collection.

To show his approval Capi waves his tail and gives his loudest bark.